Detective Strongoak and the
Case of the Dead Elf

A former biomedical research scientist, one day Terry hung up his electron microscope and started writing jokes for radio, musicals, feature films, TV and the stage. He is especially known for his political satire, writing for several series of *Rory Bremner, Who Else?*, *Bremner, Bird and Fortune*, *Dead Ringers* and *The Way It Is*. His theatre work has won the 2004 Fringe Report Drama Writer of the Year and a Headline Highlight Award, and he was made a Writer in Residence at the Canal Café theatre. Terry spends his spare time happily writing songs in his summerhouse in sunny Sussex. He can be found on Twitter @adeadelf and on Facebook at: www.facebook.com/adeadelf

Detective Strongoak and the Case of the Dead Elf

TERRY NEWMAN

HARPER
Voyager

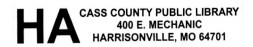

Harper*Voyager*
An imprint of HarperCollins*Publishers* Ltd
1 London Bridge Street,
London SE1 9GF

www.harpervoyagerbooks.co.uk

A Paperback Original 2015

1

First published in Great Britain in ebook format by
Harper*Voyager* 2014

Copyright © Terry Newman 2014

Terry Newman asserts the moral right to
be identified as the author of this work

A catalogue record for this book is
available from the British Library

ISBN: 978-0-00-812066-5

This novel is entirely a work of fiction.
The names, characters and incidents portrayed in it are
the work of the author's imagination. Any resemblance to
actual persons, living or dead, events or localities is
entirely coincidental.

Automatically produced by Atomik ePublisher from Easypress

MIX
Paper from
responsible sources
FSC™ C007454

For all the dreamers and those who make dreams come true, especially Susie and Sean and my editor Eleanor, for her boundless enthusiasm.

1

THE TWO FINGERS

Thunk!

The arrow hit Alderman Castleview in the middle of his right eye socket. A promising start. I took careful aim and let fly again.

Thunk!

The second arrow caught him just below the temple.

Thunk!

The final arrow buried itself plumb centre of that famous winning smile. I smirked and awarded myself a bonus point before retrieving my darts.

The picture of Alderman Castleview had occupied pride of place on my dartboard ever since he had announced his intent, the previous spring, to redevelop the Third Level and cause yet more traffic nightmares. I sat and tilted back my chair before taking aim again – but, to be honest, my heart wasn't in it. This time I left the darts abandoned in the wood and walked over to the window instead. I leant against the ledge and took in the view.

On a good day the sixteenth floor of the Two Fingers

building just poked clear of the smog that wound round the High Summer Citadel. This was a good day and I watched it from my office on the sixteenth floor.

I have never found anyone who could adequately explain why this office block was called the Two Fingers, as there was, in fact, only one. Some said the answer lay wreathed in legends, others said that the first block had simply been pulled down. Perhaps the stonemason did have bigger plans, but had forgotten his kickback to the Dwarfs Construction Guild. Nobody knew and nobody really cared, apart from me, but then again I cared about a lot of outdated edifices – like law, justice and good government. Down below I followed the various people going about their late-afternoon Citadel business. The Citadel, the city on a mountain: actually a giant granite extrusion located near where the River Everflow meets the sea. One last, remaining lonely outcrop of a mountain range, lost on the horizon like a melody in a dream. A city gift-wrapped by five towering walls, with gates that have not been closed since the songs were fresh, and you could still tell who the heroes were by their shiny swords and better complexions.

With characteristic humour, most of the population referred to the place simply as 'The Hill'. And today The Hill was sweaty and irritable.

A nasty undercurrent of violence had been evident throughout this, the hottest summer on record. *The Citadel Press*, the Hill's main news scroll, was working itself up into a lather of indignation and turning umbrage into an art form. Elections were scheduled for the autumn and all sorts of worms were crawling out of their holes. But today the heat had defeated even them. The sun was raising bubbles in the road-coat like the boils on a goblin's back, and the parchment pushers, the slogan shouters – all the ranters and ravers – seemed content to give the rest of the population some time off and sulk in whatever shade they could find. The sun was beginning to go down; nevertheless humidity was still in the nineties, which meant I was as cool as a goblin on a twenty-league route march.

I pushed my chair back from the window and sighed. It was the time of day for important decisions – more coffee or the office bottle – in the end coffee won out. I would twitch 'till midwatch; but I already knew there was little chance of sleep on a night like this. I got out of the chair and stretched, marking how the muscles in my back creaked and moaned a bit. They take to inactivity like a dragon to gargling extinguisher foam.

In common with other dwarfs, I was born to wield an axe of some variety, whether it be pick or battle. Although not particularly conceited, I am quite at home with my physique. I am tall for a dwarf, which makes me about the height of a short man – but then again we all know dwarf heights have been increasing in recent years. My mother says it's the free school milk. Musculature? Well, my current 'party piece' is cracking nuts in the crook of my elbow, an activity that always impresses the ladies, be they of the dwarf variety or otherwise. And, furthermore, like the rest of my kin, I have a wrestler's shoulders; the dwarf that needs shoulder pads in his suit jacket has yet to be born. A lot of men, particularly those more used to the company of gnomes, often forget that dwarfs and gnomes do not frequent the same tailors. Not that I have anything against gnomes; we dwarfs are simply just not built to the same scale. This has come as an unwelcome surprise to more than one would-be assailant, on a dark gloomy winter Citadel night.

I picked up the bones and walked over to the mirror, re-tied my plait in the family knots and ran a hand over my chin. I could do with my evening shave – us dwarfs have that sort of make-up. I pumped some water into the small basin and splashed my face. I do not keep much in the way of furniture in the office – some might call it sparse, I like to think of it as minimalist. The small hand basin is the only amenity, and for the rest I have to walk along the corridor.

The room is somewhat dominated by my desk, which came with the room and looks as if it was poured out of the same mould as the rest of the building. 'Monumental' is an understatement. Its legs are enough to qualify as a tourist attraction in themselves. The desktop is inlaid with a green leather that might have been taken from the butt of the worm that won the Battle of the Forgotten Mountain. Fortunately the desk has two chairs; both similarly worked, as finding a good match would have been impossible on this side of the Big Sea. I had added a chest and a small cupboard. The chest I used for papers and the cupboard contained a change of clothes, my little stove and, most importantly, all I needed for the preparation of coffee. The grinder was a new electric model. I still preferred my old mechanical one and the comforting ritual that went with it. However, far be it from me to spit in the face of progress, as it had actually been a present from a rather special lady. It's a noisy business though, and with the grinder on full, I almost missed the knock on the reception door and the whole economy-sized parcel of grief that came along with it.

I shouted a simple 'Come-In!' I know ... I know ... over-familiar, but it was out of regular office hours, and I was feeling kind of wild.

The face that peered round my inner door was pretty, but

in a world where 'pretty' tends to be a rather over-subscribed commodity, you might not think to look at it twice. If you did, however, there was a certain something around the eyes that could come back to haunt you at the most inappropriate times.

With the face there also came a mass of sandy-coloured hair, back-combed in the style that was everywhere that year. Her frame was not large but quite compact, and she radiated an air of both vulnerability and independence: an intriguing combination. She could look me straight in the eye, which, although as I mentioned I am tall for a dwarf, made her quite short for a woman. I recognised her as a receptionist from an office along the corridor.

'Are you busy, Detective Strongoak?' she asked.

'No, come in, take a seat.' I waved vaguely with the grinder.

This was the first time I had seen her out of work-wear. She had on shorts and an oversized tabard-shirt sporting the legend: 'Surf Elves – Really Out of Their Trees!' Surfing, I knew, was the unicorn's horn as far as the elfin elite were concerned: bronzed, blue-eyed young lords and ladies with enchanted boards that seemed to float forever above the waves. Like most elfin activities, it had now caught on with the Citadel men and women too. It was a trend I did not subscribe to. We dwarfs have an affinity with water a rain-wear manufacturer would hock his treasure trove to patent.

'The name's Liza, isn't it?' I said, casually, after she had settled.

'That's right, Detective Strongoak, Liza Springwater.'

'Well, would you like some coffee, Liza?' I paused with the scoop held over the percolator, pleased to have gained an attractive drinking companion.

'What I really would like is some help.'

'Sure,' I said, thinking that there was probably a chest or two that needed the application of some dwarf muscle. The sort of job I'm only too willing to help out with, especially if the grateful party has been blessed with extra helpings of cutes. Liza certainly had plenty to spare. In fact, she could probably have started a market stall and made a good living supplying cutes to women who think that men just go for the physical attributes that are easier to record with paint and brush. Not that I've anything against them either; far be it for me to play favourites.

'Can it wait until after some coffee, Liza?'

'I don't know, Detective Strongoak,' she said, very seriously.

I added an extra scoop to the percolator anyway, and set it on the small stove, which I lit with a flint. I adjusted the flame before we both passed out from heat exhaustion.

'They can never get the temperature right in this building,' I added, rather unnecessarily.

'I know, too hot in the summer and too cold in the winter. Our office is freezing from the moment the first snow starts to fall.'

'What is it you do there, Liza?'

'Nothing very exciting: take messages, scrollwork and some dictation. Occasionally I get a trip out if the boss wants a smiling face. Hers only being suited for scaring off ogres.'

'I'll remember that. Just might come in handy one day, in my line of business.'

The water was finally warming to my satisfaction, so I sat down on the business side of the desk and put on the understanding face I usually reserve for widows and orphans.

'Now, perhaps you had better tell me all about it.'

For a moment I thought she was going to cave in on me, but she had come this far and did not intend to back down now. I sort of admired that. 'It's about this boy I've been seeing, Perry Goodfellow.'

She paused, as if expecting some comment from me. If so, she was disappointed; all she got was that same old noncommittal look and the background music of the bubbling percolator. This must have been good enough, as she continued:

'He's disappeared. We were due to meet last week, but he never turned up. When I still hadn't heard anything from him the next day, I called the inn in Old Town where he worked. They said he had collected his pay and cleared out. They didn't know where he went, unfortunately. A week's gone by and I've yet to hear a word. I'm concerned, no ... actually I'm worried sick.'

She stopped and we sort of stared at each other for a while. I got up deliberately and took my time pouring the coffee. 'No milk, I'm afraid, but I could probably find some sugar.'

'No, thank you. Black, without, will be fine.' I passed her a mug and we both sipped through the, almost, too prolonged silence. Finally I said: 'You know what I have to ask?'

She shrugged. 'Sure, I wouldn't be the first girl to be kicked off the unicorn, and I'm not saying that Perry is any sort of hero. There have been other women in his past and there might well be other women in the future, I can't say; but I know Perry, Master Strongoak. And I can tell you this, whatever the reason, whatever the cause, there is one thing he would never have done, and that is leave without saying goodbye.'

It was a pretty speech, verbs and everything – the full fellowship. If Perry had run off with some other woman, I, for one, was willing to bet that he had made the mistake of his life. When the wolves come howling round my tree, this is one lady I would not mind being up there with me.

What could I say, though? The heart is a strange sorcerer, which casts its spell in the unlikeliest places and kills them on a whim. Something like that, anyway. The Lizas of this world are being lied to every day and crying their eyes out every night, unlike tough hard-bitten dwarf master detectives. They are far too canny to have trod those dangerous paths – ah, sweet Elester, where are you now with your coal-black hair, ruby-red lips and pilfering fingers in the Old Town Pension Trust? Oh yes, serving five years for fraud after I found the evidence in the false bottom of your bedside bridal hope chest. After all, dwarf, elf, human or gnome, none of us are immune. Shoot, I even saw a goblin once get mushy over a piece of skirt he picked up in a bar – and he wasn't even trying to eat her.

So it was my turn to shrug. 'Some people just don't like goodbyes.' After all, I'd had more than my fair share and I'd never got exactly fond of them. Taking another jolt of coffee, I put down the mug and reached for the security of my pipe resting in the ashcup. Something was making me edgy. Painful Memories or was the coffee simply too strong?

Just put it down to the weather and move on, Nicely. 'I can afford to pay you, Detective Strongoak. I have some savings.'

'We can talk money later,' I replied, convincingly dismissive. 'I offer special good-neighbour rates.' I paused for a moment, hoping that didn't sound suspect and scratched my chin.

'Thank you, Master Strongoak.'

I got up, decision made and topped up our cups. 'One thing I insist upon, call me "Nicely". All that "master" business went out when my forefathers traded in their pickaxes for steam hammers.'

'Nicely. I like that. It suits you. Is it your proper name?'

'My proper name has rather more consonants than folk,

other than dwarfs, can get their tongues round.'

'So, why 'Nicely'?'

'Well, I could tell you, but then I'd only have to go and make you swear a blood oath with your lips sewn by spider silk under a sickle moon ... and we all know how tiresome that can get!'

'I think we'd better leave it then, thank you, Nicely.' She relaxed a little and laughed for the first time. It was an attractive laugh, like water falling in a cave lit by magic torches.

I needed to lay off the weed and find me a lead. It didn't pay to get too sentimental.

First I reached in the drawer to get out the papers that made it all legal – next I would concentrate on obtaining the necessary background concerning young Perry Goodfellow.

Magic torches, bah!

The sun was dropping over the Third Level wall by the time Liza had left. I poured the last of the coffee into my mug and went to the window, watching the sightseers and lovers making shadows on the battlements. I bit the brew – the coffee was too strong and too stewed. I poured it into the basin, watching it drain down the hole and begin its long journey to the bay. Tonight there would be a few fishes sharing my insomnia.

2

TREE FRIEND

My wagon was in the smiths, having its shoes changed. There was also a small steam leak that I just couldn't locate. The condenser was struggling but she was losing power on hills, so I just had to bite the bullet and lay out the big buckskin to get her fixed. In the end, and in the vain hope that some exercise might burn off the caffeine and use up some surplus energy, I decided to exercise the beggar's nag and walk down the Hill to Old Town.

Tidying the desk by sweeping the contents into a drawer, I picked up my jacket, hung the 'Back Much Later' sign on the doorknob and shut up the store. I took the lift to the lobby. Old Jakes was on reception and we had a quick word, concerning the optimal watering of geraniums and the pros and cons of mulching, before I headed out into the late-afternoon heat.

If I was to get to the bottom of Perry Goodfellow's disappearance, his last place of employment sounded like a good place to start. I wasn't sure what I was looking for but hopefully it would be big and obvious and preferably have 'clue' written on it in large letters.

The walk gave me some time to review the facts regarding the life and career of Perry Goodfellow, as Liza Springwater had just related them to me. Liza and Perry had met on the beach at the Gnada Peninsula the summer of the previous year. They had been strolling-out ever since. Perry worked at an inn as an odd-job man and runner. The duties could not have been too onerous as he seemed to spend most of the time surfing. The picture Liza had brought with her, now sitting in the top pocket of my suit, showed a tanned, relaxed individual with curly black hair. It was taken on the beach. Under one arm he carried a surfboard, in his other hand he held a gold chalice. This, I was reliably informed, was the Gnada Trophy, the big prize of the surfing season, and he'd beaten an elf called Highbury to win it. The Gnada Trophy had disappeared along with Perry and this was upsetting various surfing folk. To be frank, it could have been a giant's eggcup for all I knew, but a job's a job.

Passing through Black Guard Bar – the unofficial entrance to Old Town – after a quick word with a helpful local, I soon found Perry's inn. Although Fourth-Level, it was on the right side of the Hill. It also had all the right timbers in all the right places, and anywhere else it would have been called *The Dragon and Ring*, or something equally folksy. Here, with admirable constraint, the sign declared it to be simply *The Old Inn*.

At the tail end of a hot day the lobby was a cool drink of water. A large ceiling fan irritated little piles of dust with each slow pass, but they lacked the energy to commit and settled happily after every sweep. Large wooden pillars supported massive wooden beams that could in turn have supported the odd army or two on the upper floors. Small, densely stained glass windows leaked in the evening sun; the light concealing as much as it illuminated. Although the place had obviously seen better days, it had escaped the rampant modernisation that had ravaged higher-level inns more effectively than the goblin hordes had ever managed.

The reception was empty. I hit a bell to no avail, whistled for a short while, then wandered through to find the bar. Empty tables greeted me but I noticed an aproned figure, bent over, stacking shelves with fresh bottles. I shouted a well-pitched hello. On hearing me, he straightened up, and up again, and even when he reached the rafters he did not so much stop, as throw a curve down the rest of his body. To say I was surprised to see one of the Tree Folk working in a Fourth-Level inn was something of an understatement. I had occasionally seen one of the tall, unmistakable figures striding around the Citadel, but mostly only visiting on business. They still lived in their northern forests, or what the logging industry had left of them. With their unbelievably long nut-brown limbs, craggy weather-beaten faces and huge bushy heads of hair, the colour of copper beeches, it was easy to see why many superstitious folk took them to be real live talking trees. Not the dwarfs of course, they never would have fallen for something so stupid – well, not recently anyway. The Tree Folk remain one of the strangest of the many different Citadel inhabitants.

'Ho hum,' he said slowly, that being the only way that Tree folk do things. 'I must tender you an apology, there is no receptionist to assist you at the moment. The manager enjoys a … ah … lie down in the afternoon and portions of the evening. Are you after a room for the night? If it is light refreshment or a drink that you require, then I should be able to be of some service.'

His voice was polished ebony, dark and smooth, but with incredible weight. To listen to him was to hear the wind blowing on and on through the branches of a forest that covered half the world. He continued, 'I am afraid you have caught us … somewhat distant from our best. We are … ho hum … as you might have realised, somewhat short-handed.'

'Well,' I said, climbing onto a barstool, 'as getting caught short is something we dwarfs generally get accused of, I'll just go with the drink for now.'

'Excellent notion, I must say. Very good, very good indeed. What would be your fancy, Master Dwarf?'

'Let me have a look here,' I responded, picking up the drink roster. This had not escaped the more depressing aspects of modernity. The list was depressingly hearty, playing on the fashion for all things pastoral. It contained more types of foaming flagons than any sensible drinker could ever require, all harking back to an earlier age that probably never existed, and the endnotes were punctuated by more 'thees' and 'thous' than you would hear at a village idiots' convention. I put it down with a sigh, and did my best to look the barkeep in the eye. 'And what would you recommend, Tree-friend?'

'Tree-friend, eh?' he said, his sad green eyes the colour of sunlight on a fading forest glade, looked around the supporting timbers. 'These are all the woodland folk I have for company now, and a sorry lot they are for conversation. Sad, very sad.' As if by way of confirmation, the silence settled in on us like a weight. 'At least, Master Dwarf, they have left *you* your mountains and mines.'

I knew just what he meant. We paused for a moment: a moment that might have been caught in amber, and buried beneath a mountain for half the lifetime of the planet, only to be excavated by dwarfs and looked at in awe on winter nights beneath cold stars. Then, he shook himself like an oak in a fall storm, and laughed; the sound rolled around the rafters and the moment was gone in a pixie's smile.

'A drink, you said, Master Dwarf. Ho hum. Well, let me tell you, the ale is no better than the barrel it is kept in, and that I would not burn for kindling. The wines have not travelled well, or very far for that matter, and the manager waters the distillates at night when he thinks I am sleeping. However, the good news is that I have another little speciality of the house. One that is not advertised on the roster, but is kept tucked away behind the bar for those occasions that require it.'

He pulled out an old-fashioned stone crock that wasn't bigger than an ale truck, but not that much smaller either. 'Now, this the manager knows nothing about and so I can give it my wholehearted approval.' He decanted a modest measure into a highball glass. 'I find it is best to take these things a little at a time, Master Dwarf.'

As if to put a lie to his own advice he crooked it over one elbow in the time-honoured fashion and took a draught that seemed to go on forever.

I approached my drink with a little more caution. I had heard of the gravy the Tree-friends made. Some sort of fancy water, I imagined. At first sip it did indeed seem like the purest, coolest water that had ever bubbled up from a woodland spring. I took a large mouthful and it felt like standing under a mountain waterfall. I finished the glass and it felt like getting hit by a whole damn ocean.

'What do you call this?' I gasped like a drowning man. 'I thought it was supposed to be some sort of Woodland cordial?'

'Not unless they come with fifty per cent alcohol,' he said, a smile spreading across his face like sunshine in a forest glade.

He refilled my glass. 'I can see that there is some other matter that you wish to unburden yourself of.'

I briefly wondered whether to play it cute or clever, before concluding I had left it one drink too late to be clever and, despite my mother's protestations, I suspect I may never have been what you might call conventionally cute. I put on my serious face and played it straight down the line. Well, that was what I was aiming for anyway.

I flashed my badge: 'Nicely Strongoak, Master Detective and shield-for-hire. I am looking for a body by the name of Perry Goodfellow.'

'Strongoak,' he said, with extra weight. 'A good name, but hardly dwarfish.'

'No, it was a given name.'

'Elfish, then?' He looked a bit surprised, if I am any judge of these things, which I am not, and if emotion can be read from a visage as implacable as a roof joist.

'Yes, the family were elf-friends.'

'Good, very good. I have been to Tall Trees, where the elves have now settled. I liked it well enough, but I think perhaps the elves now care less for the trees than the homes that they have built in them. However, that is as maybe. Time always sprints ahead and leaves us stranded in its wake. I am Grove. I have had other names … but Grove will do for now.'

I let him continue at his own pace until he arrived back at where I wanted. 'This Perry Goodfellow, would he be in any trouble?' he rumbled.

'No, but a young lady of his acquaintance was rather concerned at the speed of his departure.'

'And this lady, she is who exactly?'

15

'One Liza Springwater.'

'Good, very good,' he said again, making up his mind. 'I thought I might have misjudged you there for a moment, got you confused with some form of snark. However, I met Liza a few times, oh yes, took to her quicker than many a woman of these later years. There was something very ... unmanly ... about her, if you follow?'

'Yes,' I admitted, 'something about the eyes.'

He nodded agreement, like an oak tree moving in the breeze. 'And Perry, he is as decent as they come. A bit wild, but he is young, and good wood often grows on the most wayward bough. I was ... hurt when he did not say farewell.'

'You too?'

Grove gave this simple remark ample consideration; summers came and went and whole mountain ranges wore down. He scratched a twiggy chin. 'I take it he did not say goodbye to young Liza Springwater either?'

I murmured my affirmative.

'Not good, not good,' Grove continued. 'I did not know that.' He took another long pull on the crock. 'If I had known, I would have been more concerned. I would have searched for him myself, not that I would have much idea where to start looking these days. Still, there are a few friends I could perhaps have contacted, to whom the name of old Grove might still mean something. Yes, I still have a few names that I can call upon if assistance is ever required. As it is, I am very glad that Liza has the sap to organise the hunt.'

'You didn't know that Liza had called here?'

'No, she must have spoken with the manager and he has failed to pass on the intelligence – a petty revenge, probably – I do not think he took too kindly to my questioning him about Perry's departure. Seemed to think it was not my affair. Hurhm! He was almost … curt. Finally he admitted that Perry had collected his wage, cleared his room and left very quickly. I should not have trusted the man, but I was sure, if he was in any real trouble, Perry would have come to me for help. He always knew he could come to me for help.'

'And since then, no letters, no messages?' I began.

'Not a word.' Grove's concern began to be evident. 'I think I have perhaps been guilty of letting myself go a bit to rot. It is easy to stop thinking when you get out of the habit.'

Who was I to argue? 'Not thinking' – at times I'd nearly made a career out of it.

'Did Perry ever bring any elves back here, for a drink maybe?'

Now Grove certainly did look surprised as he replied: 'Elves? No, never. I'm not sure he had any particularly close friends amongst the elf kind.'

'Did he ever happen to mention any? Does the name Highbury mean anything?'

Grove slowly nodded his large shaggy head. I half expected to see a warbler or two pop out to see what all the commotion was about. 'Yes, the only elf I ever remember him mentioning at any length, the young lord called Highbury who obviously thought far too highly of himself.'

Time was moving on and I tried not to appear too hasty or, the ultimate sin, too curt.

'Would it be possible to give his old quarters the once over, if they're not occupied, of course?'

Grove gave a slow nod. 'We have not employed a new runner yet, so I do not think that will be any problem. The manager may think otherwise, but as he is not here and I am busy stacking shelves and the master key is lying on the bar, I cannot think what there is to stop you. However, I did clean out his sleeping quarters rather thoroughly, and I did not find any traces of any goods Perry may have forgotten, but then again I was not really looking for any. It is room 4-15, top floor.'

It was a lot of steps, but I felt my legs growing to meet them; marvellous stuff, that gravy the Tree-friends make.

The room itself was small, but bright and airy, and sparsely furnished. A large rug in that whirling pattern the gnomes do so well dominated the floor, with two large chests serving for storage, and a smaller chest of drawers by the bed for personal items. The large bed was wedged tightly to the wall. It stood on iron claws that barely lifted it from the floor. It all looked depressingly spotless. Grove clearly, somewhat unfortunately, took his work very seriously. I searched around anyway. The chests were as empty as Grove had promised, the drawers likewise. Nothing obvious under the mattress or the rug either. Grove, however, was not the most flexible of individuals, so I bent down to check under the bedstead as well. It was of a sturdy wooden slat-box construction and attached to the wall along one length rather than freestanding. At first sight there appeared to be a whole lot of nothing of interest underneath, but a dwarf has more refined senses at his disposal than just sight. A dwarf's nose is an appendage of great sophistication, having evolved through generations of applied excavation to recognise precious metals and gems. You don't believe it's true, then try passing off phoney coinage to a dwarf and you'll soon need to be looking for a new place to put your hat. People marvel at the vision of an elf but can they find an uncut diamond underground in the dark?

Now, with my head stuck under Perry's recently vacated bed, I was getting a very clear signal of 'gold' coming in from the nose outpost. It didn't take me long to realise that a false wall under the bed had been crudely added and behind that must be the source of the gold. This had 'clue' written all over it, just as I hoped.

I do not know if I was simply distracted by the smell of treasure trove, or maybe it was the drink, or perhaps I was guilty of not yet giving the case the attention it deserved … either way, I didn't hear the swish of the mace until the briefest of moments before it took me with it into the dark that has no name. It's like the dark that has got a name, but it was rotten to its parents and they disowned it completely, which has made it a whole lot meaner.

A rhythm section began playing on my skull's back door – a good solid bass thump with fast persistent beating timpani. Nothing too refined involving brushes or sticks with tapered shoulders and fancy tips, just good solid mallets that displaced thinking with a pulsing cavalcade of agony.

Carefully I opened my eyes. I was lying on my front on the rug. I tried to focus on it, but the gnomes' handiwork just made my head spin, so I tried my sleeve instead. When that didn't work I compromised and concentrated on my hand. As I raised it into view, a few tiny grains of sand caught the last of the evening light and fell onto the patterned flooring.

The different percussive elements at play in my noggin became identifiable: the beating was the blood returning to the pulpy spot on my head and the thumping turned into Grove's footsteps coming up the stairs four at a time. He burst into the room.

'Axes and blood, I thought you were gone too long!'

Grove helped me carefully to my feet. Whatever had been under the bed was long gone, as was my attacker. Grove then picked me up and carried me down the stairs, which would have been embarrassing if I could have got there any other way. As it was I didn't complain. He put another large glass of his special gravy inside me. This made me feel, not so much better, as just rather less. A third, however, had me wanting to go hunting dragons with a fruit knife. Instead we opted to go looking for managers, as they were now suspiciously overdue.

We found him unceremoniously dumped, tied up in a storeroom, assailant unseen and unknown. A busy officious man, he wanted someone to blame. He decided I would do, which I didn't need, so I quickly helped myself to what passes for fresh air at that time of year in the Citadel. Before I departed I pledged to keep Grove informed of my findings. Grove, in turn, said he would pull in a few favours and see if there had been any word concerning young Goodfellow's departure. He would also try to get more information from the manager, when he was in a better mood. Grove slipped a small bottle of his special gravy into my pocket, in case the pain returned. We shook on it. He had the kind of grip that reminds you of how tree roots are supposed to be able to split stone, given the time and the inclination, but he held my calloused mitt as carefully as a first-time mother holds a baby. I felt so secure I almost burst into tears. Then again, three of those drinks will do that to anybody.

Things were beginning to buzz and the nightworms were moving when I left *The Old Inn* and hit the cobbles. Lights appeared on everything that wasn't moving and quite a few things that were; blue elf lights of iris-popping purity, yellow dwarf lights, homely and welcoming, and red wizard lamps, glowing with hidden power and slightly sinister, like a prophet with a hard-on. And everywhere multicoloured gnome lights

– instant party-time for Hill folk. Evening vendors were out early to catch those homeward bound. Spice sausage and burnt-blood pudding, cold taffies and the prince of pickles, a heady cocktail for the nose and instant indigestion for the over-stressed Citadel shuttle worker. And all mixed together with the smoke and choke of too many folks, in too little space, driving too many wagons. Representatives from every corner of Widergard: men and elves, dwarfs and gnomes, goblins and trolls, most minding their own business, some minding other people's business and no small number looking for business.

The night-time Citadel clocking on for the summer evening shift.

The roads to Old Town were as packed as I had ever seen them. Citadel guards, in warm-weather outfits of short-sleeved tabards and dark visors, were directing traffic with the air of tired magicians, to the music of a thousand over-worked steam-powered fans. I was making far better time than anyone stuck in a wagon, boilers and tempers over-heating. Old Town is not actually any older than anywhere else in the Citadel, the Hill being built all of a period, as it were. It just so happens that the High Council thinks it's a good idea to corral all the visitors and tourists into one particular area – makes it easier to get at their bulging purses. I pushed my way through rubber dragons, battle-axe keyrings and various other tasteful knick-knacks until I ended up by a small pavement inn at the corner of Twelve Trees and Mine, and it was there that I ran into the march and the reason why traffic was backing up.

Demonstrations were the big thing of that year's election campaigns. All the major parties had been out and about, airing their views and bad haircuts. Near riots had accompanied some of the more volatile pairings as rival supporters met and clashed. This march, however, was not of that ilk. This was forged from a different metal. In front of me a new force in Citadel politics was flexing its muscles.

My progress interrupted, I got myself a glass of something dark and sticky from a roadside vendor and sat and watched the free entertainment. I could see the placards above the heads of the watching crowd, carried by members of the newly convened Citadel Alliance Party. The placards were all very neatly written, on good parchment, stretched over well-constructed frames. The message seemed to be one of co-operation and 'getting folk together'. The majority of demonstrators, though, were men, although the leaders seemed to be Lower Elves. They're the elves that don't get invited to all the very best elf parties, but they still look down their collective perfectly shaped noses at the rest of the population. There were even a few dwarf brothers who should have known better. They all walked neatly by, two by two. Everyone wore the shirts of the party's sky blue, all neatly ironed. There was no ranting and no raving and indeed an unnatural silence fell upon the normally vocal bystanders as they passed. Nobody shouted, nobody even heckled from the sidelines. The few children that cried out of turn were hushed by their mothers. The whole march passed by without an incident. This worried me more than anything else. I immediately finished my drink, and left, feeling distinctly uneasy.

The crowds began to thin and I soon found myself walking through the Wizard's Gate, one of the huge sets of ironclad doors built into the walls that separate the different levels of the Hill. The imposing blackness of the gate and the impressive strength of the cladding had been somewhat spoilt by a scribbled legend in faded white paint informing us that 'Bertold loves Lucer.' I hoped that Bertold's intrepidity had been rewarded all those years ago and that Lucer had succumbed to his charms (and climbing ability) and they were now happily living in domestic bliss in the Bay suburbs. Well, that's assuming the wizards had not found him first and made something far less appealing out of him, of course.

I started humming the children's skipping song:

Walls of the Citadel,
One to Ten,
One for the elves,
And one for the men,
One for the wizards,
And the Keepers of the Trees,
One for the dwarfs,
But none for the pixies.
Round and round the Hillside,
Round and round the town,
Keep them hid,
Or the walls come down.

It was a surprisingly subtle little rhyme piece, with a built-in offbeat on the pixie line deliberately contrived to lure the unwary into the twirling rope. I had never worked out why, when there were only five walls to the Citadel, the children's song said one to ten. Still, you're on a hiding to nothing if you go looking for the truth in children's nursery rhymes.

My rooms are in a converted armoury on lower fifth; not particularly fashionable, not particularly smart, but very secure. In my line of business you do not wish to encourage home visits.

I waved at Bes, the watchman at the desk, and made for the lift; the effect of the Tree Friend's gravy was wearing off. My quarters are at the very top of the building, not handy if the lift is out of action, but giving excellent access to outside space.

Being an ex-armoury, at least the place is basically of extremely sound construction with good thick walls and strong foundations. Taken together with my very own battlements, it has a lot going for it. The front door I had added myself. It is made from ironwood with riveted brass banding, to discourage those more adventurous callers. The locks are of the best dwarf construction and guaranteed to three thousand feet. Still, as I pushed the great door back, I promised myself one day I really would do something to make the place just a little more homely.

I moved one pile of papers and introduced it to another matching pile, and carried a tray of dead dishes through to the scullery. With trepidation I approached the cold box. It didn't look great, but at least it contained something that was green in all the right places and still had enough nutrients for a body that had, after all, developed in a world largely lacking in sunlight. Sometimes this works to a dwarf's advantage – we synthesise many of our own vital factors, which means we only have to drink fruit juice through choice (usually fermented and then distilled) and as an added bonus we don't get many colds. Our make-up also means that we grow body hair at a rate that requires we shave at least twice a day, especially when in female company, lest you risk complaint. Furthermore, we need to take in a lot of iron. This explains some of the more, well, bloodthirsty stories you may have heard about our eating and drinking habits.

Many are exaggerated, of course. Many are not.

There was also a large stash of coffee beans in the cold box, which was a relief. Coffee has an important, if not pivotal role in Nicely Strongoak's life. In the morning I drink it white and frothy and in copious quantities. At midwatch in the day I tend to take it filtered. As the shadows lengthen I take it black and percolated. Come night it's as dark as the pit, measured in thimbles and would stir a petrified troll. I made a double and poured out an apple brandy to accompany it.

A bit of a breeze had now picked up and, despite recent temperature extremes, out on the battlements it was about as perfect as it can be without being taxed. Feet up on a crenel, I took in the view. I watched the molten silver of the river Everflow run across the plain of Rhavona and join with the opal iridescence of the bay. Small boats struggled upstream against the tide, engines chugging and smoking, their paddle wheels making spray that caught the sun, throwing up prismatic jewels. I lit a pipe and sat musing for a while about the missing boy and his most attractive lady and must have nodded off … wakening to find a night sky and a sudden chill in the air.

I went inside to put my head down and do the sleep business properly.

3

ON THE BEACH

I collected my wagon early the next day. It's a racing-green Dragonette '57 convertible; the last model with the little wings and the air-trimmed front end. Daddy's pride and joy, with marble interior finish and leather ragtop. It did my heart good just to touch her. Sceech the grease goblin had done a good job on the shoes, and I took off in a reasonable frame of mind. I had slept pretty well and though I didn't feel like a million crowns, well at least I didn't look like buried treasure. Silver linings and all that.

The morning rush had yet to start and I made it round the Hill in record time. I decided to cross the Everflow at the Troll's End Bridge. Normally I would avoid this like the plague, as it is one of the worst bottlenecks in the Greater Citadel, but as the roads were still reasonably clear I gave it a go.

The suspension bridge looked like a web spun by one of the monster spiders of legend, dew still shining on the mighty struts and wires. Traffic was building up in the other lane as I drove across the bridge that spanned the Everflow Chasm. Down below I could see the rapids where the Great Troll was said to have met his end and the massive rocks that legend dictates are his remains. As tradition requires, I spat for good luck and sailed right through without any problems. Maybe tradition has something going for it after all.

It's always a relief to be out of the summer Citadel and the air tastes better with the ragtop down. There are still small pockets of greenery to be found and these get more common the farther from the Hill that you travel. By the time you hit the Gnada Peninsula things look pretty good. Of course, it is no coincidence that the holiday homes of the White and Wise are all found in this region; the White and Wise, and the Surf Elves too, of course. I spotted an attractive-looking provisioner's called *Dolores* and, hungry after having missed a meal, stopped off for some warm breakbread to go with the flask of coffee I had safely stowed in the glove compartment. There was a black Battledore '83 pulled up in the wagon-park gently letting off some steam. That was a serious beast: expensive, big, and fast enough to give my Dragonette serious competition on the straight. I'd take him on the corners, though.

I opened the door and the smell of fresh baking hit my nose in a tidal wave of scrummy. I breathed deeply and tried not to dribble – never an attractive feature in a dwarf, dribbling, even without a full beard. There was only one other customer ahead of me – a man – and, well, he did not look like the sort to be out for an early morning drive in his Battledore '83. I nodded politely and he ignored me impolitely, refusing to make eye contact. Force of habit made me give him the once over, but between the pulled-down brim of his hat and the turned-up collar of his coat there wasn't much to see. His posture spoke volumes, however. I don't think I'd ever seen anybody stand that straight without artificial aids. He certainly looked like an ex-foot soldier to me. Throwing some coin onto the counter, he snatched up his purchases and left, not waiting for change. My eyes followed him as he exited, jumped into the Batttledore, gave it some steam, and headed back to the Citadel with an unpleasant squeal of tyres.

The girl serving, dressed in a fetching white apron, smiled at me and shook her head. 'Not a local,' she explained.

'As long as he's left plenty of that wonderful-smelling breakbread!'

She assured me there was plenty and I stocked up for the duration. 'You can't be over-provided for', has become my motto. I paid up and, resisting the urge to nibble, got back into my wagon and carried on to the north coast.

The sun was well risen over the hills before I heard the sound of breaking surf. I drove on down a well-maintained side road and soon got my first view of the sea. This was not the South Side with its oil refineries and petrochemical works that make the Bay area unfit for bathing; this was the real thing.

Large rollers tumbled in from the Big Sea onto a shoreline that mixed large sandy beaches and small hidden coves in the most tasteful manner. Wooded slopes ran down to the shoreline from the summer homes of the councillors and other High Folk. No tent sites or holiday camps here or any of those nasty work-related activities.

Well, at least it keeps the sea clean.

I followed the directions that Liza Springwater had given to me, found the beach road and drove down it carefully, mindful of the Dragonette's springs. I spotted some buildings with a flagpole and pulled up nearby. It was busy on the strand, even at this early hour. Plenty of boards and riders were out taking advantage of the morning swell – both elves and men, and their ladies.

I carried on driving to a less-crowded part of the beach, where one lone surfer, garbed in a canary-yellow wetsuit with a matching surf cap, was slowly paddling out past the breakwater. I parked and walked across the sand dunes. At this moment I did not want an audience; even in my light-weight linen attire I felt conspicuously overdressed.

I sat on some driftwood and admired the surfer's dexterity. A slim figure, obviously elf, with that deceptively tough, almost impossibly willowy frame that gives them a grace many other folk envy. I'm no elf expert but from the height, around the size of a tall man, I'd guess the surfer was a Higher Elf: the Lords and Ladies of the Hidden Lands. The Lower Elves tend to fetch up a smidgen shorter, are more compact, and have much more humble origins. I've heard it said that somewhere there are Middle Elves, but they're far too embarrassed about the name and don't get out much.

The elf was dancing the full length of the board, poised between the wind and water. Despite myself, I couldn't help but be impressed. If only the whole exercise wasn't so, well, wet.

Suddenly the surfer was knocked off the board and didn't appear to get up. I ran across the wet sand to the water's edge, though I wasn't sure what help I could offer. Fortunately I was saved any difficult decision. A yellow surf-capped head bobbed up close to the shore, further down the beach, and swam the last few strokes in to retrieve the errant board. I guess those light elfin bones make drowning almost an impossibility.

'You all right?' I hollered across the roar of the surf. I got a nod as the wetsuited figure picked up the board and headed in my direction.

'Mind if I have a word, son?'

'I can think of a few, Master Dwarf,' replied the young elfess, taking off her surf-cap and letting her long blonde hair flow before I had a chance to correct my error.

'Sorry, lady – my pardon. It's a bit difficult to make such distinctions with all the surf gear on.'

This got me a stony glance from those fierce sky-blue elfin eyes. Clearly I hadn't really clocked the way she filled the suit either. I went on anyway.

'I was just hoping that you could help me with an enquiry concerning Surf Elves.'

The sky-blue eyes turned stormy and the knuckles of the hand holding the board turned white. It appeared I had compounded my error. This was not going well.

'If you are another quill-stiff from the press, then the words you are looking for have existed in the common tongue since the earliest ages.'

I took a deep ozone-filled breath and sighed. 'Look, lady, I'm no scribe, just a dwarf detective with a job to do, and a bruise on his head bigger than a troll's wart. Now, I have said my apologies, and if you accept them gracefully, I have fresh breakbread and a flask of coffee in the wagon. So if you have not yet broken your fast, I would be delighted if you could join me.'

It was quite a speech for that time of the day, and the young elfess looked at me closely before her face broke into a grin. 'All right, Master Dwarf Detective, glad to see you are not too big to admit your shortcomings.'

I let her have that one, it seemed only fair, and matched her grin. Together we walked back up the beach to where my Dragonette was perched like some strange mutated dune insect. I laid out a rug and she threw herself down on it.

'So, apology accepted, Master Detective. I admit these wetsuits are not exactly flattering to the figure.' She unzipped the front of her suit, and released the more than adequate form constrained within. I was glad she had on another bathing top underneath. Axes and blood, of course I wasn't really.

'I am rather hungry,' she continued, shaking loose her hair and sending my blood singing. 'So I will join you and your provisions. However, I am not sure whether I can be of any assistance. Contrary to appearances, I am not a subscriber to the Surf Elf philosophy.'

I mused over that one while I fetched the provisions from the wagon's trunk. We set up breakfast on her board and for a while just munched on the light, fluffy rolls and sipped coffee, whilst we took in the ocean. I had to admit it was some sight. Sky and sea of a blue they just cannot quite replicate in house-paint colours, sand like dusted gold and gulls soaring like spirits freed from the Necromancer's Pits, crying out thanks for their liberation ... or, more precisely, just their desire for some breakfast.

'Good breakbread,' I said finally.

'Yes, from *Delores*, if I'm not mistaken. Best breakbread on the Peninsula.'

'Know the region well, do you?'

She wasn't fooled by my mock innocence. 'Back to work already, Master Detective?' she said, her eyes still fixed on the ocean. 'Don't I even get a chance to finish breakfast?'

I looked her over surreptitiously. My work did not lead

me to mix with elf folk much. My clientele was mainly at the opposite end of the social spectrum. One thing I had noticed, though, was how different, and yet how very much the same they were – especially the ladies. Some had curves that would make a tree blush, but others, well, here was this tall, fair, blue-eyed lass with pipe-cleaner arms, every bit as elf-like as some twilight enchantress. Don't get me wrong, I've not got a fey fixation like so many of my kin, but neither am I made of stone. I've read all about those tricky scents they give off, but we're all mortal. Or, rather, only some of us are, I reminded myself.

'Right, sorry, your ladyship.' I knocked the ball back into her half. 'Let's just finish breakfast, then I'll go drown myself. It should be easy. We dwarfs swim almost as well as some elves surf.'

'That last wave was just bad fortune,' she cried, defensively. 'If I had not been distracted by the sight of an overdressed dwarf, in a cheap linen suit, walking down the sands, I would never have lost my balance.'

'Now that I object to,' I said, butting in. 'This suit is by Gaspar Halftoken, and was hand-cut by at least a dozen gnomes!'

She gave me the full-beam elf smile for the first time, and I felt something go fluttery inside. 'Gaspar Halftoken! In that case, Master Dwarf, I am very sorry. It is a fine suit.'

'And the name is Nicely,' I said, handing her a card, 'Nicely Strongoak.' She took the card and examined it closely. Satisfied, she replied:

'Well, I am Thelen, and I will answer your questions if you answer me one first.'

'Fire away,' I said.

'Who are you working for?'

'A young lady who has lost a boyfriend; I thought at first he had just ditched her, but now I am not so sure.'

She picked up a handful of sand and let it slip through her long graceful fingers. 'This boyfriend, not Perry Goodfellow by any chance?'

'The same. Did you know him?'

'By sight and reputation. One of the best surfers around – had to be to win the Gnada Trophy.'

'So it's that prestigious?'

'Sure.' She shrugged. 'Mind you, not everyone feels the need to enter competitions.'

'Like you?'

She regarded me solemnly. 'I know you have never surfed, Master Strongoak, so it is difficult to explain. Out there it's just you and the big blue ocean. Total communion, total involvement. When I am on the board I feel free, like I imagine they felt in our ancestors' times, when the world was still wide and the sky unbounded. That's what it's about, not trinkets.'

'But Perry thought differently?'

'I suppose he thought he had something to prove. He was very aware of the gulf that many say exists between the elves and the men of the Citadel.'

'Go tell it to the gnomes, lady.'

'Sure, but gnomes do not go surfing.'

'Did anyone bother to invite them?'

'Yes, an interesting point. That would really upset Highbury. Gnomes on his precious beach.'

'And who is this Highbury?'

'He is the self-appointed leader of the Surf Elves faction.'

'Faction? I thought the Surf Elves were really just something invented by the tabard-shirt manufacturers.'

Thelen began picking up small pebbles and throwing them at a piece of driftwood, punctuating her speech with each direct hit. 'Oh no, Master Dwarf, it's about more than T-shirts. I would not grace it with the name of philosophy, let us just call it an attitude. An attitude of elfin elitism calculated to annoy most right-thinking members of the community.'

'And it annoyed Perry?'

'I am not really sure; as I said, I did not actually know him well. When he came to the Gnada and started surfing, I think at first perhaps he was flattered by the attention of the elves. It was obvious that he was a natural on the board. Later, when he started getting rather too accomplished for the likes of Highbury and his friends, he may have felt their displeasure.'

'Would it have been enough for him to have quit the beach and run out on Liza, perhaps to prove himself elsewhere?'

'See this board, Master Strongoak,' she said, knocking our breakfast table and appearing to change the subject. 'It is made of myrtle, a superb wood. It is wonderfully light, but extremely hard. It can be worked, but only by a craftsman, and in consequence it is very expensive and only the elves can afford them. Perry Goodfellow might have done a lot of things for one of these, but he would not have left his lady for a goldmine full of them. It was just not in his nature. And remember, he wasn't the only one with something to prove.'

'What, Highbury and the Surf Elves?'

'Yes. The relationship soured on both sides. He had, after all, won the Gnada Trophy, and was, incidentally, the first man to do so. The Surf Elves like having followers, but they are not so keen on being on equal terms with mortals. And Highbury, well, let us say he has ambitions which encompass more than simply the sporting arena.'

'You sound as if you do not altogether approve?'

She scored another direct hit on the driftwood. 'No, I do not approve. I do not like elites, elfin or any other variety. The Surf Elves strut around with their air of superiority, and their silly blue shirts and badges, as if the whole of Widergard was arranged for their convenience. It annoys me considerably, as well as giving the rest of us a bad name. We are all in this place together, there's no Never-Neverland left over the Big Sea, and so we had all better get on with each other. The last thing we need is a group of blue-eyed, blond egoists running around, causing racial tension and getting up people's noses.'

I had to agree with her. I would feel the same if it was young dwarfs. Mind you, half the population of the Citadel don't want to look like young dwarfs, but that's their problem.

'But this Highbury body, elf or not, he is, after all, just some kind of dune drifter, isn't he? I don't know what these ambitions of his may be, but at best he is just a half-baked athlete.'

'Do not underestimate the appeal of the Surf Elves,' Thelen responded. 'These half-baked athletes, as you call them, have a considerable following among the younger men and women of the Citadel. They are, after all, the modern heroes in a world where heroes are thin on the ground, and have been since the times that men dismiss as myths.'

I thought about this for a bit. The elfess had a point. Since the voting age had been lowered, the Citadel youth seemed to have had an inordinate effect upon the proceedings of the place.

'How did this Highbury take Perry's victory?'

She laughed beautifully. It made me want to run off and

become a comedian, just to perform for her and hear it every day.

'Lord Highbury Evergleaming was absolutely furious. He had won the Gnada Trophy the previous three years and was beginning to consider it his own property. He went into the Surf Elves' beach dwelling and did not come out for a week. It was wonderful.'

Her laughter was replaced by a look of concern. 'And now Perry is missing and presumably the Gnada trophy with him?'

I nodded to her: 'It seems that way.'

'I know which one will concern the Surf Elves the most! Highbury wants that cup back on his trophy shelf. '

Thelen got up with an ease I wish I could match. She turned to face me. 'So, Master Detective, as you can probably gather, I will be delighted to help you in any way I can, especially if it adds to Highbury's discomfiture.'

I got out one of the little leather-bound notebooks I use for this sort of business – a hangover from my days in the Citadel Guards, but good practices are best not forgotten. I soon had all the background on the Surf Elves that I needed. I left the lady with my business card and drove down the beach. She offered to teach me to surf. I said I would keep that in the cold store.

4

SURF ELVES

Thelen had directed me to the right part of the beach; the Surf Elves' headquarters were the collection of ranch-style huts built into the dunes I had previously spotted. The surrounding sand was covered with dumbbells and weights and everything else for the body beautiful. The Surf Elves were easy to spot with their pointy ears, perfect noses, clean, lean, hairless limbs and cheekbones higher than a juiced-up eagle. Some still wore cropped blue beach jackets that sported a crossed leaf-and-sword motif. This was also the design flying on the flag above the huts. I had seen it sprayed up round the Hill all summer without taking in what it stood for.

I didn't like it.

The device had a nasty military feel to it. From what I could gather there wasn't much about these guys to like at all. My opinion was not about to change.

I drove the Dragonette onto the Strand, chancing any injurious effects of salt spray on the bodywork. I took out a spyglass from the glove compartment and scanned the area. It was interesting to see Higher and Lower Elves up close together. The differences, especially in height, were obvious, but they still shared that undeniable quality of elvishness.

There were a lot of boards out on the water and the riders all looked good at what they did. I tried to identify young Lord Highbury. It wasn't difficult. I spotted him as soon as he came out of the surf. Who else would expect or court a round of applause? The admirers were elves with some of the Citadel's better-looking men and (mostly) women. Even from that distance he had that elf glow, like gold straight from the forge, as if lit by internal fires. Overrated, if you ask me.

I got out of my wagon and propped myself up on the hood of the Dragonette. I had managed to attract quite a crowd myself until Lord Highbury realised he was in danger of losing his audience and sauntered off in my direction. Nobody had yet felt inclined to break the silence and I wasn't exactly feeling verbose myself, so I just continued to help myself to some of those negative ions I've read so much about – turns out, they're overrated too.

Highbury approached. 'Good morrow, Master Dwarf. It is many years since one of your race was seen on the Gnada Peninsula.' The guy spoke like someone from a badly scripted rolling picture.

'I like to stay open to new experiences,' I replied.

Highbury shook himself lightly and water fell off as if by magic. I wished I could do that. However, dwarf body hair has an absorbency index roughly equivalent to that of blotting paper. One smaller elf, who had been standing by with a towel, looked so crestfallen I thought he was going to burst into tears. As if sensing his distress, Highbury took the towel and made the young elf's day, if not his life. He only wiped his hands though; a gesture I felt was solely for my benefit.

Highbury continued: 'Your race is not, however, renowned for its love of water.' This race business was beginning to get to me already.

He handed back the towel as if bestowing some kind of gift, then ran a hand through his expertly mussed blond locks. I thought the smaller elf was going to swoon. Taking my time, I got off the Dragonette and examined it for imaginary marks, before I turned to face the elf lord again. 'Well, you know what these legends are like. You should not believe anything unless it's carved in stone.'

'Oh,' said Highbury, his blue eyes twinkling. 'Perhaps you have come to surf, then.' His fan club appreciated this example of their leader's wit. Another round of applause. I mean … please!

I scratched my stubble thoughtfully. 'No, perhaps I'll just have a swim.' This soon shut the lords and ladies up. Highbury was equal to it, though. 'A swim!' he said. 'Truly, wonders do still walk Widergard – a swimming dwarf!' He winked at his audience, something elves actually find very hard to do. 'Perhaps you would care for a little race, then?'

What I did not care for was where he put his emphasis, and I thought of a place where I would like to put his board. The renewed applause that greeted his suggestion soon stopped, though, when I accepted his challenge. Highbury's blue eyes took on a steely look. 'Then how about a wager, oh Son of Stone, on this swim?'

'Why not? As long as I choose the distance.'

'Even better, I will give you fifty strides' start to the water, but be careful, as the beach drops away very suddenly.'

'Oh', I said patronisingly, 'I'll be very careful.'

'Then what shall we wager?' He was playing to the crowd

again. 'I think if I win I would rather like your fine suit.' And the crowd was loving it. I, however, was playing for slightly different stakes. 'If I win, I think I will settle for the answers to a few simple questions.'

This strategy caught his attention and he looked at me strangely. 'Agreed. Perhaps, then, we should find you some beachwear.'

'It's all right,' I said, walking over to the dunes. 'I don't think you boys would have anything my size.'

Cheap shot, but frankly, what had they done to deserve better?

I carefully folded up my beloved Gaspar Halftoken hand-cut linen suit and left it by the weights. I was wearing boxers, the big baggy kind with pockets. They had a rather natty little green-dragon design. As I strolled back I dared anyone to laugh; mercifully no one did.

'Now, Master Dwarf,' said Highbury. 'What about a destination? We usually go around the yellow buoy, but the choice is yours.'

'How about here,' I said, taking the small hand weight I had picked up while disrobing, and throwing it like a disc over the crashing surf. It skipped like a stone for a bit and then sank. Not a bad throw; not as good as the throw which won me the Darrow Games, and is still I believe in the record books, but good enough.

'And just to make sure we do not have any cheating, we will make it the first one to bring back that weight. Now,' I continued, before anyone could raise a complaint, 'I will take that fifty strides you so sportingly offered.'

He was a trier; I'll give him that. Even before I was over the shock of the cold water he was past me. A wonderfully relaxed crawl, grabbing handfuls of water with no apparent effort. I was stuck with the rather ineffectual breaststroke I had been forced to learn when on Bay Patrol with the Citadel Guards. Mandatory, I'm now glad to say.

Highbury must have attempted to reach bottom at least a dozen times before I even made it to the spot where the weight went down. I saw his blond head bobbing up and down like a frenzied fisherman's float. Such a shame; those wonderful elfin bones that make them so light and nimble, and do such wonders for the legs and cheekbones, do also make them so incredibly buoyant. Pity, really. We dwarfs, on the other hand, tend to sink like bricks. Add to that lungs like a blacksmith's bellows and night vision that would shame a cat – well, it was so easy I didn't even have to use the spare weight I had hidden in my shorts' pocket – just in case.

By the time we both got back to the beach, Highbury's blue eyes were bulging from exertion and his style was a bit more ragged. I had to help him out past the tide mark and he lay there panting.

'Now, elf,' I said, brandishing the weight for all to see. 'I think you owe me a few answers.' Still gasping for breath, he nodded his head. So, I said: 'What can you tell me about Perry Goodfellow?'

'Why?' he managed.

'Just answer the question.'

'A young man of dubious honour and undistinguished parentage, who worked for a living in an inn somewhere in the Citadel.'

'And an excellent surfer, so I hear.' When that did not elicit a response I continued: 'But why do you question his honour?'

'I heard he additionally moonlighted as a runner for some

dubious industrialist. From what I gather, he left there under somewhat clouded circumstances.'

'Meaning what, exactly?'

'Meaning, I do not make it a habit to listen to the gossip of mortals.' He had managed to expel most of what he had swallowed from the Gnada and was re-emerging, cocksure once more. 'I think that is about your limit on the questions, Master Dwarf.'

'Just one more, Goldy. Can you tell me where Perry Goodfellow is now?'

I thought I saw a trace of relief pass over his face, a small cloud passing over his sunny personality. I sucked on my teeth. I know elves are not supposed to be able to lie – 'live elves don't lie', as the saying goes – but there is more than one way of not telling the truth, and I didn't trust this guy further than I could throw a troll – four strides, I know, I've tried it. He fixed me with calm blue eyes. 'No, Master Dwarf, I do not know where Perry Goodfellow is.'

That seemed to be as reasonable a time to leave as any. I went back up the beach to collect my clothes. Nobody was there to offer me a towel, so I took one anyway, from the little elf who had been so obliging to Highbury. He was staring at his pole-axed hero, disbelief written large all over his face. I tried to offer a conciliatory smile, but nothing was going to mend that particular broken heart.

Dusting the beach from between my pinkies, I got back into my wagon. I checked the reflection in the vanity mirror: hey, looking even better for a touch of those ultra-violet rays, Nicely, but still, I left the Gnada with the nagging feeling that I had missed something very important.

5

MRS HARDWOOD

It was well past midwatch when I made it back to the Two Fingers. The bright, sunny Gnada morning had turned into sweaty, sullen Citadel afternoon. The roads were choked with steaming wagons and their steaming drivers. I was not in the best of tempers, still plagued by a nagging doubt, and hardly ready for the surprise I found waiting for me on my return.

I had already let myself into the office from the corridor before I noticed someone in the reception room. Opening the adjoining door to invite them in, it being the help's day off, I found myself taking a breath even deeper than Highbury had mustered out on the beach. If you were to think I was unused to seeing stunning women, dripping jewels and wearing the latest in high fashion, waiting in one of my rooms, well, you would be right. She unwrapped legs longer than my treasure house deficit and stood up.

'You keep irregular hours, Detective Strongoak.'

'The sign on the door says "waiting", lady, but it ain't compulsory.'

'It does not seem likely to encourage custom.'

'Custom tends to find me, one way or another.'

'Are you going to at least invite me in?'

'Lady, the place is yours.' And it probably could be, with just one little stone from one perfectly manicured finger.

She strode across the room like an expensive racehorse. Her hair was as black as the deepest dwarf mine, and piled up high in a topknot, with some escaping down like a mane. I was willing to bet that pulling out just one pin from the complete, carefully contrived concoction would cause a whole cascade down her back. Thoughts like that can put a fire in your grate on long winter evenings.

'And how was the beach, Detective Strongoak?'

'The beach was just fine.'

'Is that why you brought so much of it back with you?'

I looked down at myself. Yes, she had a point. Offering her a seat, I got myself behind the business end of the desk and tried to instil the proceedings with just a little dignity.

'Look, lady, this is a lot of fun, and I'm sure we could keep it up all day, but how about you just tell me what the matter is and I'll tell you if I can help?'

She ignored the offer of the seat and decided to keep on prowling.

'But Detective Strongoak, I was so enjoying it, and I do tend to want more of what I enjoy.' Finally she parked a perfectly formed rear on my desk and leaned towards me. 'You do believe that, don't you, De-tec-tive?'

I must admit until she said it I did not know the word had so many syllables, but she pronounced each one perfectly and each one sounded like a sin. But she didn't know who she was dealing with; after all, I'd just had my Citadel Guards 100 strides swimming certificate updated.

'Lady, I'll be willing to believe that Princess Panaline and the Dwarf Brothers were just good friends, if you're footing the bill. Negotiations have yet to reach that point though, so how about I peel you off my lapels and put you into a seat?'

This I did with the maximum of grace and the minimum of bodily contact. She still seemed unwilling to get to the point. From her new vantage point she surveyed the rest of the room.

'You do not decorate your offices in the height of fashion, Detective Strongoak.'

Fashion was obviously something she knew all about. She was wearing a dark-blue dress that buttoned at the front like a man's double-breasted jacket. The effect was disorientating. Her long elegant hands held white pixie-lace gloves. She played with them, her only trace of nervousness.

'Discussing hem lines would also be fun, lady, but I have a living to make.'

'And what sort of living would that be?'

'It keeps the wolves from the tree and fills the occasional pipe.'

'Your manner is a trifle short, Sir,' she observed, putting her gloves upon my desk.

'I've heard them all before, lady. So come on, why don't you put your cards on the table as well as those gloves, which you can't quite stop yourself fiddling with?'

I am not quite sure why I was doing the tough-guy routine, except that maybe she was expecting it. Certainly I seemed to have passed some unseen test, because she finally got to what was on her mind.

'My name is Hardwood; you may have heard of my husband.'

The amount of emotion I revealed wouldn't have filled a pixie's purse. 'Yes, I've heard of him.'

Who hadn't? Hardwood was one of the wealthiest industrialists in the Citadel, a real financial wizard. He owned half the petrochemical plants that added so much to the Bay area – and the Bay itself. The word was that he bought Councillors and traded in Aldermen, being one himself.

'But then again, I've heard of Dofu the Dragon Herder.'

'I don't think Dofu the Dragon Herder ever owned the Hardwood emerald.'

'No, I don't believe he ever did.'

'Well I do, and it's gone missing.' She dropped her head, making her expression unreadable.

'Lady, if that means "stolen", then you should try the Citadel Guards. The Cits aren't quite the fools they are made out to be.' I got up out of my chair and walked round the desk. I slowly sat down on its edge in front of her.

'If "missing" means something else, then I think you probably want one of the big First-Level outfits, because this sounds out of my league. Why choose me? Apart from my big brown eyes, of course.'

Face still hidden, she said: 'I need someone who knows about gems. Who can recognise the real thing.' That sounded reasonable.

'And,' I added, lifting up her face to meet my own.

'And,' she said, as we matched lights, 'I need someone who can be discreet. I cannot risk a large company. As I said, the stone is only missing. It disappeared from my home and no one from outside could have stolen it. I just want it returned and I am willing to pay.'

'What makes you think that whoever "missed" this sparkler for you will want to part with it?'

'I just think they will; I think they will. With the right middle-man, or middle-dwarf.' Something in her expression

46

had gone overseas and she was as unreadable as the goblin alphabet. Decision time for dwarf detectives. I flipped a mental half-a-crown and it came up shields – all right, Nicely!

I got up off the desk and sat back on the hired help's side and opened a drawer. 'I'll get a contract drawn up.'

'Is that necessary?'

'Oh yes, I have tax returns to fill in so that I can give the Citadel authorities something to laugh about at Cit Hall. Also I'll need a list naming all your staff, plus any that have left in the last year, and their reasons for leaving.'

She said she would have it ready the next day, and if I wanted to come round to Hardwood House at cocktail time she would see that I received it. I promised to bring the contract round at the same time and told her, while she was at it, to lay on lots of those little cheesy biscuits. She said she preferred to lie on mattresses but was willing to try anything once. We left it at that: points even, Nicely to throw next.

6

TRUETOUCH

I probably should have enjoyed a quiet supper and gone directly to bed or maybe practised my paper-folding skills, but, still edgy from the beach, I put the wagon into first and headed on out. If a stone like the Hardwood Emerald goes missing, it has got to turn up somewhere. However, the kind of collector who dabbles in that sort of gem is not likely to advertise in *Stones and Stonemen*, but the merchandise still has to be moved. There are middlemen with minders, negotiators and evaluators. Leaks happen. When in doubt go and listen to the talk on the streets – but if there was any talk, it can't have been in the five languages I spoke. In the end, of course, I didn't have to go looking for trouble; it found me. I have a talent for trouble.

I was sitting in a skin joint named the *Gally-trot-a-Go-Go* keeping a pot of muddled ale company. The owner of this establishment dedicated to the disrobing arts, one Snatchpole Sidling, owed me a favour. I had sorted out some trouble for him, a little problem with under-age gnomes, fresh from Little Hundred, trying to improve their knowledge of other-race anatomy. I hoped that he might be able to clear the debt tonight. He always kept one finger on the Citadel's pulse, but it was not yet payback time. Snatchpole had not heard a single whisper from his various sources about the illicit marketing of an expensive piece of pre-loved treasure trove.

Some bored-looking 'Jane the Wad' was taking her clothes off on the platform, with all the enthusiasm of a patient about to undergo an unwanted internal examination from a physic with cold hands. She was billed as Elsie the Enchanted Elfess, but with a wig like that she was not fooling anyone. Certainly elfin clothing is not renowned for quite so many frills, garters, bows and inspection vents.

The music came courtesy of a three-piece band that probably thought they were a four-piece band, judging by all the gaps they were leaving in the tunes. Still, the drink was good, although I would not be willing to guess what the paying guests were consuming, and how much it was costing. I had seen and heard enough, and certainly drunk enough, when I noticed a halfway familiar elfin face enter, scanning the stalls. I was on my way out, but I put my hat down again. The young elf saw me at about the same time and came over in a hurry. He was wearing a lightweight linen summer coat with pearl buttons over a raw silk scoop-neck top and ankle-hugging five-pleat trousers. Very natty; he had certainly not been dressed by his mother! But the confidence displayed in his dress was not matched in his manner. The normal elfin air of self-possession had been replaced by something approaching nervousness.

'You are hard to track down, Master Dwarf.'

I finally placed him, one of the Surf Elves; Highbury's young towel guardian. 'I get around,' I ventured, not at all sure what he might want from me.

'Can we go somewhere to talk?' he continued, glancing around, fingers playing with loose change in his trouser pocket and his foot tapping impatiently; as worried as an elf is ever capable of getting. I looked around too; was there something else agitating him? Something other than Elsie the Enchanted Elfess, now down to her silks and satins?

'What's wrong, don't you like the surroundings? Snatchpole spent a small fortune getting exactly that right combination of glamour and grime.'

'It is not the sort of place an elf should really be seen in,' he said, obviously not fooled by Elsie the Enchanted Elfess's ample charms, finally being revealed in all their glory. I thought of mentioning this fine example of elf femininity, but my essential good nature got the better of me. After all, this could be the break I had been waiting for.

'I take it that this is more than a social call, elf?'

'Perhaps we can leave that conversation until later, somewhere else?'

I nodded and followed the young elf out, missing Elsie's finale and what in the business I believe is called a 'bowstring'. The things women will put on to attract a mate, when really just a smile is all they need to wear. Elsie certainly wasn't wearing one of those as she slipped behind the curtain.

At the door I threw a salute to Snatchpole and then together the elf and I went to collect my wagon. It was parked nearby and it was only a short walk. The elf seemed to relax as soon as we were out in the open air and when he saw my wagon he got positively animated.

'Dragonette '57? That's the last model they made with the wings and the air trimming, isn't it?'

I nodded an affirmative.

'They should never have gone over to foils, big mistake. Dragonettes were never the same after that.'

So, the elf knew his way round a wagon and also dressed with dash. I was beginning to warm to him, but would never put something like that in writing.

I opened the door for him and he ran one hand appreciatively over the milkwood trim with a contented sigh. Yes, definitively warming to him. We drove off together into the clammy, clinging, high-summer Citadel night.

Now he had started to talk it was hard to shut the elf up. After a few more comments on the current sorry state of wagon production and some observations on how badly traffic was handled in the Citadel, I got a detailed elf-centric analysis of the economic woes of Widergard in general, and then, finally, an introduction.

'My name is Truetouch.'

'Nicely Strongoak, but you probably caught that on the beach when you were with your Surf Elf buddies.'

'Yes, Strongoak – a good name.'

'Didn't elves ever consider that, maybe now, they should, just perhaps, consider investing in some last names as well?'

This earned me a somewhat restrained laugh.

'My dear, Detective Strongoak, it is the duty of an elf to give names to things, not to be named ourselves.'

I had to laugh. 'Hardly an attitude to endear yourselves to the postal service?'

'Perhaps not. But have you ever seen an elf post a letter?'

I tapped the steering wheel, more than slightly irritated. 'Well, didn't elves ever consider that, maybe now, they should, just perhaps, stop being such almighty, self-important, pains in the posterior?'

Truetouch didn't have an answer for this one. It shut him up for a while, though.

I had kept the ragtop up, as discretion seemed the better part of not attracting attention. It was still warm and the air that climbed into the half-opened windows from the narrow streets and back alleys spoke of the heat of spicy food, overworked machinery and sweating bodies. I followed the elf's directions and he navigated us by a tortuous route to the Fifth Level. Truetouch certainly knew his way around the Citadel and we passed some interesting places where one might while away the odd lifetime or two. That's one thing you can say about the Citadel: around every corner is a new way of endangering your health. I do not know if Truetouch thought we were being shadowed, but he had done a very good job of losing anyone who might have been trying to follow.

We finally pulled up at a place just outside the Fifth Level, some distance from my quarters in the armoury on the other side of the Citadel. It was an undistinguished building in an area I was not familiar with. I looked out of the driver's window; if this was the Inn Truetouch was recommending. I could not see the attraction of the establishment. There was no sign and no modern cold-light tubes. I suppose in its own way the building was actually quite remarkable, one of those rare places in the Citadel that looked as if history had passed it by. Solid stonework, in need of some mortar, and good ironwood shingles, all with no signs of the damage that combat and canon fire can impart. Nothing special had ever happened here, nobody important had been born here, no one important had died here either, and in a place like the Citadel, believe me, that is remarkable.

The elf stepped nimbly from my Dragonette, as they have a

tendency to do. He beckoned, but I paused before following.

'Is there a problem, Master Strongoak?'

'No, I always follow strange elves into places unknown where their disaffected brethren might be waiting to welcome me with a stout staff made from the wood they value so much.'

Truetouch seemed genuinely surprised by the comment. I know elves are supposed to have difficulty lying, but that is another part of their self-promotion I have trouble believing. That and the whole five-day sex business.

'Well, Truetouch, is it the sort of invitation you always accept?'

He thought a moment and a genuinely winning smile came to his lips. 'Master Detective, I have seen from your suits and hats that you are indeed an expert of matters sartorial. Do you really think that if I had intended you harm tonight I would have worn a linen summer coat with pearl buttons?'

'That,' I said, with a matching grin, 'was the best answer you could have given. Lead on!' No doubt about it, I was most definitely warming.

We went down some badly lit steps that had seen some traffic over the years. At the bottom there was a crude board with the legend *The Twilight Alehouse* written in chalk. The elf knocked twice on the door and we were let in by a greybeard who had seen it all before, and hadn't enjoyed it the first time.

Nobody looked up as we walked in, and nobody said anything as we sat down. The customers were a strange mix. The lighting was low enough for most men to be sent stumbling, and even my mine-adapted vision found it oppressive. Two Brothers got up as I entered and left without a sign – which was strange; obviously they were on some business which was not necessarily all 'above ground'. A couple of characters, boasting hairlines that had moved south to invade their eyebrows, looked like men from way out of town. They carried themselves with the swagger of pathfinders. A couple of others, pumping some goblin blood by their eyes and dentition, might be the local muscle. They were sharing a table with a straight-backed individual who could have given a pillar lessons in posture. Something about him was familiar but a large hood hid any features. I even thought I saw a couple more elves in one corner. No gnomes, but what's new?

The elf went to fetch the drinks. I studied him at the bar. He certainly looked like one of the Lower Elves; those left behind when the Higher Elves disappeared off in a sulk back to the Hidden Lands all those years ago. There was something a little different about him though, maybe the sense of humour. Elves are as renowned for their sense of humour as they are for their humility and big bushy beards. Truetouch returned with two full glasses and an extra bottle. My sort of round. He almost dropped the tray as he sat down. Nerves, surely not? Where was that famous elf composure now?

I knocked my wine back quickly. I'd drunk worse, but I can say that most places I go. Truetouch sat, toying awkwardly with his glass. At last he spoke. 'Master Strongoak, I saw the way you handled Highbury at the Gnada, and it was very impressive.' He gave that winning smile another airing. It suited him. 'You would not believe the uproar on the beach after you drove off.'

'Oh, I think I could! I've seen a five year old throw a tantrum before.'

'One might be half inclined to believe, Master Dwarf, that

you do not hold my brethren and myself in very high regard?'

'Not at all! Some of my best friends are elves ... oh no they're not.'

This got the winning smile a final outing before he grew serious again.

'So Master Detective Strongoak ... to the point ... I would like to hire you.'

'Suppose I'm not for hire.' This was a turn of events that obviously had not occurred to him.

'But you must be!' he blurted.

'No "must" about it, Truetouch,' I replied. 'I have two clients at this moment and I like to give customer satisfaction; unless you can give me a good reason why I should think otherwise.'

'I can pay you.'

'Generally a sound first move; however, in this case, not good enough.'

Truetouch finished his drink, and hurriedly poured another. That soon went the way of the first, and he collected another one to keep them both company. I followed on at a more sedate pace now.

'But I need ... I need protection,' he finally admitted.

'And whom might you need protection from?' Was there disharmony amongst the Surf Elves? Could he have seen something in connection with Perry, perhaps? This might be even better than a clue. This just might be a lead.

Truetouch drummed his fingers on the table and tried a change of tack. 'I could provide you with something, something of value, that I think you might find very interesting.'

It felt like he was playing me here, so I proceeded with some caution. '"Something of value"? That's a rather vague term, Truetouch – sort of politician's words. You running for office this year?'

Truetouch found this a pretty funny idea and it raised a snort of derision. 'That is a pretty spiteful thing to say to an elf that just bought you a drink.'

'You're right, I take it back, but the sentiment still remains.'

'Shall we say "material germane to your investigation" instead?' he continued.

'You can, Truetouch. Me, I don't use gold-coin words when I can be straight with a body.' I poured myself another large helping of gravy and soaked some of it up while the elf considered his options.

'Look,' I said finally, feigning disinterest, 'as the old Da use to say: if it's getting too hot, get off the dragon.' And, indeed, it was actually hot in the bar. We were both sweating like goblins. I glanced around. The place had pretty much emptied.

'Maybe I can help you take me seriously. Have you a quill?' I passed him my pen, wondering when everyone with blond hair and pointy ears would finally learn to speak the common tongue like the rest of us. He fished out a scrap of card from the inside pocket of his rather lovely linen coat. He scribbled something rapidly and passed it over to me. It was a picture giveaway from a pipeleaf packet, a horse of all things. On the script side, in one corner, he had written an outer Citadel number. 'Give me a blast on the horn at this number tomorrow at midwatch and I assure you that you will not be disappointed.'

'Why wait until tomorrow? What's the game, Truetouch?'

'The game is bigger than you can imagine, Master Detective. Much bigger! Tomorrow I will have something in my possession that I think you will be very pleased to see. It will more than recompense you for your services and should warrant a bonus too. Just as long as you can keep me safe!'

Truetouch was looking around him, his sky-blue eyes darting back and forth. The remaining customers were not paying us the slightest attention. I wondered who he was looking for: friend or foe? Beads of perspiration were gathering on his brow, like spray from the sea. He was not looking at all well. Mind you, I wasn't feeling too great either. Something was not as it should be.

I looked Truetouch in his clear elfin eyes. The eyes were big, blue and round. The biggest bluest eyes I had ever seen. They got bigger and rounder, as large and inviting as two swimming pools shimmering on a hot summer's day. It was so warm I almost felt like going for a dip. I was trying to remember why this might be a bad idea, but it was too late and I could already feel myself diving, down, down and down. The swimming-pool eyes opened even wider with surprise and slowly, slowly ... I went under.

7

WET WORK

I was drowning. I was seated behind the steering wheel of my wagon, seatbelt tied, and I was drowning. There was salt water in my mouth and I was sinking fast.

The plan would probably have worked with any other race, but there is not anything you can put in a dwarf's drink that he will not recover from after that initial splash of cold water. I grabbed a last lungful of air as the water reached the roof and the drowning-clock started running. I tried the door, but the weight of water was too much. Then a little voice from inside reminded me: I drove a convertible. The catch on the roof would not work, though, and even dwarf-muscled hands could not get the material to part.

I had one chance – if only they had left me my hand axe.

It proved easy to find. It was in the head of the young elf sitting next to me with a shooter in his hand. His lovely linen coat had not passed the evening intact after all. Truetouch had gone west in a big way. If I was not to join him I had to do something fast.

Removing my axe was not pleasant, and even my

capacious dwarf lungs were beginning to scream as I went to work on the roofing. The material now tore easily; mercifully I keep my axe sharp. Wielding it was a bit harder though, but I quickly made a hole just big enough to squeeze through. I slipped the axe strap over my hand, pocketed the shooter, and struck out for the city lights that were glimmering through the water above. I barely had the power to make it to the surface, but reserve tank banging on zero, I finally broke the surface and could put some puff back in the machine.

My beautiful Dragonette had been run straight off a quay-side and I was not that far from the shore. I would make it in one piece; if the various poisons that our industry pumps into the Bay did not get to me first. They had made a mistake there, whoever had sent us for this unwelcome dip. They should have just pushed the wagon off a cliff somewhere and let us both fry.

However, that maybe would not have fitted with the little picture that they were trying to paint. Instead, they tried to fit me too closely in the frame. They had tried to be too clever and when you try to be too clever ... you get unlucky. That was their first mistake; the second was making me angry. I'm not exactly saying we were kindred spirits, but there was something about Truetouch that I'd liked, something other than his taste in summer outfits. The elf had come to me for help. I had not actually struck the deal and now I never would, but there was an obligation there and dwarfs take their obligations very seriously. Somebody was going to find out just how seriously. The split skull of the helpless Truetouch was now Illustration Number One in my Big Book of Nightmares and it was going to take some work before I could rip the picture out and throw it away.

It was a long walk back to the armoury. I went by the back streets, and little-known staircases, as I could not afford to be seen. It gave me plenty of time to try to think, but powders and a dunking don't promote my best work. What did Truetouch know about Perry and the Surf Elves that could get him wraithed in such a spectacularly unpleasant manner? We had both been drinking the same wine, unless it was Truetouch who had slipped something in my glass and had subsequently been betrayed by whoever wanted me out of the way. It was possible, but was it likely? Who had been the target here and who was the innocent bystander? The questions rattled around my head but answers ... there were none.

I made it to the armoury unseen; the new doorman was fast asleep on the reception coach. Dawn was just sending its first outriders around the Hill walls, announcing it was going to be another hot one. By that time a combination of intensive seething and the still warm night air had dried me off completely so I would not be leaving any telltale pools. My damp suit would never be the same, though. Exhausted and still befuddled by the liquid macing, I slowly climbed up the back stairs and finally made it to my rooms. Letting myself in quietly, I found a hastily scribbled note that had been pushed under the door. Two words only: 'RING RALPH!'

I rang Ralph, but he was not at his desk. The desk duty officer asked if I wanted to leave a message. I hesitated; a message would get logged – did I want that? I decided it could do no harm, and so I told him that Nicely Strongoak had called and could he get back to me. I needed coffee so badly my taste buds were considering suing for abuse. I saw to the percolator and then went and stood under the

shower until I felt that my pores were free from the filth of
the Bay. I came round a fraction and had just slipped into a
robe when there was a knock on the door that immediately
spoke to me of the Citadel Guards. I opened up and there
stood Sergeant-at-Arms, Ralph Fieldfull.

'Little late for bathing, isn't it – personal hygiene problem?'
he remarked, and came on in uninvited, followed by an
impressively uniformed scout he offhandedly announced as
'Telfine'.

Not that Ralph needed any invitation. I had known
Ralph since our earliest undercover days in the Citadel
Intelligence Agency. After that he went public and entered
the Citadel Guards. I had tried it for a while, but then
entered the private sector. Ralph made it to Sergeant-at-
Arms in record time, but then got stuck. The rumour was
that he could not be entirely trusted – trusted to do what
the department dictated, rather than what the law required.
Me, I am still working the same streets, but at least I know
which side the bad guys are on – most of the time. The
young scout had a razor-shaven, flat-top 'yes-sire' haircut
and a manner that demanded a tickle with something sharp.
He was obviously well on his way up the soapy staircase
and keen to make an impression with the gold badges.
About as benign as a nettle poultice, he knew all the right
handshakes, went to the right parties and was not going
to get stuck at Sergeant.

'Maybe he's been for a dip in the Bay?' the scout said,
not as stupid as he looked.

'It's been a warm night,' I said, drying my plait and doing
my best to ignore the scout and concentrate on Ralph, to
attempt to gauge the wind direction, as it were. 'Looks like
he's been warned about our visit,' popped in the eager scout

again.

'Now who would want to do that and why?' I wondered aloud, following them into my rooms.

Ralph threw himself on my old settle. It groaned a little, unused to the extra weight. He carefully took off his cap and put it down next to him. Married life and three children had added the inches to his waist, but he still had the rugged features of an outdoors man. I sat on a bentwood armchair I had made myself during my recovery from the knifing that had left the scar that looked like the results of a botched second-rate kidney procedure. The scout just paced. He was good at pacing. He obviously equated pacing with good detective work. He would probably pace his way to the top-of-the-tree and then drop dead two days after retiring. His tombstone would read: Citadel Guard Commander Telfine. 'He came, he saw, he paced.' I tried not to stare at the bathroom door and the damp suit, with Ralph's note in the pocket, which lay behind it.

'Understand, you've been trying to reach me, Nicely.' Ralph took out his pipe and offered me his pouch, but my lungs still contained a bit too much of the Bay. I finished tying my plait.

'Sure, I called you on the old horn a couple of times, wanted to report my wagon missing.'

'What time would this be?'

'Can't say exactly. I was scouting various drinking holes last night, must have got in a shade after midwatch. I tried to sleep, tossed around for a while – hot and bothered – and then decided a shower and some coffee might help. When I got up, I glanced out of the window and noticed the wagon was missing. That's when I first tried to reach you. I tried again after my shower and when you still weren't there I left a message—'

'We weren't there,' the scout interrupted, 'because we were busy pulling your wagon out of the Bay!' He seemed to think this had earned him a point or two.

'Oh dear,' I said, concerned. 'Barrel-riders, I suppose, probably kids. I hope it's not in too bad a condition.'

'It's in better condition than the occupant!'

Ralph smoked his pipe. He smoked with a determined air, giving it his full concentration. It must have been taking all his attention, because in the meantime he was letting the new boy give me the whole story. But Ralph just sat there, impassively, while the scout made every mistake in the book. Maybe even funny handshakes were not going to make this man's career after all.

'Well, it is quite a difficult wagon to drive, the Dragonette,' I remarked, matter-of-factly. 'Very fast.'

'Fast, nothing!' The scout stopped and glowered down at me. 'This particular barrel-rider was the passenger and he did not get injured going into the Bay, not unless an axe fell onto his head from the vanity mirror! A dwarf axe, from the looks of it, rammed into an elf head.'

'And you have the axe?' I asked.

'No we don't, as you very well know, which is why you're still sitting there and not sucking in air in the Citadel slammer!'

Yes, this one was a real charmer. I caught Ralph's eye and lifted one brow. The scout was stomping around now like a hobgoblin on heat.

'Do you know what happens when an elf dies on the Hill, dwarf? What happens is we get more shit coming down on our heads than you would if you lived on a dragon's flight path. So don't you get cute with me! We've got a dead elf, and he was seen earlier leaving the *Gally-trot-a-Go-Go*, talking with a dwarf, so you look like a pretty good fix for his murder. What happened? You two argue, so you axed him, lost control of the wagon and ended up in the Bay? I think maybe we should just take a little look round here.' He headed for the bathroom and the incriminating suit with my wet axe on top.

'I think that is probably enough, Scout Telfine,' said Ralph, in the nick of time. 'You cannot go searching the rooms of law-abiding folk without a warrant, and as for the accusation, I think you will be very lucky if Master Strongoak here does not post charges,' Ralph added as he arose from the settle, intercepting Telfine and firmly shutting the bathroom door. 'He is a licensed detective and an ex-member of the Citadel Guards himself. I think the best thing we can do now, scout, is offer an apology and ask Master Strongoak, politely, if he would kindly give us details of his whereabouts last night, so we can do some checking before we go around wielding accusations like irate pikemen.'

The scout, stopped in his tracks, looked at us both. 'I get it, some kind of old boys' act, is it? I've been warned about you, Fieldfull. Well, I'm telling you, I wasn't just shat from no fellhound. I'm not going to end up stuck at Sergeant-at-arms!' With that he charged from my rooms, slamming the door behind him.

'Talented lad, should go far,' I remarked.

'Can't be far enough.' He sat and sucked at his pipe again. 'It's the quality of applicant we get these days. I blame the rolling pictures, they make the job look glamorous, instead of what it is: an exercise in hobyah herding.'

'Was ever that way.'

'All the same, Nicely, I am going to need that statement from you.'

'Sure,' I said. 'You check with Snatchpole, the keeper at the *Gally-trot-a-Go-Go*, he'll be able to tell you it wasn't me.' Ralph eyed me up slowly, picking up his cap from the sofa.

'I guess you know what you're doing, but Telfine, my much-esteemed junior colleague, is giving it straight from the bow. There is going to be some real heat about this from the elves, so you had better stick around the Hill for a while – and I could do with that statement sometime soon – very, very soon.'

'How soon?'

'Now soon.' He stood up and stretched, stifling a yawn.

'Sure thing,' I said. 'Now tomorrow soon enough?' I asked. He nodded and gave in to the yawn before getting up to leave.

'How's the wife and kids, Ralph?'

'Still need clothes and three square meals a day.'

He paused at the door and turned back round. 'Don't spit in the eye of any dragons, Nicely. Hear me? It's looking like it might be a bad time to be out there without a magic sword.' And then with a last wave, and a last yawn, he was gone.

I collected my over-stewed coffee and sat slowly back down, trying yet again to get my thoughts in order. Who exactly had axed Truetouch? Could it have been the hooded stranger and his goblin chums? Was Truetouch about to dish some dirt on Highbury or did he know the whereabouts of the missing Perry Goodfellow and the Gnada Trophy? Thelen had said Highbury wanted to regain the trophy pretty badly, but neither of these reasons seemed to warrant such a permanent sanction as Truetouch had received. And what light did any of this throw on Perry's disappearance? Plus, where is The Lost Gold of Galliposs, how deep is The Bottomless Pit of Doom and if you're being stalked by letters of the alphabet, do the 'i's follow you around the room? These and other such imponderables I would have to leave until the morning.

I managed to catch a few hours' sleep. I obviously needed them, because it was only after I rolled off the bed that I remembered the number written down for me by Truetouch. I rummaged through the damp pile of clothes – Gaspar was going to have a fit, he was very protective about his stitching – and finally I found the dead elf's pipeleaf card. As I feared, the ink had run and the number was all but illegible. I reached for the horn and tried a few combinations of digits that might once have been inscribed on the card, but with no joy.

The card itself, though, was interesting. I made a large coffee and examined it closer. It was indeed a pipeleaf card, the kind they give away free in a packet of pipeleaf and children then trade. It had obviously been carted around for some time, and had seen better days, even before its trip to the Bay. Number 16 in a series of Famous Track Winners. It portrayed a large black horse with a distinctive white mark on its muzzle. The legend read: 'Rosebud'. I suppose the mark could have passed for a rosebud, with a little imagination. I waved it dry and pocketed it thoughtfully. It was not much to go on, but, by Hograx the Uneven's hairy one, it was at least a clue and that's what us detectives love most of all. Give us a clue and we're as happy as a pixie in a poppy field. Unless, of course, it turns out to only be a bit of waste paper lurking in an elf's favourite coat.

My musings were rudely interrupted by a blast from the horn on the table behind my head. I picked it up: 'Nicely Strongoak, Shield-for-Hire,' I said, forgetting for the moment that I was not in the office.

'I saw your race with Highbury. It was wonderful. I cannot

remember the last time I laughed so much.'

Even in my sleep fug I recognised the voice at the end of the line as belonging to Thelen, the elfess from the beach. The thought of her laughing made my toes curl and the rest of me feel much better. 'Thanks,' I replied. 'How did Golden Boy seem to take it?'

'Livid, apoplectic. We have a very good word in elfish for it; unfortunately it does not translate.'

'Shame, maybe you could teach me it, in case I run into him again.'

'That's why I was calling. Did you get the information about Perry Goodfellow that you required?'

'Yes and no. Why?'

'I was wondering if you would relish the opportunity for another go at Lord Highbury?'

'Lady, I think you might have got the wrong idea about me. I'm always left foot forward when I dance.'

She laughed down the horn. 'I meant keep him on the boil, as it were. And no, I don't think I've got the wrong idea about you at all, Master Strongoak.'

'Fine – sounds interesting then. What did you have in mind?'

'A friend of mine has two tickets for a big Charity Ball; all the White and Wise will be there. Unfortunately my friend has been taken ill and I wondered how you would feel about accompanying me tonight. I have it on good authority that a certain other party will be there.'

'And me without a thing to wear.'

'I am sure you will think of something, Master Strongoak. You strike me as pretty resourceful.' She rang off before I had a chance to ask how she had found my home number. I am not listed in the books and I do not print it on my business cards. Interesting.

I finished my coffee and went to the closet to see what outfit I could get ruined today. I chose a suit in tan buck leather, so light you wouldn't raise a sweat at a troll's barbecue, but suitably restrained for a visit to Citadel Central Archive.

The Citadel Central Archive entrance is on the Second Level, but the vaults themselves, dark labyrinths, delve deep into the mountainside. When I first came to the Citadel I would visit the archive if I felt homesick. Leaning on the revolving door, I entered and passed through the entrance hall into what has become known as the Widergard Gallery. This large round room is the hub from which the various tunnels that contain the Citadel records radiate. The Widergard Gallery – now only containing the information stall – still has on its walls the famous friezes. The whole history of Widergard carved in stone. Or rather the official history, with dwarfs featuring far too infrequently for my liking and the pix never getting a look-in. I do not blame the mason, though, as it is expertly hewn. You've got to love rock!

Unlike many of the Citadel buildings, the lighting here is excellent. Sconces line the tunnels and downlights mark the intersections. The whole effect is subdued, but studious. I am sure they must have had dwarf help. I found a tome on famous gems. I looked up the Hardwood Emerald and was surprised at the paucity of the entry. The ring was very old, that much was certain; made by men in some time lost in antiquity, when all such rings were said to be 'magic'. The story went that it was given to the Ancestral Hardwood at the time of the Old Wars, for some forgotten act of valour. Strangely, there was not a single picture, so I went searching for the stacks concerned with the Great Citadel Families.

The entries chronicling the Hardwoods and the current

Alderman Hardwood were not that much more extensive than those concerning the emerald of that name. Much was alluded to but little documented. I was surprised at his range of interests, and not just in the business world – not simply a financial wizard, it appeared. More fingers in more pies than a blind man in a bakehouse.

I carried on searching and found an interesting article in a low-circulation, once well-respected, but now defunct periodical called *The Green Book*. The scribe, one Renfield Crew, implied that Hardwood was the backer of more than one slightly suspect political figure, with ideas not exactly contrary to the interests of big business. No big surprise there, but these politicos were also often a few gods short of the full wolf pack. Some of their views made the Great Despot of Dangenheim look like an expert in man management.

Interestingly, *The Green Book* had ceased printing the month after this article was written. Coincidence, or something else?

I scribbled the scribe's name down and kept searching.

There were no recent pictures of Mr Hardwood; he had made privacy into an art form. The one picture I could find, taken many, many years ago, showed a young man in sporting attire who obviously could not wait for middle age. From his youth Hardwood looked like he was longing for the air of wisdom and sagacity that only advancing years can give. The long Hardwood face was crying out for the first whiskers of a beard and the hairline was already waving its goodbyes. Even his knees looked uncomfortable without the comfort of a cover of good tailoring. How he had ended up with a woman as incendiary as his current wife was anybody's guess.

I put the book back on the shelf and made my way to a very

different section of the Archive. The stacks concerned with the bloodlines of racehorses outnumbered those concerned with the Citadel great families by about two to one. This just shows you where the Citadel's priorities lie. There were lots of fact and figures concerning every race Rosebud had ever run; where he was placed, and whether the ground was fast or slow, or green or brown, or up or down, but it was all in some kind of specialised sports code that might as well have been Higher Elvish as far as I was concerned. It was the horse on the card, though. I was expecting to find some pictures of Rosebud galloping though the winning tape, but although there were some nice stills of him looking suitably handsome, in a very horsey way, there was nothing in the way of action shots, a disappointment I would just somehow have to live with.

I next took a street-train from there to the lock-up built into the fifth ring where Sceech, my grease goblin, plied his trade. He sympathised with my circumstance and loaned me a replacement wagon, a big old Helmington. Who would have thought, before the anti-discrimination laws and positive employment, that the goblins would have become such a vital component in the industrial life of the Citadel? I suppose all those generations spent taking folk apart had given them a natural inclination for engineering. It was just conversion from the living to the mechanical that was required. Whatever, there was little doubt that they were the best mechanics around now, and no self-respecting wagon stop was without its grease goblin. Old habits die hard, though, and there were still enough goblins around who preferred their more traditional forms of employment – that is thuggery, butchery and larceny. Damn good mechanics, though.

8

ROSEBUD

It was after midwatch when I made it out to the stud farm where the racing pedigree scrolls had informed me that Rosebud was currently domiciled. The stud stable was just off the Great East Road – on the very outskirts of the Greater Citadel where the Plain of Rhavona begins and the land prices allow for such activities. I parked, walked up to the open gates, and rang the small bell. The afternoon was hot and very still. In the stable yards even the flies were taking a break. I wandered in and hollered, but all I disturbed was the dust. There were a lot of horses (not a big surprise), but this did not put me at ease, as I have never been big on equine recreations.

To be honest, I loathe horse racing and all that is associated with the track. I have found it attracts all the bad sorts of every folk and race. It brings out the worst in all of them – everyone looking for the lucky break that will change their lives. Spitting into a gold mine, I call it. If it really is the sport of kings, I say they should have got rid of it too, at the same time as they dumped all the crowns and coronets.

Not that I blame the horses themselves; they just make me nervous. Today they seemed to be immune to the post-midwatch heat and several were pacing restlessly in their stalls. Pride of place seemed to be given to a pure black stallion in a fancy stall covered with rosettes. I headed towards him, but he didn't exactly seem to welcome the company and reared up suddenly. I backed off quickly from the kicking animal and reversed into a mountain. At least it felt like a mountain; it certainly was the size of a mountain and the shadow it threw could have been cast from one. I turned and found, instead of the igneous stuff with the snow on top, simply the tallest man I have ever set my eyes upon. Axes and Blood, he was almost the size of one of the Tree Friends!

'Clubbin,' he said by way of introduction. 'And you are?'

'Strongoak, Nicely Strongoak.'

'And that is The Dark Lancer,' he said, in a low singsong voice, pointing with a staff the size of the trunk of an oak. 'He was the winner of every classic in the book and the sire of a half dozen other winners, and you had better have a good reason for being this close. A very good reason.'

He planted the staff down expressly into the ground.

'Because if you do not have a good reason, and if the boss finds out I let anyone in here, I'll be out on my arse before sundown. And as I am very fond of this job, I would not take that too well.' He now twirled the staff effortlessly in one hand, looking like a deregulated windmill.

'Just trying to find some help,' I said nervously, missing my axe. 'I rang the bell, and called out, hardly the act of a sneak thief.'

'That is true.' He relaxed slightly. 'So, here is the help.'

'I am actually interested in a horse named Rosebud.'

'Rosebud!' He sounded genuinely surprised. 'I had no idea that dwarfs took much interest in the track.'

'To be honest, all I know about horses could be engraved on a pixie's tiepin. It's for a client,' I explained, showing him my shield. This seemed to satisfy.

'Well, well, old Rosebud, eh? He is currently stabled out this way. Come have a look, he enjoys having visitors.'

He led on. I followed, failing to match his long stride and trying not to break into a run. The stud farm was large, and in an obviously less-favoured spot we found the horse with the distinctive marking, taking his ease in the shade. 'Go on then, introduce yourself,' said the tall stable man.

I edged forward nervously, not sure if this was some sort of test, and was delighted to find the horse soon nuzzling my outstretched hand, big brown eyes staring in mine. 'Hey, he likes me!'

'Yup, old Rosebud likes a bit of male company.'

'Not like The Dark Lancer?'

'The Lancer's a good sort in his own way, but there's a mare in heat around, one he's booked for later. Makes him kind of frisky.'

'I noticed!'

'And the mare's owners have put down a king's ransom in corn for the pleasure, which is why I am a bit cautious.'

'I guess Rosebud must pay his way, him being a big winner too.'

A low chuckle escaped from somewhere deep in the chest of the stable man and he passed me some sugar for the horse. 'Well you're right, he did win a few. I never saw him run myself, but I gather he was something in his day. He, though, was what we call a "chancer", a one-off, no pedigree. Not like The Lancer; he's from a line of winners as long as your arm, or my arm, even. This makes any investment in Rosebud's bloodline very chancey as well. Still, he should have been worth something for stud, if it wasn't for the other couple of problems.'

'Which were?'

'Well, for a first, in his last outing Rosebud is said to have run out of legs. Happens to horses sometimes, they just lose form. Big race too: The Helm Handicap, with him favourite. Quite a stink it made at the time, as I recall. A lot of money on him. I remember I lost a few crowns myself.'

'Hmm, and the other problem?'

Again the chuckle. 'You still not caught on? I just told you there's a mare in heat, and every other stallion in the stable is straining fit to burst, and here's Rosebud gently nuzzling sugar from your hand.' I began to feel some sympathy for the horse. 'You mean, he paid a little visit to the physic with the scissors when he was a lad.'

'Oh, no. The equipment's all there. It's more a matter of what he wants to do with it.'

Daylight, rather belatedly, began to break.

'He's just not one for the ladies.'

'Really!' I said, pulling back a bit too quick; the big horsey brown eyes looked down at me accusingly.

'Yup, happens with horses, same as most other flesh. Does not command the highest fee, though!' He strode forward and rubbed the horse's head and ears. 'He's a good lad, though, no trouble at all, but if your clients are interested in any little Rosebuds, I'm afraid they won't be blooming.'

Rather taken aback by this lesson in equine behaviour, I failed to notice the implication, so he put it to me straight. 'So, now that I've cleared that up, does your client have some other interest?' A question that deserved a straight answer;

shame I could not deliver. Delivering straight answers is not exactly a number-one detective priority, unless they're along the lines of 'Black, no sugar', 'A little to the right' and 'Just give me ten minutes.'

'It's rather involved, Clubbin. I'm looking for someone who may have owned the horse at one time, or been associated with him.'

We walked away from Rosebud's stall and headed to the gate. 'We've got the stud record, but really you want to talk to Leo.'

'Leo?'

'Leo Courtkey, he was always Rosebud's rider.'

'Is he around?'

'No, he left about the same time Rosebud went out to stud.' He let out one of his big chuckles at his choice of expression. 'I think his heart wasn't in it any more.'

'A man, was he?'

A snort of derision greeted this comment. 'Of course he was, all the best riders are. I was rather good myself as a lad, until I sprang up somewhat.' He stretched and took a piece of the sky.

'What about elves? I thought they were great riders?'

'Oh, sure, the elves are good. They do not take to using a saddle, though, always ride bareback. But, more to the point, they aren't happy dirtying their hands at the track. This, of course, makes them next to useless as far as the racing business is concerned.'

'Did Rosebud ever have an elfin owner?'

'No, like I said, they don't touch the track; that goes for owning race horses, as well as riding them.'

'Could we check the stud record, anyway?'

The big man shrugged; it was all the same to him. He led

75

me to a small office, full of pictures of winning horses and proud owners. The stable man pulled down the studbook. Rosebud's owner went by the name of Merrymead. The man said I had better get the address through the Owners' Stock Book, as it was not really done to give out that sort of information. He was able to get me an address and number for Leo Courtkey, him just being the hired help.

'I don't suppose you would have a picture of young Leo around here anywhere, would you?'

'I should imagine so.' He went back into the office. 'We always keep a scrapbook of photographs taken at race wins. He wasn't a bad rider, very good with the horses, although he was inclined to be light with the whip, which meant he didn't win as many races as he might. Him and Rosebud were quite a pairing, as I recall.'

Books and scrolls got moved around but with no success.

'That's typical. I swear I had it just the other day.' He even went round the pictures on the office walls, but again no luck. He gave me a description of the rider, though. A particularly lucid physical portrait: small and light. Well, that was clearly not going to help me find any buried treasure. A visit to Master Courtkey was going to be required. Maybe he could tell me why an elf was carrying round a pipeleaf card with Rosebud on the front.

I left the stable man my card, and he promised to do what he could to help. I thanked him and left the stable, waving a goodbye to Rosebud.

I drove slowly back to the Two Fingers, getting caught up in the traffic. The walls of the Citadel came into view. Walls around the city, which were really just rings. Rings around the Hill. Rings, rings, rings; rings within rings, and what about the Hardwood Emerald? The children's rhyme came back into my head:

Walls of the Citadel,
One to ten,
One for the elves,
And one for the men,
One for the wizards,
And the Keeper of the trees,
One for the dwarfs,
But none for the pixie.
Round and round the hillside,
Round and round the town,
Keep them hid,
Or the walls come down.

Even in New Iron Town we had played the game that went with this song. All the children in Widergard probably did, except maybe the gnomes, who did not seem to get a look-in, as per normal. A lot of nonsense it seemed at first, like most children's rhymes. Sure, there were walls around the Citadel, and they were more than just decorative. There were only five, though, not the ten that the song mentioned. I dragged my mind back to thoughts concerning rings, and magic rings came to mind. I suddenly felt the need to know a lot more about them. And when you wanted the low-down on that sort of jewellery, you needed a wizard, and fortunately I knew just where to find one. First, though, I needed to get hold of somebody even more important than a wizard: my tailor.

I took the wagon round the Hill to where my tailor Gaspar Halftoken has his new premises. He was coming up in the world, in all senses. I made it there just before closing time.

I have had a fixed account with Gaspar ever since he left the Craft School – potential spotted early – I am glad to say, as I could not afford his prices now. Gaspar had a fit when I told him where I was going – and my pressing need for some new, appropriately styled, threads. How could I not give him at least six moons' notice? I explained the situation and he quietened down. I didn't have the heart to tell him about his previous creation that was still waiting, soaked, in a laundry trunk in my bathroom. Nothing like the threat of decapitation from the authorities to make you forget about personal grooming. But I needed something special for tonight.

Gaspar was working on two suits for me at that time, both practically ready for me to pick up. One of them, with a few alterations, he was sure would be ideal for my evening with the elfess Thelen. I waited while he worked his usual miracles with a needle.

'Hey Gaspar, where do you keep your fashion scrolls?'

The young gnome popped his clean-shaven, curly brown head out from the store cupboard where he was currently searching for some small black opal buttons, cut as sleeping dragons, which I simply had to have.

'My dear boy,' he said, round a mouthful of pins. 'I hope you're not going all elf queen on me; my opinion is usually good enough! But if you just want something to keep your eyes busy, you are practically sitting on them!'

I lifted the cover of the daybed that Gaspar keeps for his special clients, and did indeed see half a dozen stuffed unceremoniously underneath. After a quick search I hit upon exactly what I was after and read the front page out loud: 'Mrs Hardwood seen at the opening of the Grassmere Gallery in a stunningly simple one-piece silver dress.'

An interested Gaspar came out of the storeroom carrying my suit and the buttons. He was small, even for a gnome, barely one head higher than my hairy belly button. However, every inch of his characteristically slight frame was dressed to perfection. Applying his precept that a tailor has to be his own best display, he wore buckle-bottom trousers with matching boots and a multicoloured weskit beautifully embroidered with woodland animals. Unlike some men who wear loud waistcoats because they lack a personality, Gaspar wore his like a ceremonial robe – he had earned it.

'Ah yes, dear boy! I remember the occasion well; more White and Wise than you could wave a wand at. And only "stunningly simple" if you happen to have a dragon's hoard of dwarf silver thread at hand.'

I looked at the dress again with extra respect. My aged great-father used to tell me stories about the famous dwarf-silver thread when I was small; I had never heard of that much thread going into one outfit. Dwarf silver was the only metal ductile enough to produce twine suitable for making into cloth. Kingdoms have been bought and sold for less than that dress must have cost.

'I would never have thought she was your type, dear boy,' Gaspar said, staring down at the photograph, before reconsidering. 'Mind you, she's fully ambulatory and has still got the use of all her limbs, so I suppose she qualifies.'

He cleverly leapt over the cushion I threw at him with a standing jump that took him to the top of a chest that was taller than he was. With equal agility, and the nimbleness displayed by his entire race, he did a front summersault in the air and headed back to the storeroom, leaving me to my scrollwork. And inspired work it was. Detective Strongoak, some days you almost earn your fee. There inside the scroll, in a small insert picture was 'The famous Hardwood Emerald.' My first glimpse of what all the fuss was about. I whistled silently. Even with that much dwarf-silver around, the Hardwood Emerald looked anything but outclassed. I checked the date on the scroll – recent. Interesting.

Gaspar came back with my suit and I asked if I could remove the page.

'Of course, dear boy! As long as you don't get a copy of the dress run up. It is very, very much not your colour, do take my word on this.'

9

THE EVENING FORGET-ME-NOT

I had spent rather longer than I had intended at the archive and stables, and I'd needed to visit the florist's after Gaspar's, so when I finally did head on out to meet Thelen I was cutting it fine. I had on the suit Gaspar had sorted out for me: a very dark charcoal double-breasted jacket, with a glisten like anthracite; low fitting with a plain back and lapels no wider than a moneylender's smile. On the trousers, instead of satin trim ('Tacky, Nicely, tacky!') he had worked in just a few threads of dwarf silver. For, as he said, 'Not enough looks too cheap and too much appears vulgar.' Mind you, that amount wouldn't have sewn the hem on the dress that Mrs Hardwood wore.

I was showered and freshly shaved, my plait tied dwarf fashion in the family knots. I had on a suit made by a master and a scent that cost more per peck than I normally made in a week. Even the Helmington purred along in fine voice. I was feeling good, too, and what's wrong with feeling good once in a while? As long as it's not habit forming. So what if you've got a murder charge hanging over your head, Nicely,

81

and still no closer to solving your case. For tonight at least I felt invincible!

The ball was being held at Citadel Hall, Top of the Hill; as far as you can go before banging into some sky. The cause: placating the poor and homeless, or 'outer ring redevelopment' as it is better known. The summer's unrest had precipitated a bout of serious purse waving from moneyed folk in the direction of the needy – or maybe just call me Detective Disenchanted.

The ball also provided an ideal opportunity for all the prospective Councillors to fall over themselves vying in the concerned stakes, prior to the forthcoming elections. All the White and Wise were indeed there, many decked out in colours displaying their political allegiance. I spotted the familiar white, gold and green of the established parties and, more common than I would have thought, the sky-blue of the Citadel Alliance Party. CAP were gaining credibility, given that when they started off they didn't even seem politically potty trained. I'd bet a sizeable sum that it was their 'get-tough' response to all the recent troubles that was resulting in their rise in popularity. It was interesting how, if this was an 'alliance', it seemed to manage to exclude about ninety per cent of the Citadel's population. I wondered if they'd ever bothered looking up the meaning of the term.

Not that I was about to let that spoil my fun. Steward parking was the order of the evening. The boy's eyes did not exactly light up when he saw the Helmington, so I slipped him a half-crown and told him to leave the wagon near the gateway. I realised that everyone else was going to be doing the same thing, but he looked a good lad and he had an honest haircut.

The Hall is not the most impressive of the Citadel's

buildings. It does not have the most impressive facade or the highest ceilings or even the biggest dome. It does not have stained glass or brilliant chandeliers. What it does have is age. It seems incontrovertible that the Hall was one of the first, if not *the* first, building constructed after the founding of the Citadel. And you can feel its age, too. I have been in some of the deepest, darkest places in the world and some of them did not feel half as old as this simple building that has been at the centre of so many of the most crucial events in the history of Widergard.

I fair leapt up the steps leading to the Hall and met with Thelen in the bar as arranged.

How do they do it?

Elves, I mean. It was only white silk, of that I am pretty sure, and there are only so many ways of wrapping a length of white silk. Thelen, though, stole the breath deep from the bottom of your lungs, leaving you gasping for something a little more than air, probably something that has not been found in Widergard for an age, and then only in the depths of an enchanted forest.

'Master Strongoak, you look simply marvellous. I really must congratulate you on your taste in matters of the cloth.'

I think I blushed. Of course I blushed! She'd managed to get her compliment in first, leaving me with my bottom lip flapping like a yokel. Fortunately where words fail, actions will sometimes make recompense. Bowing low, from behind my back I pulled out the flowers I had picked up earlier: ariethiah (the evening forget-me-not, in the common tongue). There are flowers more exotic, there are flowers more perfumed, but none have a blue of such depth and purity.

'Why, Master Strongoak, a corsage, how very romantic of you.' Her voice showed amusement, but did not hide how touched she was. 'Ariethiah: the evening forget-me-not. These are sometimes called "Elfhome", Nicely. They are said to be the colour of the sky in the Lost Lands. Did you know that?'

I shook my head. 'Where I come from they are known as "Winter's Longing". It is said to reflect the desire of the dwarfs in the coldest and darkest months of winter for the light of the summer skies.'

She raised an eyebrow. 'I did not even know that dwarfs relished the sunlight.'

'Why, lady, you should not believe it, if it's not carved in stone. Just because us dwarfs have lived for so many years in the farthest north, where the temperatures would make even the most hardy elf run for the shelter of a warm cave, it does not mean we have turned our backs on the sun. We are workers with light; we frame it with rock in the windows of our summer halls, we work it in our lanterns, bending it with prisms, and we release it from the deep hearts of gems.'

'And now a poet, Master Strongoak! I had better watch you carefully. There is obviously a lot more to you than meets the eye.'

'A lot more, my lady.'

We walked on into the main hall. If the expected fury amongst elfin kind following Truetouch's death was about to engulf the Citadel, Thelen obviously hadn't been informed. Neither had any other of the elves there present. Maybe Ralph and the Cits had managed to keep a tighter lid on the matter than they had anticipated. That could only be to my benefit. The longer I had to sort things out, the happier I was.

The evening began to look even better after Thelen described the nature of the entertainment. As befitted its intentions, the music was drawn from all of the Citadel's peoples. What the White and the Wise would make of the *All-Star Syncopated Gnome Home Jump Band* would be anyone's guess.

Thelen led us to our seats and almost magically a path opened up in front of her. The stewards kept bowing and politely waving us through. You could get to like this, Nicely old lad, they are spoiling you. Our seats in fact turned out to be in a small, very pleasantly outfitted box.

'Well, shame about your friend,' I said, making myself comfortable, feeling like I'd just stolen the dragon's gold. Thelen looked puzzled. I reminded her: 'You know, your friend, the one who's ill, the lady who's given us the tickets.'

'Oh yes, last-minute thing,' said Thelen, taking out a small spyglass and scanning the crowd.

'She must be very rich or well connected.' Thelen, however, was not to be distracted from her crowd watching and only muttered something in heavily accented elfish.

'There!' she said, triumphantly. 'Could not be better.' I followed her gaze and saw a recognisable face amongst a group of elves and High Born seated in a large box opposite. Certainly top-of-the-tree, no spear-carriers, or towel-carriers for that matter. I borrowed the spyglass, and soon those oh-so-handsome features sprang into view.

'Good evening, Highbury. How is the Golden Boy?' I said quietly, to no one in particular.

The Golden Boy looked fine. Gone was the muscled-athlete look so evident on the Gnada. The sun-bleached hair was now styled by an expert, short at the sides, tapered at the back and high on top; less tousled surf divinity, more squeaky-clean confidant, and even I had to admire the way he was dressed. It was no dune drifter sitting there; damn it, this elf looked like a politician.

'Nice suit,' I said, passing the glasses back to Thelen.

There was only one problem with it as far as I could see. On the lapel were pinned the sky-blue colours of the Citadel Alliance Party, which now I thought about it, was the same blue that the Surf Elves wore. I pointed out this apparent coincidence to Thelen.

'Why, yes! Now, that is interesting,' she smiled a little grimly. 'Though he won't be the only elf wearing the sky-blue this fall. I have heard a lot of my younger kin expressing their displeasure with the politics of their elders. The Citadel Alliance Party provides a home for the dissatisfied of many persuasions. All it needs is someone with the charisma of a Highbury to act as a focal point and they may have to be taken very seriously.'

'Surely not enough to worry either the Branch and Leaf or the Hand in Heart?' I questioned, referring to the two longest-established Citadel political organisations.

'Well, you have to remember, Nicely, these parties have been in existence for a great span, even by elfin standards. Perhaps people might think that it is time for a change.'

'Still, I can't believe that they will amass enough votes to cause an upset in the result.'

'They don't have to, Nicely. If the result looks like being close, and remember the polls say there does not seem to be very much to choose between them at the moment, then the CAP might well hold the balance of power. Who knows, there may even be some kind of pact?'

'What, with the elves of the Branch and Leaf?'

'Probably not, but the men of the Hand in Heart are more pragmatic.'

I realised she was right. A lot of the Citadel population

shared an unconscious feeling that elves were somehow automatically destined to be the ruling elite.

Citadel politics was a sorry do, no doubt about it. As I pondered I continued my surveillance of the elf Highbury – potential Citadel leader?

'Don't make it too obvious, Nicely,' Thelen said. 'He'll notice you.'

'I do believe, my lady, that that is the nature of the game at the moment.' And very soon, in fact, I saw one of his party point towards me. Highbury took out a pair of glasses and turned them in my direction. I lowered mine and waved, giving him my best pleased-to-see-you grin. Much to my disappointment, he did not seem pleased to see me. Those perfectly proportioned features managed to arrange themselves in a less-than-pleasant array – I tried not to let it break my heart. Sadly, or not, I do not think I had added to his enjoyment of the evening, but was this the face of someone who was surprised to see me still alive? Had Highbury some reason for axing the Lower Elf when he thought he was about to cough to me? Those damn elves can be so hard to read, sometimes I think they should make special glasses just for that.

Anyway, for a dwarf potentially about to be charged with the Big One, I had me a great time. In fact it was during a rousing encore by the *All-Star Syncopated Gnome Home Jump Band* (quietly loathed by everyone there with pointy ears – excluding Thelen, I'm pleased to say) that I noticed Highbury had slipped out. Thelen reckoned that he was very unlikely to miss the post-concert reception, as this was the time that counted with the Wise and White. Me, I just kept jumping in my seat like I was born for it.

Sadly, the music at the reception did not reach the same

heights, all elf toots and flutes and lutes and harps, but there was plenty to sup and it was free, and with what Thelen told me the tickets were costing, it should have been.

Perhaps it was the nature of the occasion, it all being in aid of the poor and needy, but eating and drinking seemed to be frowned upon. Not by me; we dwarfs invented optimal foraging. And not by the *All-Star Syncopated Gnome Home Jump Band* either – 'great rhythm, great attack and yet great swing' and even greater appetites, come to mention it.

The food steward was no more impressed by the attitudes of the High Born than I was: 'enough food to feed the lower levels for a week, and to look at this lot you would think trolls had been drooling all over it.' Thelen was no slouch when it came to tucking away the victuals either, which I've always found an attractive trait in the female of whatever race.

The bar steward was similarly depressed by the lack of action. A true exponent of his art, he was only too pleased to rise to a challenge. I therefore introduced him to Thelen. I then introduced Thelen to the delights of the *Darrow Bomb* and then *The Necromancer*, followed by a *Baby Dragon's Breath*. She in turn introduced me to the *Elfin Sling* and *The Twilight Gleaming*, and we all got together and had a jolly good time.

I kept a weather eye open for Highbury, but he was not in evidence for the schmoozing. When he was still not around for the speeches, a wise move as it turned out – too much stuff about tolerance from people who probably wouldn't let a gnome take out their garbage – Thelen and I split up and went out searching for him in all of the Hall's dark little recesses. I would have thought he would have liked to be more visible, but as it turned out I was wrong. Upon spotting a dark figure about to depart from a small alcove, my curiosity was aroused. I had struck gold and I decided to personally excavate it.

'Well, if it isn't Highbury, the well-known master of the surf!' I aimed a shot at him to see how he would take it: 'Where are all your little elf chums?' This didn't so much as make an eyebrow twitch. Uninvited, I nevertheless sat, to the elf's obvious consternation.

'Can't have you getting lonely. This isn't like you, Highbury, old chap, ensconced in the dark. What's the matter, developed a nasty skin condition?' I sprawled all over the seat next to him, effectively trapping him between me, table and wall. 'Oh no, I forgot, you don't have that sort of problem, do you? Perfect skin, perfect teeth. Tell me, how does it feel to be so perfect?'

Highbury flinched. 'I do not know what you are doing here, Son of Stone, but I wish you would go away as far as it is possible to go in these circumstances.'

'Hey, haven't you heard, it's a democracy, Goldy, old boy? Isn't that what you elves are always saying? Free speech and equality for all. Of course, maybe your Citadel Alliance Party has different ideas. Not many gnomes in the CAP from what I hear, not that many dwarfs either, eh?! Maybe I should join up! What have you got to offer today's modern dwarf? A one-way ticket back to New Iron Town?' I gestured a little too wildly with my cocktail glass and sprayed the elf with its contents.

Highbury tried to maintain his air of superiority, but was having some difficulty maintaining his composure with half of my *Necromancer* spilling down his suit. 'I believe you have had too much to drink, Son of Stone,' he said from between teeth that were as gritted as elf teeth can grit.

'Yup, but at least I have a choice about making an ass of myself.' He didn't get it. As I thought, Old Blue Eye's talents did not run to a sense of humour. No surprise there. Name me one good elf comedian and I'll show you a dragon in loafers. I continued my friendly drunk act because I was enjoying it and he wasn't. 'Come on, lighten up, Shrubbery, old boy. Can't you take a joke? What do you say, let's be buddies? Forgive and forget. All bones under the troll-bridge.'

Highbury stood up, his perpetual tan now coloured by something more like excessive blood pressure. I swear I could see little wisps of smoke coming off the tips of those pointy ears. 'The name is Highbury. I have nothing to say to you, dwarf, and I do not forgive or forget anything, and if that is not clear enough for you, in words you may understand: Get out of my face!'

Great parting speech, a pity its delivery was rather spoilt by the fact that he was simultaneously attempting to climb over me to get out from the table. For some reason, certainly beyond my control, this did not prove easy. Then from across the room I heard an unexpected voice: 'Why, Master Detective, aren't you going to introduce me to your friend?'

I turned to see Mrs Hardwood, carrying one drink in her hand and several more on the inside. With a little forethought I would have realised I stood every chance of crossing her tracks. This type of get-together would be meat and drink for her.

The lady was also wearing white, as befitted the occasion, but half of the dress must already have been donated to charity, judging by how little was left. Mind you, it didn't matter how white the dress was; she still looked dirty.

'I am just leaving, Lady Hardwood,' said Highbury, taking

advantage of the interruption to disentangle himself from my legs, but kicking over the table in the process. A lot of people looked on and he coloured an even deeper shade of irate. This was not the way he liked to get attention. He eventually strode off in the direction of the main hall, dignity left somewhere in the Desolate Wastes, while I righted the furniture.

Mrs Hardwood sat opposite, put down her glass and then drank most of mine. 'Hmm, tasty.' She had another go. 'Very tasty. So, who's that with the cheekbones and the pointy bits?' she added, conversationally.

'I'm surprised you don't know him, Mrs Hardwood. I would have thought there were few influential people who escaped your notice.'

She shrugged a bit, used her little cocktail onion to wipe round her glass and then put it on her tongue. She let it hang there for a while before swallowing it whole. I've probably seen more provocative party tricks, but I don't recall when.

'It depends what you mean by "influential", Master Detective. My husband owns as much land and as many industries as a middling-sized kingdom. You know, in days gone by he would have been called a king. Now, in that class, "influential" means a whole different thing.'

I took her point.

'Well, Mrs Hardwood, the elf with the personality by-pass was Highbury, self-styled leader of the Surf Elves and, if I am reading the runes correctly, potential Citadel Alliance Party Councillor.'

'His manners could do with some attention.'

'Don't mind him. Big problem.'

'Such as?'

'Small dick.'

Unfortunately it caught her just as she was taking a sample out of the cocktail. Coughs and fits do not a lady make, but she handled it pretty well. A lot more people did look on, though. 'And I thought that was you,' she said, after recovering. 'The small dick.'

I raised one eyebrow.

'Hey lady, don't you know what they say about dwarfs?'

'I know they say a lot of things about dwarfs, Master Detective.'

'Could be at least one of them is true.'

She wiped the remains of the cocktail from her face. 'Like to talk dirty, do you, Master Dick-tective?'

'Just stating an anatomical fact, lady.'

'Oh my, the things you can learn on a night out in the Citadel!' She took out a compact from a small vanity purse, perused her reflection and was not impressed. 'I had better go and put on my party face. People always expect the best.' She rose effortlessly. 'Don't forget drinks tomorrow. You can talk dirty all you like then.'

The walk to the ladies' room was a masterpiece of application; an awful lot of work had gone into getting it right and an awful lot of folk of the male persuasion appreciated it; she had this walking business off to a fine art. 'Petrochemical industries,' I muttered to her departing back. Dirtiest thing I could think of to say.

Thelen slipped into the vacant seat.

'Who was the woman, and how come her mother never told her to wear an undervest out in the evenings? It can get chilly even in summer.'

I smiled. 'That was a client. Name of Mrs Hardwood.'

'Oh yes, *the* Mrs Hardwood, I've heard of her, but have not had the pleasure.'

'Highbury knew her, but I don't think he's had the pleasure either.'

Thelen liked that one.

'She didn't admit to knowing him, though, which is interesting, as I think one of them was lying.'

We tried to get back into the swing of things, but the fizz had gone out of the party. We decided to cut our losses and leave. The night was fine and clear and pleasant after the day's heat. The stars were doing what stars do best and the moon hung like an opal set in jet. We decided to leave the wagon and walk through what are, after all, some of the oldest and most famous landmarks of the Citadel. The Tower of the Guard, the Sepulchre, the Forever Fountain, the Courtyard of the Trees, all laid out before us, floodlit as the tourists never see them. I had liberated a bottle of something sticky from our friendly bar steward and we showed suitable deference to our thousands of years of heritage by waltzing a few times round the Courtyard of the Trees and dipping our pinkies in the Forever Fountain. By the time we had made it down to the Third Level where Thelen was staying, things were humming again. Arm in arm, we passed between the shadows, making no more noise than sneak thieves looking for a dragon's hoard.

'I would ask you in, Nicely,' said Thelen, as we reached her door, 'but to be honest I am absolutely exhausted.'

'That's fine, lady. Why spoil a perfect evening with us getting tangled up in each other's chain mail?'

She gave me that particular elfin look, the one like an X-ray machine on overdrive. There are lots of strange things about elves, at least to my way of thinking – some good, some not quite so good, or at least not as good as they like to advertise them. That look, though, is particularly unnerving.

Elves seem to have the capability of giving you one hundred per cent of their attention – whereas the most other peoples can normally manage is about forty to sixty. For that one moment you are the only thing that seems to matter to them in the whole of Widergard – scary.

'You are a strange one, Nicely Strongoak,' Thelen continued. 'A peculiar mixture, like those cocktails you are so fond of drinking – a dash of this, a measure of that. I do not think you quite know what you want to be.'

We made our goodnights quickly after that and I hurried on my way; too much perception can be dangerous.

10

PETAL

It had been an almost perfect evening, some dancing, some romancing and some elf baiting. Not bad at all. The night was still balmy, the stars still alive and, as I searched for a hire wagon, I ticked off the constellations. I recognised the Wizard's Staff, the Two Princes, the Flying Dragon and the Silver Tree, but I failed completely to spot the Over-Confident Dwarf.

I was heading down a side street when the wagon pulled up. It was big and black. At first I thought I had found my ride and I leaned into the cab, only to find myself facing a shooter. The bouquet of steel and machine oil brought me round like smelling salts.

'The chief wants to see you.'

I stared down a barrel as big as a drainpipe, at a face fit only for scaring children.

'Tell him to make an appointment.'

'He did, it's for now. You're late, get in.'

The grunt with the shooter motioned me into the back and I sat sandwiched between his compatriots, watching quietly as the lower levels of the Hill slipped by. My two muscle-bound bookends were the usual mixed-bloods, hoodlums very much of the third division; three-ring boxers and wrestlers, slightly past their prime. The armed one, he was different, he was the real thing. Big and broad, he wore gloves to save him skinning his knuckles on the cobblestones, a pure-blooded goblin of the old school. The three of them did not have the charm of a paper bag, but what they lacked in pedigree and refinement they more than made up for in height and width – probably all that free school milk again. They were certainly too many for me, so I sank back into the softness of the seat.

We passed over the Dwarfs' Dike, the outer boundary of the original Citadel proper, and slipped through the suburbs as silent as wraiths. Soon we were heading out towards the docks.

As we hit the Bay area they slipped a mask on me. I had one last quick look round before the bag was put over my head, but I didn't really recognise anywhere and the rest of the journey passed in blackness. After what seemed an age, the wagon finally stopped and they pulled me none too smoothly out. I took a deep breath. The smell of salt, industrial plant and sealeaf was a distinct improvement from the atmosphere in the wagon; goblins and personal hygiene travel in separate stagecoaches. It was a smell I could recognise again. These goblins didn't know their dwarfs.

They shook me down, relieved me of my wallet and shield and then pushed me up some stairs, helping me catch my shin on the metal as I went. I owed somebody for that. Next: into a room, through another door, into another room, which felt heated even at this time of the year, then a new voice.

'All right, lads, you can take off his blindfold.'

I blinked a few times. I seemed to be in some sort of office. The walls were covered with charts and cheap calendars from engineering concerns, featuring pneumatically improved women and seeking to sell pneumatic tyres; shredded paperwork was strewn over the floor. A large antique desk with a finely polished surface dominated the room, and the desk was dominated by a large seated goblin.

His was not a type I had familiarity with; some kind of grunt, I supposed. He was fat, but there was no mistaking the muscle beneath. Even his huge head had rolls of fat congregating at the collar beneath lank hair the colour of steel, soaked in skull-oil and parted down the centre in a line; axe sharp. Massive shoulders came with equally impressive arms, displayed beyond rolled shirtsleeves. His chest was barely contained by a check waistcoat that would have given Gaspar nightmares for a month and he carried a watch chain that might once have held a ship's anchor. As ugly as a voluntary violation of the marriage bed, his face hinted at knife work, both of the reformational and bar-room variety: the slant eyes were regulation, but if he was born with that nose then I am a pixie's poorboy. It was the teeth that were the real give-away. I have yet to see a goblin with a full set. Normally, they are rotten, brown, cracked and stained and big – the sort that makes a dental hygienist wake up early in the morning with the icy sweats. These, though, were white and gleaming, with square, neat incisors and, when he smiled, instead of fangs I spotted neatly pointed canines. A lot of work had gone on in there; I just pitied whoever had been paid to do it. Nobody should need money that bad.

He puffed on a large leaf-stick and blew a smoke ring. 'I

take it he's clean.'

'As an elf queen's undies, boss,' replied the driver, throwing my wallet and shield on the desk. 'Not that he could hide anything in a suit like that.'

The big grunt chortled. I think he was still getting the hang of the teeth, as small drops of saliva formed at the corners of his slit-like mouth every time he spoke.

'Don't listen to him, dwarf. The suit is fine.'

'From you I should take that as a compliment?' I said, opening my innings.

'What's the matter, don't ya like checks?'

'Only the sort with my name on and somebody else's seal at the bottom.'

The new teeth went for another outing that I now guessed was really some form of smile. 'I can see you and me is going to get on fine,' he spat.

'Uh huh,' said Master Noncommittal Detective, 'look, I'm all for integration and I have my wagon serviced by the best grease goblin in the Citadel, who is as hard working as they come, but let's face it, there is not exactly a history of great love between our two folks.'

'Well flog my ring, and call me a lordling, but I do believe the Master Detective is jumping to a seriously wrong conclusion.' He got up on thick bandy legs, came round to where I was still standing and loomed over me – he was definitely a good loomer. Me? I was an indifferent loom-ee, so I shrugged instead.

'See that sign, Short Stuff?' he continued, gesturing behind his desk. I looked up at what appeared to be some form of diploma, taking pride of place amongst the girly calendars. 'That is a Certificate of Racial Purity.' When this didn't cause the anticipated response he went on: 'It states that for the last seven generations – two more, I hasten to add, than is legally required – my ancestors have been traced as unsullied, impeccably pure men.'

'Men?'

'Men. You take my point.' How could I miss it? It was about three hands long, made from finest steel and held directly at my throat.

He continued: 'It's just that I happen to come from a pretty ugly family, which is not a crime even under elf law. I was the youngest of eighteen children and was therefore both a burden and a joy to my mother – may her bones never be dug up for soup. You following this, dwarf?'

I nodded very slightly. Which, considering the position of the knife, was the wisest choice.

My captor continued: 'So, since I was so much more attractive than my brothers and sisters, you know what she called me, dwarf?'

'No – man.'

'She called me Petal. You find that funny, Dwarf?'

'Uh, huh.'

'No?'

'No. I really don't find it funny,' I insisted. Petal took the knife from my throat and went back to his desk, examining my shield. 'Nicely Strongoak. Master Detective Nicely Strongoak. Maybe with a handle like that, Petal don't seem too funny after all.'

The ex-goblin and newly, at least to me, reclassified 'man' let himself down on a suitably reinforced office chair.

'So sit!' he directed.

I sat. He continued examining my credentials. 'Shield-for-Hire. Bit of an old-fashioned sound in this day and age, don't yer think? Shield-for-Hire – guess it's an honourable profession – all the way back to the days when there was always some poor village full of us poor folk, needing protecting from, oh goblins, or even worse.' He looked across the desk at me, but I didn't bat an eyelid. Petal proceeded to clean his nails with the knife. 'Well, it's not the good old days now, Master Shield-for-Hire, times change, they get more complicated and sometimes the little folk do not really know what is good for them.'

'I don't think there is much new about that particular argument.'

'Meaning what?'

'Meaning that there's always been people around who think they can make other people's decisions, better than they can make them for themselves, that is.'

'That's what all this democracy business is about, ain't it, dwarf? Getting someone else to make your decisions for you.'

'Correct me if I'm wrong, but I seem to remember that there was supposed to be some voting process involved, something about little crosses on a piece of parchment.'

'So, they vote to hand over their thinking to someone else. I'm saving them the problem of one more decision – sort of cutting out the middle man.' Petal gestured wildly with the knife and then – almost quicker than I could follow – it was in the air and heading for my head. I swear I heard the very air itself part, as it zipped past my left ear, and embedded itself into the door.

I did not so much as flinch – probably because it had all been too quick.

'Can't stand those damned blood-sucking, flying para-sites!' Petal continued nonchalantly, opening the top drawer of his desk, taking out a knife that was the twin of the one he had just thrown.

'Now where were we?' he continued, attending to his manicure again.

'You were telling me about your interest in helping others shoulder some of the burden of civic responsibilities?'

'Oh yeah ...'

'Does that include persuasion with sharp pointy things?'

The goblin shrugged massive shoulders. 'Just underlining the point.'

'What about innocent bystanders?'

'Master Detective, Widergard is full of innocent bystanders. We've got plenty enough.'

'No, I still have the feeling you have missed a vital aspect of the democracy business.'

'Well, isn't that the marvellous thing about our free society, everyone is entitled to their own opinion, even those amongst us who make it their business to interfere in other citizens' business.'

'Meaning?'

He picked up my wallet and shield and threw them across the desk. 'Meaning that one dwarf detective has been poking his nose far too far into matters which are none of his business.'

'What if I make them my business?' I said, bending to pick up my shield.

'Then your business goes out of business.' With that he stabbed his current knife, hard and fast, at the desk, sending the point deep into the surface, just a hand away from my face. I straightened up slowly and looked him in his squint eyes. 'Now look what you went and made me go and do,' he said, speaking very slowly. 'I went and ruined my desk. And I care about this desk, so just think what I could do to you, 'cos I don't care a pixie's fart about you.' He eyed the damaged top with what looked like genuine regret. 'Take the great detective away and give him something to help him remember us, lads. Hurt him, but don't spoil his looks too much.'

I turned quickly, but the three bruisers from the wagon were already there. I struggled because that sort of thing is expected from a tough guy like myself. Eventually, they marched me across the room. As they bundled me through the door, I caught sight of the embedded knife and a red smear that had been some particularly nasty flying insect. They slipped on the hood again, which was probably good news, as it indicated that I was not so likely to have an early introduction to the Bay marine life. We drove a short distance, and then I was dragged out again. A blow to the gut caught me unawares. I doubled up, gasping for breath on the floor, and as I breathed in something was pushed into the hood and I was coughing and spluttering in the dark. There was a tingle in my nose and throat: a smell of ice, a frozen lake on a winter's night. By the time recognition sank in and I scrambled at the hood it was too late; they had powdered me with Moondust.

Moondust is a narcotic, and as such is off-limits to all of Widergard; unless you are an elf. The story goes that what is for them a mild stimulant, enhancing certain 'creative' faculties, is, for the general population, the ultimate good-time party powder. That is unless it's taken in large doses, when it just kills the brain, leaving the body to fend for itself. If the gnome's pipeleaf leads to a mellow glow, then Moondust is a strobe light in the skull. The wormheads – those cobblestone stimulant enthusiasts with skulls full of flying dragons, just love it, which is why it is illegal. Dwarfs don't touch it; we get to the party just as the lights are going out.

I fumbled at the hood with fingers the size of a dragon's talons and managed to make a little light, but it was at the end of a long, long corridor full of folk, laughing and singing. Men, elves, Tree-friends and even a few casual-suited wizards were having the time of their lives. For some reason they didn't want me to get to the door. There were arms and legs everywhere, but they were only mine, and they didn't work, and I wasn't going anywhere anyway and then the party was over.

I got to the office early. More exactly, I was dumped unceremoniously in the Two Fingers' reception early. I think it was Petal's way of saying: 'We know where you live.' Old Jakes found me there, woke me up, or tried to, and then helped me into the lift and eventually onto the office bedroll.

I tried to say a thank you, but I have a feeling I simply delivered the recipe for my mother's famous beetroot and boggle stew. It's a fabulous dish but you have to have really fresh boggle; however, I got the feeling that Jakes wasn't that interested and then I passed out again.

It was really late, nearly midwatch, by the time I woke up, but I wasn't going to beat myself up about it – not when everybody else seemed to be getting into a queue to do the job. Mindless violence is all very well for taking an opponent out – he may not be able to run far with a broken leg, after all – but he can still think. I couldn't move and also could barely remember my name.

Goblins are not just mindless thugs. There is always room at the cooking cauldron for one or two like Petal, the kind with the extra brain space necessary for organising things. The seriousness of his warning was clear, but as to what he was warning me away from, I didn't really have that much of a clue; certainly not in my current state.

I splashed water on my face but didn't feel much better. I tried drinking some water and that didn't help either. I was considering my other water-related options when I remembered the Tree-friend's gravy that I had left in my drawer yesterday, or a million years ago, as it was now called. I went for it like a hungry baby to the teat and the rewards were just as immediate. My brain played join-up-the-dots with the departments in charge of legs, arms and feet, fired them up into activity and I felt new life flow into my veins. Ha, foiled you, Petal. Invulnerable Wonder Dwarf was back.

The problem came back into focus too: why would his kind of goblin be concerned about my investigation of a missing barkeep and the death of a surfing elf? Something wasn't adding up here.

I took a clean shirt out of the trunk that I keep for these occasions and put on the spare hat that usually hangs on the back of the door. I winced slightly as I pushed the hat on; even with the Tree-friend's drink safely inside of me I could still feel the soft spot where I had been maced at *The Old Inn*. It takes a lot to dent a dwarf skull; whoever had wielded the blow knew what they were doing. And as they had been dragging sand around with them, I guessed it must have been Highbury, or one of his minions. I also suspected that they had found what they were after: the golden Gnada Trophy, hidden safely away by Perry Goodfellow. If he had made himself scarce, why had he not taken his famous trophy with him?

I needed some hot food and a nice smile to look at.

I needed to call Liza Springwater.

I picked up the horn and rang her office number: 'Hi, Liza. Nicely, here.'

'Good morning, Sir. What can I do to help you?'

'Well, how about you drop the formalities?'

'I am not sure. My supervisor is here. Shall I see if she can help?' Liza responded in her best official manner.

'I get the idea, sorry to put you out. How about you come round my office an hour after midwatch? That is, if you get time off for good behaviour.'

'I'm sure that can be arranged.'

'I'll put some coffee on and we'll call it lunch.'

'I'm sure that will be satisfactory. Thank you very much for your enquiry, good Sir.'

I hung the horn up and headed on out to buy a few provisions. I found myself whistling. The head was feeling better and, despite the assaults upon my person, I was in a frame of mind I could only describe as cheerful. I made a mental note to check with my physic and see if this was likely to be detrimental to my normal state of being. Or was I just developing a worrying exotic gravy dependency? Another bad habit, just what I needed.

I picked up the goodies and made it back to the Two Fingers in record time, my purchases still warm in their brown bag beds, the smell of baking going before me like an advance guard of goodness. I found Liza waiting on the office doorstep, clutching consumables as well.

'Great minds,' we said in unison and both laughed. 'Sorry about the problem with the supervisor,' said Liza, as I opened the door. 'The boss is a bit of a dragon, not too keen on the personal calls.'

'Never mind. How long a break does the Old Worm give you, then?'

'Oh, don't worry about that. The Old Worm is out for the rest of the day and I have someone covering for me.'

'Good, then we'll take our provisions to the Secret Garden.'

'Secret Garden. I've never heard of that!'

'Which is why,' I said, looking smug, 'it is a secret.'

We collected our coffee, I locked the office, put the 'BACK MUCH LATER' sign up, and we headed to the lift. Instead of going down to the lobby I pressed 'roof'. When we debarked, I took Liza to a little-used staircase, which led up to a stout wooden door.

'It's locked,' said Liza, who was in front.

'I know, which is why I have the key.' I passed it to her and she unlocked the door and swung it wide open. The effect was rather as I hoped.

'Oh Nicely, it's wonderful!' And indeed it was.

The door opened onto a grotto that would not have been out of place in an elf's summer garden, if elves actually put gardens on roofs of buildings and not just up trees. Delicately leafed willows rose from hidden containers beside a small stream that was in fact the recycling overspill of the building's water tower. A wealth of flowers covered every available surface, except a small gravel path that wandered in and out of the greenery, becoming small stepping stones at the stream edge.

We stepped out; the trees provided some welcome shade on what was yet another sweltering Citadel High-Summer day.

'Who would have guessed that this was here? How in Widergard did you get it up here? Is it all yours?'

Liza was like a small child in her enthusiasm.

'One question at a time please,' I insisted. We followed the gravel path to the stepping stones. A pleasant breeze curled around the willows, shaking them gently.

'Now, to take your last question first. Sadly, I cannot claim ownership of this delightful spot, or even take credit for it.

To take you into a confidence, the instigator was Jakes the watchman. Although I should get you to swear an oath of secrecy on that.'

'Honestly,' she said, bending down to admire some delicate light-blue elfin lights, 'my lips are sewn. But Jakes, how did he manage all this?'

'As Jakes tells the story, it all started in a small way. He began to rescue all the office plants that people threw away, usually after public holiday neglect, and discovered he had one green finger, if not yet a complete handful. When his back room became a little crowded he moved some out onto the roof. Then he began to need more soil, so he began separating out the rubbish and started a compost heap up here. People were always throwing out furniture, so he began to add a few bits and pieces, here and there. One day, after a particularly heavy winter storm, the water butt overran and he found that the drainage channels made rather a pleasant stream, so he just added a small wind-powered pump. Then seeds started blowing in and so on.'

'So where did you come into the picture?'

'About the time the roof started bowing! Jakes needed a bit of structural support, as it were. So, together we shored up the roof, and I am pleased to say that you could probably land a squadron of dragons on the top of the old Two Fingers now without so much as a creak. After that, we both took over the upkeep, and I got a key to the door. And here we are now at the picnic spot: Look-out Leap.'

We had in fact arrived at the edge of the building. A park bench and a solid guardrail made for a great spot to share a pipe or lunch. We leant on it and took the air. 'What a view, Nicely.' Indeed, to the west the sea was an unbroken blue blanket tucked up neatly to the green hills of Tall Trees in the south. Even the Bay area did not look too bad from this distance.

'Do you like it then?'

'Oh yes. One of the things I enjoy most about living in the Citadel is the views. I always think that it must be like living on a mountain.'

'And that appeals?'

'Very much so. All that clean air and sunlight, then huddling up for the winter.'

'Just like the dwarfs.'

'I suppose so, but I always think of dwarfs as living underground.'

'We do live underground, but in mountains. It's the obvious answer. Combines all our interests: mining, scenery, and terrific illumination possibilities. Not to mention the convenient summer pastures for our grazing animals.'

'Animals? What, sheep and goats?'

'Yes. You didn't think we lived on coal, did you?'

She blushed rather fetchingly. 'I'm sorry. I guess I don't know much about dwarfs.'

'You and the rest of the Citadel.' I smiled to show no offence had been taken. 'I think I must have spent half of my childhood leaping around the hillsides after some irascible goat – if I wasn't too busy rescuing sheep from briar patches.'

She laughed. 'I can't quite picture you as a lonely goatherd. Did you have a pipe to play?'

'Err, no. To be honest, I took a small wireless with me. A crystal set. I spent most of my day listening to strange music from far-off places.'

'So, even then you wanted to travel?'

'Oh, yes. Even then I had the dwarfs' wanderlust. The desire to travel to foreign places, to find great riches, get drunk a lot and sing interminable songs about how much we miss home, and how great it was and why did we ever leave?'

I was doing well; she laughed again. 'I always wanted to travel as well. My mother was the same, always telling stories about far-off lands and old times. But she has never left the Citadel. Never even as far as Gnada. At least I've managed that.' She got all wistful.

'It's not exactly too late, you know,' I chided gently.

'No, I suppose not.' She picked herself up. 'Did you know,' she said, pointing south, 'did you know that they say that way over there, where Tall Trees is now, there once was another Citadel? As large as this.'

'No,' I answered, 'I did not. If that was the case, where is it now?'

'Well, the story goes that it became a place of great evil; full of goblins and trolls and worse. And then there was a great battle between the two Citadels, and the men and elves pulled the evil Citadel down, so not even a stone remained. The elves then planted their tall trees there so that evil would never threaten this Citadel again.'

'Good story.'

'Yes.'

'No dwarfs, though.'

We both laughed at this one, then set about divvying up the provisions. Liza had only been able to find a couple of watchman's lunches. As she said, how the watchman managed to walk all day on a bit of hard sausage and a pickle was beyond her. But, with my breakbread as well, we managed all right. A few cheeky birds, the common spaggers, landed to keep us company. 'The spaggers are coming,' I said softly to myself, but still broke off some crumbs and encouraged them onto the seat next to me.

'That's a pretty one,' said Liza, pitching a bit of sausage to a new arrival.

'What, the one with the big beak? Back home we call that a "bald griff", and those little ones are "men of cleat".'

'How about that one?' she said, pointing again.

'Well, I don't know what it is in the common tongue, but we call them "candied tuffs".'

'I must confess, I don't know any of the names in any tongue! The only birds I ever recognise are the spaggers and the seagulls. There were always lots of gulls out at the Gnada Peninsula.' She was waxing wistful again and it didn't take a wizard to work out what was on her mind.

I didn't know if this was the right time to tell her of my suspicions, that the Gnada Trophy had still been in Perry's rooms at *The Old Inn* and it was unlikely that he would have left town without it; voluntarily, at least.

'Thinking about Perry?' I said finally.

'Sorry, am I that easy to read?'

'Well, you do have reason to be concerned, after all.'

'It's just that every time I begin to feel normal, or have a good time, or even laugh, I remember Perry and I feel terrible. I am sure something awful has happened.'

I threw a last few crumbs to the birds. This was getting difficult, to say the least. 'That's just guilt, Liza. People always get that when their life, especially after bad news, seems to be going on as normal. Not ...' I added quickly, '... that we have had bad news, nothing for certain. It's early days yet, after all. But whatever, you've been hurt and that takes time to recover from – another old story, I know, but it just happens to be true.'

'I suppose so, but as they always say in those old stories, I just wish there was something I could do.'

'Maybe there is. Tell me everything you know about the elf, Highbury.'

It was pretty much as Thelen had suggested; although Perry and Highbury had been big buddies, they'd had a falling out. Liza thought it was probably over surfing, although she suggested something else may also have been going on. When I wondered out loud whether another woman could have been involved, the temperature fell rapidly. I changed the subject and by the time we went back to work she had warmed up again. I hadn't managed to mention the Gnada Trophy.

The office felt cramped after the great outdoors, or the roof-garden version of it. I contacted my answering service, but there were no messages. I threw open the windows to get some air in, and tried to do a few bits of routine business to fill in the time before my appointment at Hardwood House. The scrollwork proved too much and I ended up playing 'pitch and toss' with the crumpled pages. Then I tried to balance my books, but they fell off the edge of the desk. Eventually I gave up and headed on out. First I gave Liza another call, just to leave my home number in case anything cropped up later. No other reason, of course.

I took the lift downstairs, hoping to see Jakes and thank him for hauling my butt upstairs the previous evening, and tell him his work had another admirer as well. Unfortunately he was not on duty and I didn't know the new man well, so I just waved and stepped out to keep my appointment with the flamboyant and always superbly packaged Mrs Hardwood.

11

HARDWOOD HOUSE

Hardwood House is on the north side of the Bay area: Cliff
Tops, as it is known. This area was one of the first settled
Off-Hill. Before the introduction of motorised transport it
must have seemed far removed from the noise and bustle
of the Citadel, and hence it became the exclusive domain
of the old families; men, that is. When the elves returned
they chose to live in the wooded area, now known as High
Trees, way to the south. Cliff Tops was still exclusive, but
the advent of the motorised wagon brought it within easy
commuting distance.

I tried for the suspension bridge and caught the start of
the early evening rush for my trouble. It looked like I might
be late for the cocktail hour, but as I had no idea of its
precise timing for the smart set, I was not too sure. All I do
know is when I pulled up in front of Hardwood House, the
reception was not what I had been anticipating.

The Hardwood House estate was all right, if you like that
sort of thing. You know, guard lodges, ice houses, stables,
orangeries, greeneries – more outbuildings than you could

find a function for anyway. The gardens had all the trappings of wealth: arched avenues, immaculate lawns – the only difference between the lake and the pool was that the latter had a diving board. But nobody walked on the lawns and nobody swam in the pool.

The house wasn't a castle, because castles usually have fewer towers and a lot less battlements. Castles only have to keep out the ravening hordes. Hardwood House was designed to keep out busybodies and members of the newsgathering professions. It looked about as cosy as chainmail underwear and a great place to live, as long as you remembered to carry a map to get from the library to the ballroom. Not that the occupants of Hardwood House would do anything as crass as walking from one room to another. Good lord, they had staff to do that sort of thing!

One of the Hardwood stewards met me at the front door. He was dressed in a heavy tabard with the Hardwood family crest on it (white horse rampart and a rising star on a sable background), stood straighter than a load-bearing timber and looked like he might have been fabricated along with the building. With hair now all salt and no pepper, ashcup eyes and matching skin, he was a conspiracy of grey. Obviously perspiring freely in all his regalia, he looked hot, but not at all bothered. I don't think much bothered him at all. From his expression I could tell he was not sure if I was even at the right door. I felt his gaze slide past me to the courtyard and the hire wagon. I'm sure it did nothing to add to my social standing. I put on the award-winning smile, gave him a card and said I was expected. He ushered me into a small side room, then returned quickly to ask if I had brought the contract. He carried a tray, probably designed for this very purpose: the silver contract tray from the contract tray cupboard. I put my contract on the tray, and then had to kick my heels for what seemed like an age. Just as I was about to go find the lady of the house for myself, the steward returned, with a signed contract and, just as I had requested, the staff lists – enough people to run a small kingdom out east. I mentioned that I was expecting to see Mrs Hardwood and was told that the family were at dinner with guests and could not be disturbed.

I took a good look at the steward's face, but it was unreadable. I asked his name.

'Goodenough,' he replied.

'Goodenough,' said I. He did not move a perfectly turned-out eyebrow. I kind of suspected he had heard them all before.

'Well, Goodenough, may I ask what duties you have with regard to Mrs Hardwood, and to what degree you share in her confidence?'

He replied, without a trace of smugness, that as Steward of the House he was both Mrs Hardwood's aide and chief executor of her desires. Hmmm … he should be so lucky.

'So you know why I am here?'

'Mrs Hardwood has just informed me of your involvement in the matter at hand.'

'To which you are privy?'

'Indeed, I was the first to know.'

'But of which Mr Hardwood is still unaware?'

'That I could not say, Master Detective.'

'However, if he does know, it's not from your lips?'

'As you say, not from these lips.'

It was a bit like trying to interrogate a statue. 'If I am to carry out these duties to which we allude, Goodenough, I am going to need to have a little look around, and in the absence of the lady of the house, I'm going to have to request your help. Any problem with that?'

Goodenough had obviously been given instructions along those lines, even if he was not sure exactly how much leeway this gave him – and me. He eventually made up his mind.

'I will endeavour to assist in what small way I can.'

'What more can a Master Detective ask for? So, Goodenough, how about we tippy-toe like we're sporting our best invisibility caps and make our way to your lady's chamber, while it's all quiet and peaceful, like.'

'Is that strictly necessary, sir?'

'Does a firbolg throw boulders?'

'I really wouldn't know, sir. Is it important to find out?'

'Not necessary, Goodenough, it's just something I throw in for no extra charge. However, I really do need to see where the article in question was kept, prior to its loss.'

We went by the back ways. Through a maze of servants' tunnels, connected by tiny stairs. Considering the size of the staff list, it was all very quiet. At one point we could hear the sounds of laughter and chinking glasses. It was eerie, like a ride through someone else's dream. Even with my highly developed dwarfish sense of direction, I soon realised I would be hard put to find the way back again. We came out into corridors resplendent with walls of burnished elm panels. They were adorned with huge tapestries of goblins and men, locked in mortal struggle. Both the combatants and the colours had bled over the ages and I couldn't tell who was winning; probably time, I reckoned – it usually does. Still, the tapestries were fine works and probably worth their weight in gold. Closer examination made me realise, with shock, that they were probably originals, dating from the actual Goblin Wars.

Goodenough led me further down this remarkable

gallery. Mrs Hardwood's bedroom and dressing rooms were off the corridor, which I found rather surprising. It was not my idea of an appropriate setting for sleeping quarters; however, the rooms were suitably opulent. They were decorated in the style one would expect from any great lady. Silks and flowers dominated, in the colours of an early fall, lifted wholesale from one of the Great Forests of the far north. Discreet lighting gave it a timeless feel. It was as phoney as a Citadel treasure map. Mrs Hardwood may sleep here but I would put good money on the rest of her recreational activities being carried out in some other, more fitting, environs.

'And where was the emerald kept?' I asked Goodenough, tired of any pretence.

'In here,' he said, leading me into a small curtained alcove. My heart missed a beat when faced with the gem-work therein – hey, I may have gone into detective work, but heredity still counts for something. It was quite a collection, too much to take in at a glance and all open to public view. Goodenough must have been reading my mind.

'Do not be taken in by the apparent lack of security. There are watchers, both seen and unseen, and you would have been apprehended long ago, if you were not with me and the correct procedures had not been carried out.'

The alcove was windowless. I went back into the main bedroom. Large drop-glass doors led onto a balcony, over-looking further outbuildings. I opened them and walked out. Ivy grew right up to the roofing, an easy enough route for any nimble thief. Superficial examination did not reveal any broken branches and the floor of the surround appeared unscuffed. Still, it all seemed very easy work for a professional.

'You will have to take my word for it, Master Detective, no outside agent could get this far.'

'But someone on the inside?'

'A different matter.'

'What are those?' I said, pointing to the nearby outbuildings.

'Stables,' replied Goodenough. 'We keep some horses here, just for hacking on the estate.'

I took out my pipe, but when I caught Goodenough's expression I did not light it. 'So, what do you think, Goodenough?'

'Sir, it is not my place to think.'

'*No,*' I thought, '*it probably isn't, but I bet that doesn't stop you.*' Still, if there is some serious thinking to be done, why not hire someone to do it. 'All right, Goodenough. Where are Mr Hardwood's rooms?'

'Is it important to know?'

'Vital, Goodenough, vital.'

He paused before saying: 'In the next wing.'

Vital? Maybe not, but interesting it was, Goodenough. Very interesting, oh yes.

I decided to take his word on the security side of things for now and get on with the possibility that it was an inside job. I was not happy doing that but I was happy to earn their money. We went back to the courtyard by a different route, one that did not involve the front door. Goodenough then walked me to my wagon.

'Ah yes, the Helmington – a good … well, solid choice of ride, sir.'

I grunted without enthusiasm.

'So much more reliable than those speedy soft tops.'

I grumpily put my hat on, wincing slightly courtesy of the bump that yesterday's macing had left me with, a reaction not missed by Goodenough.

'Has the Master Detective been in an accident?' he unwound enough to ask.

'No,' I replied, 'I've been in an on-purpose.'

'I see. Those are indeed the difficult ones. And it seems they can happen anywhere, any time. I did once read that nine out of ten "on-purposes" happen in the home – which I do find food for thought.'

I chewed that over too as I reversed out of the courtyard. Something else Goodenough had just said was important and I was on the verge of striking gold when a face at an upstairs tower window, viewed in my rear mirror, distracted me. I recognised the face as belonging to Mr Hardwood. He had a book in his hand and I somehow guessed he wasn't sharing starters with any family guests. He looked just like the photograph from the Citadel Archive had prophesied. The beard and polished bald pate had arrived on schedule, even if the remaining hair was somewhat longer at the back than I might have expected. For that brief moment I knew I had his full attention. The eyes in the wagon mirror seemed to take me in, weigh me, catalogue me and then discard me as not being worthy of any more regard. The work of a moment such as that was all a busy man like him could be expected to spare me.

Hardwood turned away and me and the Helmington drove off, spitting drive gravel all over his lawns on the way out. Take that expensive, immaculately mown and cultivated grassland. Ha. I could not say I exactly felt cheated of my cocktail and the chance of someone soft sitting on my lap, but I had been looking forward to those cheesy little biscuits.

I made my way back to the Hill by the scenic route to

give myself some essential thinking time. The road curved its way around the cliffs with precipitous drops at every bend. Round and round I drove but my destination never looked like it was getting any closer.

Back in the office, my feet up on the desk and a large meditation juice in my hand, I took stock. It was all well and good to have top-of-the-tree clients, but a full purse was not going to do me much good if I was languishing in one of the newly renovated dungeons that were now the alternative to beheading if leniency was considered appropriate. How lenient they might feel about elf splitting I didn't like to consider. I needed to have another look at the *Twilight Alehouse* as quickly as possible. Truetouch might well have been a regular there. The more I could find out about him, without alerting the elf establishment, the better. I owed the poor elf that much at least. It was time for some serious detecting, and failing that, to cash in some favours.

Not that Doroty, at Criminal Records, owed me any favours. I knew her from my time in the Citadel Guards. She had taken a shine to me, and although I must have been twice her age, she cast a maternal eye over my activities. I guess she never did altogether approve of me going private, but she was astute enough to know that in the Citadel there were some things that the Cits were not best qualified to deal with. She therefore saw it as part of her civic duty to give me the same access to records offered to other detectives. I, in turn, promised to brush my teeth, change my socks and try not to leave my axe-head anywhere it should not be found. Oops, not my fault, Doroty.

After swapping the usual pleasantries with her I got onto the business of the Hardwood list. It was made up of two parts: present staff and those that had moved on over the last few years. Given the recent picture I had seen of Mrs Hardwood in the fashion press, in which she was still wearing the famous gem, I decided, initially, to rule out all ex-staff and get cracking on with those still indentured. I read the list through for Doroty and she promised to see what she could find.

Josh Corncrack was a man who did owe me a few favours, but we had such a frequent exchange of this currency that it was hard to keep a score. I also knew him from my time at the Cits. A police photographer by trade, holed up in a small dark room in the depths of the Guard Watchtower, he had a certain magic with an image caught in glass that made him invaluable. He consequently also had a semi-legit trade as a freelance for a number of major Citadel news scrolls. I had helped him out with many a good story, and with his connections at the Citadel Press, he was an excellent source of information for me from that direction.

Some of his seniors reckoned Josh had a discipline problem. As he pointed out to them, how could he have a discipline problem when he had no discipline? Yep, me and Josh got on just fine.

I had his direct number at Guard Central. I spun it and got an immediate reply.

'You've reached the number of Josh Corncrack. I am currently doing something much more important than talking to you. Leave a message and I'll scrub it along with all the others, so quit bothering me.'

'Josh Corncrack, I am delighted to inform you that you have won 1,000 thousand crowns this instant if you can answer this simple question. What was …'

'What? Who?' Josh spluttered, taken by surprise.

'Ah, got you!' I said, laughing.

'Strongoak, you little carpet creeper! Still not getting on the dangerous fairground rides?'

'Yeah, you must have seen me there, Josh – you were on break from working as an exhibit in the House of Horrors.'

'I've squashed bigger than you with a fly swat.'

'And I've seen squashed flies that looked prettier than you.'

Pleasantries done, we got on with the serious business of the Hardwood list.

'Has this got anything to do with the little matter that is making your name about as popular round here as a firbolg's fart?'

'Maybe Josh, I'm not too sure anymore.'

'That's a shame, Nicely. I'd welcome a little opportunity to get up the noses of a few of the gold badges. They're running round like they've got a kobold's pick up their arses and they're currently making life unpleasant for a lot of us, including your ex-partner Ralph. One of them even had the nerve to say I should be filling in a time sheet!'

'Sorry for that, Josh. To be honest, I'm surprised they haven't had me in for an extended sweating.'

'Well, something's stirred the dragon, Nicely, and that's for sure. I just don't think anybody knows how to deal with it. In the meantime running about looking very concerned seems to be the order of the day.'

Fine with me! I wasn't going to worry, not while I was still in the clear. Josh promised to stroke a few of his contacts and see if any of the names on the Hardwood list had been featuring in any reports or gossip. I thanked him and promised to take him out for a hogget bun next time I was in the neighbourhood.

Five minutes later I'd picked up the Helmington from the Two Fingers' handy underground wagon park and headed on out to revisit *The Twilight Alehouse*. Although the recently departed elf had driven me all around the Hill, my dwarf direction bump had rarely failed me before. After a frustrating hour I began to think that this time I just might have come unstuck. Maybe it was the Moondust, or the macing – it couldn't be the exotic gravy, of course.

I parked the Helmington in what I judged to be the correct neighbourhood and took to foot. In the daylight, the area seemed even more commonplace. The rocks of the houses were all clean of moss and the steps were washed, but nobody much was at home. Bright drapes lit up the windows and small brass fittings were common on the doors. A lot of homelification had recently gone on and it seemed that all the useful older folk had been moved on. Nowhere could I see any indication of the alehouse I had spent time in with the dead elf. I tried talking to the locals, but they were of the 'we-mind-our-own-business' variety that is the bane of detectives everywhere. Even the local traders were not spectacularly garrulous. I did get an unpleasant sneer when I asked for directions from a butcher, but that might have been his need for a new personality.

I returned to the wagon and worried a nail. Whoever was trying to put me in the frame either had some sort of magical powers or alternatively an awful lot of clout. I hoped it was the clout, because even though I wasn't sure whether I actually believed in all that sorcery malarkey, I knew I would surely be out-gunned in that department. I thought about the other options available to me and felt in my inside pocket for the pipeleaf picture of Rosebud. I examined it again, looking for something I may have missed. The driver of a delivery wagon was leaning on his horn behind me. All of the Hill available and he wanted the space my wagon occupied. I took it as a sign and pulled out.

My headache was returning and I decided I needed something a bit solid inside me to put some more fuel in the boiler. I went to a gnome joint I knew called *The Side of Beef*. I chased the ribs down with something dark and sticky I had not realised I'd wanted. I then chewed on a toothpick, whilst planning my next move. Before anything else I decided to make my peace with the Citadel Guard, so I took the Helmington down to Guard Central on Fifth. It knew it would be a waste of time for all concerned at this stage, but it had to be done. From what Josh had said, my credit with the gold badges was fast running out.

I walked into the entrance hall and straight into Scout Telfine. He had been practising curling his upper lip especially for me.

'I hear from around that you used to be hot stuff, dwarf?'

'I don't know if I can make any such claim, Scout Telfine. I think I was just lucky in the quality of my workmates at the time.' Telfine added a sneer to his lip curl – an impressive achievement in facial manipulation. 'Yes, laugh it up, ground hugger! I'll tell you something for nothing, though: things are about to change around here. You just wait and see! We'll have proper law enforcement, a place suitable for men, with no favours, corn spreading or special treatments!'

'And there I was, thinking that is what we had already?'

'Maybe that's because you used to be one of the folk handing out the favours and spreading the corn! Times change though, dwarf! See you around!'

Telfine stormed on out, the creases on his trousers sharp enough to hobble unsuspecting walkers on the cobblestones ahead of him. I don't know who had pickled his pixie, but he was going to do himself a mischief if he wasn't careful.

Unless I got there first, of course.

The Cits who conducted my interview were also new but at least house-trained. I played the indignant law-abiding dwarf, unused to the big-city ways and still with coal dust behind his ears. They were the put-upon professionals, just trying to do their duty. We danced around like this for a while. No one was fooled. I'm just glad nobody else recognised me at the station; they would have laughed themselves stupid. I checked the roster; Ralph was just coming off duty and I caught him in the wagon park. Snatchpole at the *Gally-trot-a-Go-Go* had given the Cits a description of the dwarf seen with Truetouch: short, bright-red hair, a waist-length beard and walked with a limp. As this did not tally with my physique – tall, dark-brown hair and twelve-hour stubble – I was in the clear for the moment, but Ralph again reminded me about not leaving the Citadel. I thanked him and let him get home to the wife and children while I returned to the office.

Since Snatchpole was not in fact visually impaired, I could take it that this was one big favour repaid. I somehow did not think anyone was going to come forward voluntarily from the back-alley inn that Truetouch had dragged me to, so I felt safe on that front. However, I did not kid myself that I was in the clear yet. Ralph and Snatchpole had helped buy me some time, but I needed to use it wisely. Most of all, at that moment, I needed the help of a wizard.

It's not that easy to find a wizard in the Citadel. It is not as if you can just look one up in the white pages. I had to go all the way to directory enquiries. I caught him on the way out and we arranged to meet the next evening - wizards aren't too good in daylight. They say it's something to do with magic working better at night. I think they are just slug-a-beds and can't get up in the morning.

Me, I was ready for bed and so I took myself home and slept the sleep of the blameless and untainted. I don't think that eight hours of uninterrupted slumber would necessarily be a good defence in a court of law. Not with the axeman already sharpening the blade.

12

AN UNEXPECTED LUNCH DATE

This hearty and clean-living dwarf was up early. An evening without being poisoned, beaten or powdered will do that for a body. So, I gave the body the treat of a steaming hot tub of water and managed to get a good start to the day. I made it up to the Two Fingers early, hoping to catch Liza, but she had pasted me a note to say she was off for the morning, visiting her kin at their home over on Helm and Rhavona. She had left me a number so I gave her a blast on the horn.

The woman that answered could have been Liza, if she was capable of spitting acid. The irate mother first wanted to know if I was 'this no-good so-called boyfriend'. When I answered in the negative she was very keen on knowing exactly why I was bothering her daughter. I tried to explain without mentioning the word 'detective', but I made the mistake of mentioning the word 'dwarf'. I thought I knew what 'my kind' was, but up until then I was not aware 'my kind' should keep away from the daughters of law-abiding Citadel men and women. Furthermore, she had heard all about 'my kind' and our filthy habits and if I didn't desist in bothering her daughter the Citadel Guards would be informed of my deviancy.

It looked like my chances of being invited round for a nice family supper had gone west big time.

I rested my aching ear and sat to write up some notes and clear my desk, binning a few bills and sending off a few of my own, hoping my clients would not extend mine the same consideration.

At what seemed like a reasonable hour, I called Mrs Hardwood's scribe and made an appointment for lunch. I wasn't going to be put off that easy.

A few more calls, touching base with my scouts, and then I drove off to visit the address I had obtained for Leo Courtkey from the stableman Clubbin. It was in a so-so part of town: one of those places that never seem to quite establish their own identity, neither poor nor rich, fashion-able nor unfashionable, it clung to the edge of the Hill like a barnacle on a sea elf's boat. Leo Courtkey's rooms were on the top floor of a building that was seeing the first of the homelification that had improved or ravished many parts of the Citadel, depending on your point of view. Gutters were being emptied and drainpipes fixed, which was all to the good, but windows and doors were being replaced without much thought and some of the fabrics at the windows would have made a transvestite troll blush. Unfortunately, for me at least, the address was way out of date. The current owners had no idea what had happened to the previous tenants and made it pretty clear that they cared even less. They also seemed less than happy about having a dwarf strutting around the quarter, like I was suddenly going to send the house prices plummeting.

On my way back to the wagon I looked out for the blind-twitcher. Every place like this still with its share of old folks has one. Sure enough, there was the sign: the give-away moving of slats that marked the ever-inquisitive neighbour. I went and knocked. The door had more bolts than a dwarf king's treasure chest. I waited patiently. Eventually, door still on a last chain, one gimlet eye was put to the resulting crack and a voice as sharp as an axe edge said: 'Yes?'

I showed her my shield and explained that I just wanted to have a few words about some old neighbours. She gave the shield a slow once over that would not have shamed the Citadel Guard's finest, and then said I had better come in.

'Dwarf, eh?' she said, leading me into a spotless parlour. 'Don't see many dwarfs in this part of the Citadel. I suppose you'll be wanting ale?' I said it was a bit early and coffee would be fine.

'Nonsense, I know what dwarfs are like.' She walked into a roomy pantry lined with stone flagons, and brought out a particularly large one. 'And just so you don't think I'm antisocial, I had better join you.'

She gestured me to a seat next to a cheery little hearth in which logs were already stacked, awaiting winter. I duly took my appointed place. She went back into the pantry, returning with some pots. 'I make it all myself, you know. That's why they call me Mother Crock.' Parking herself in a rocker that looked like it had seen some service, Mother Crock poured out ale and words in equal measure.

And what a mine of information she was. The problem was keeping her from wandering off the vein I wanted dug. A further problem was the strength of the ale. As she'd mentioned, it was all made to her own recipe, and what the ingredients could be, was anyone's guess – blasting powder, maybe? The result, though, was smoother than a baby drag-on's belly and more dangerous than its mother. After we had put Widergard to rights (she put a lot of blame on the councillors and aldermen and looked forward to the next elections with glee: 'heads will roll'), we finally got round to the subject of Leo Courtkey. The Courtkeys, as it turned out to be, for the address belonged originally to Leo's mother and father. They had died some years before and Leo had sold on the house and had pretty much cut his ties with the neighbourhood. I told her I was trying to find him to ask about a horse he had once ridden. I wondered why this made me feel uncomfortable. Of course, I was telling the truth! It was the novelty of the situation.

'I remember him best as a boy,' said Mother Crock. 'He was a strange one, he never really fitted into that family. His father was a lamplighter, as I remember. Mother sewed, and well; all very worthy, but to be honest, more than a bit dull. Leo, an only child, was different.' She pulled herself out of the rocker, had a little walk and did a quick survey through her parlour window. Happily updated, she took her seat again, and picked up her ale and the thread of the conversation.

'Leo was very small as a boy and hardly said a word. Always being picked on by the other boys. I took pity on the poor thing, and many a time he sat just where you are sitting, and I would tell him stories of the old days in the Citadel. He loved the old stories, especially the ones with horses in them. They made him really smile apparently. He loved horses, he did, and I was so pleased when he got a chance to become a rider. Of course, his build was with him, you see, and he did have a wonderful way with the horses, one you can seldom find in men. Oh, they make very good riders, but they say they don't have the empathy you might find in an elf.'

'How about after he stopped racing?'

Here Mother Crock looked more agitated. 'I don't know, he seemed to lose part of himself. Some say he fell in with a bad lot – not that he dropped by much after that, so I am mostly going by what I've heard. Eventually he stopped visiting at all.' She stopped rocking for a moment and had a think.

'I did see him once more, but in the market. I hardly recognised him and he didn't seem very keen to talk to me. He looked very out of sorts. Very pale.' She leant forward in that conspiratorial fashion that people adopt, even if there is nobody there to overhear them.

'I was worried about powders and potions, you know. They say a lot of that goes on now.'

I had to agree with Mother Crock – far too much of that goes on now.

She sighed and continued: 'I think he was probably trying to find something to replace the riding. I am just grateful that the Hardwoods kept him on at the house.'

'The Hardwoods!' I blurted. My astonishment was genuine and immense; I was completely trolled by this turn of events.

Mother Crock realised as much. 'Yes, didn't you know he raced for Mr Hardwood?'

I struggled to recover my composure. My credibility in the detective stakes was rapidly heading westwards. 'But surely Leo rode Rosebud, owned by the Merrymeads?'

'I don't know all about that. It was Rosebud all right though, that was his favourite, but it was the Hardwoods who paid him his purse – I'm sure.'

Well, here was quillwork for the scribes and no mistake.

'And before that it was the King of the Desolate Wastes,'

she added triumphantly.

'King of the Desolate Wastes?' I said, now really wondering where this was all heading.

'Without any doubt. Leo's mother was always going on about it.' She tutted quietly. 'For a hugely dull woman she could go on. He moved in there, of course, and if you ask me that's where his problems first started, they did! Never the same after that, restless he was. Only visited me once and he couldn't keep still. Something changed there!'

'Did he ever mention any elves? One in particular, called Truetouch?'

'Elves?' Mother Crook rocked and thought. 'No elves by name, but he loved the stories with elves in them. Those were always his favourites, the elf stories – mind you, what child doesn't?'

I didn't like to suggest, pretty much every young dwarf that was ever told a bedtime story, as that might have seemed a bit undignified.

The tie-in with the Hardwoods had taken the power from my pick, that was for sure, and what to make of the royal connection was anyone's guess. The rest of her tale rather passed me by as my wits wandered westward. It was time to be moving on. I gave my thanks and said as speedy a farewell as manners and her continuing monologue would allow.

Mother Crock had given me a lot to think about. She had also given me a flagon of her homemade ale, which I put safely in the back of the wagon. What she had not been able to give me was a current address for Leo Courtkey. I waved to her, perched on the doorstep as I drove away, and promised to look after Leo if I found him; really I should have had more important things to do than chase after a fallen rider and, I suspected, wormhead. Like trying to find whoever was putting me in the frame for a very nasty murder. I mean, there was no way that Perry's increasingly worrying absence, the dead elf and the Hardwood gem could be connected, was there?

I made my way back to the Two Fingers and I was at the desk just in time for a call from Mrs Hardwood's secretary: Mrs Hardwood would not be able to make lunch today after all, and no, Mrs Hardwood would not be taking any calls today either. I did not even have time to get disappointed before the horn tooted again.

'Master Strongoak, this is Thelen.'

I resisted the temptation to say 'Thelen who?'

'Could we meet, perhaps for lunch please, Nicely?'

I said that, as luck would have it, I was available and knew the perfect place. We agreed to meet at midwatch. I'd arranged to meet Mrs Hardwood at a very new and exclusive eatery called *The Sea Star* run mainly for the White and Wise. In typical elf style, it seemed that the more they took out of the setting, the more they took out of your purse too! *The Sea Star* was minimal to the point that you wondered if perhaps you should come back after the decorators had been in. The walls were coloured in those shades of white that have names like lace-white and shell-white and elf-white but still just look like white to me. Everything was in such good taste it put my teeth on edge and made me want to go wild with a pot of lava-red paint and a hefty book of gold leaf.

Thelen was suitably impressed.

I admit that I had intended putting this on Mrs Hardwood's expenses and I shuddered slightly when I saw the prices, because there was no way I would put this on Liza's tab instead. Oh well, speculate to accumulate, they say. I just hoped there might be some elucidation and illumination too.

'I have heard of this place,' said Thelen, 'it must have been difficult to get a table at such short notice.'

I shrugged in what I hoped was a 'dwarf-of-the-world' fashion and, feeling suitably smug, I ordered a wine I had only heard whispered about before. We chose the food with the sort of attention I normally reserve for juggling vipers and when the wine arrived, in its own silver handcart, we traded appreciative noises, obeying the 'no business while eating' rule of the elves. Actually, dwarfs have a related rule: 'whenever possible try to be eating and doing business.' It explains why so many dwarfs have been so financially successful, but also why the dwarf waist measurement is, well, let's just say certain eating disorders are a most rare phenomenon.

The food was in the 'new style' so beloved by the elves. All wonderful colours and beautifully arranged, and really subtle flavours, but nothing that could kick-start the wagon on a cold morning. Thelen, though, was absolutely in raptures, and that was OK with me. I could get used to Thelen-style raptures.

I had seen the young elfess in her wetsuit, looking almost boyish, and also at the ball looking like a princess. Today she was much more businesslike, wearing an outfit which would not have looked out of place on Mrs Hardwood: a dress cut to resemble the top of a gentleman's suit, double breasted, buttoning down to the waist, but then opening into a slit skirt. This one was blue, with a discreet, narrow stripe, and the effect was both elegant and disconcerting, probably because it reminded me a little too much of the other lady. The business it brought to mind had nothing to do with finance.

Thelen was considering the dessert menu, holding it in one hand, her long tapering fingers and nails showing a natural manicure that, just for once, made me slightly self-conscious of my own workman-like spades. A fresh-berry confection safely put away, we then sat over coffee and finally discussed what had occurred since I last saw her. Her main tale concerned the recovery of the Gnada Trophy. I didn't let on that I had been preoccupied with getting my head stoved in while it was being 'recovered'.

I listened keenly to the full three volumes. The reappearance of the cup, back in the main hall of the Gnada Surfing Club, was greeted, it was fair to say, with some relief, as the date of this year's competition was fast approaching. Although there was a rumour that Perry had been seen delivering the trophy, Thelen felt that this had been started deliberately, and had heard a whisper that Highbury was involved in its return. She wouldn't reveal her source, and I did not push too hard; in her position I would have done the same thing.

I then told her about my run-in with Petal. I wanted her to be on her very pretty and well-formed toes and to look out for all lurking goblins with perfect dentition.

'But why a warning? A warning against what?' she asked, quite reasonably.

I had to admit my ignorance, never easy for a detective. We all like to pretend we have some idea about what's going on, no matter how much of our lives we actually do spend totally mystified. It helps us feel better about our shiny badges and hourly rates.

'All because of a missing barkeep and a lost trophy?' She raised one perfectly shaped (for an elf) eyebrow. 'Or is there something else currently engaging your attentions that may have caught their attention too?'

From where I was sitting there was a lot engaging my attentions, but I didn't think it gallant to mention it. This also did not seem like the right time to casually mention my predicament with regard to a recently deceased member of her own kin, and since she hadn't mentioned anything either, I decided that somebody was indeed really keeping a very tight lid on matters. The only problem was that it you kept a lid on a pot too tightly, and then keep adding more heat, you generally end up with a very messy explosion indeed.

I tried a different approach. 'Maybe Highbury keeps more dishonourable company than we have considered? One quiet word in the right ear can kill as surely as an arrow.'

'That's a very unpleasant thought. All this sporadic violence that keeps breaking out around the Citadel, do you think perhaps it's not quite as spontaneous as it seems?'

'Ouch!' I said. 'That is an even more mean and cynical idea than I was contemplating and I think it's a vein we should dig a great deal deeper.'

Thelen sighed, 'I find it hard to believe that my own kin could behave in such a fashion.'

'Lady,' I replied, 'nothing has surprised me since I did a body search on a Witch Queen and found a wand in a place it had no right to be.'

Thelen had a further appointment, so she made her apologies and left, while I stayed for another perfectly brewed coffee. I left the restaurant feeling strangely unsatisfied, though, and it was not just about the size of their portions. I thought it was about time I got back on the offensive. I had been everybody's favourite punch-bag and it was beginning to sour. It was time to take the dragon by the tail, or a least poke him a bit with a very long stick from a very long way away.

I found a street-horn nearby, put a few calls through and then kick-started part two into operation. For my next step I needed some more background. I was not sure who to connect with, but when in doubt ask the Citadel Guard. Ralph was at his desk when I called, and I got straight through.

'Hi Ralph, Nicely here. How's my wagon, any chance of seeing it again this side of winter?'

'I am sorry, sir,' came the reply. 'I am afraid you will have to make that request through the appropriate channel, and no, sorry, I will not be available for comment later, as I have to visit my dental technician concerning some bridgework.'

So, someone was now breathing that close down Ralph's neck as well. Or was my speech-horn style in need of some attention? Interesting, especially given Doroty's earlier reticence. There was something that Ralph wanted to tell me – he'd given me our secret password. The bridgework he had mentioned had nothing to do with dentistry. The bridge in question was over the River Everflow.

The Dwarfholm Bridge is the last of the great bridges that span the Everflow as it makes its way past the Hill down to the Bay. It is a combination of drawbridge and suspension elements and a mighty fine piece of engineering. The four structural towers would not be out of place in a grand fortress and they have more pointy bits than is strictly necessary for crossing a river. But an abundance of pointy bits can never be a bad thing on a building, it's like the wings on my Dragonette, it just wouldn't look right without them.

Some years before, when we were both still with the CIA, Ralph and I had been responsible for busting a 'dust ring' based there. The once bustling Dwarfholm Bridge area was, at that time, pretty derelict, with empty storehouses made obsolete by the new docks opening up further down in the Bay. The 'dust ring' had set up business in rooms built into the very foundations of the bridge. Being of dwarfish construction, the rooms could only be opened by key-and-code. By some oversight, Ralph and I had both ended up with keys to one of the secret doors, and we both kept forgetting to hand them in long after the investigation was over. What are the chances of that, I ask you?

It was a fair step to the Dwarfholm Bridge and I had not been out there for some time. A lot of change was happening. Storehouses were being taken over by bright young things from the upper levels and being converted into dwellings. Stockshops and knife-and-finger joints were reopening as licensed provisioners and rather smart little eateries. I hardly recognised the old place. Fortunately, the Bridge itself was still home to nothing more than a few bottle-boys and worm-heads, and they had more things to worry about than one lone dwarf out for a stroll by the riverside. I still double-locked the Helmington and kept a careful look over my shoulder as I entered the combination and undid the lock to the Bridge Room.

There were a lot of steps up to our little secret hideaway in one of the two main towers that house the hydraulics and engines that lift the leaves of the drawbridge. After the steam engines were upgraded the near-bank tower had become largely superfluous to needs, but as a hideaway it could not be beaten.

Ralph was already halfway down his first pipe when I entered. Lit only by the glow from his bowl and the glow from Citadel street-lamps, he looked like some weathered hero from days gone by, more suited to guarding against the ravages of goblins and trolls than dealing with the politics of modern-age detective work.

I lit a pipe and looked out of the Tower window, which gives an unbeatable view upstream along the Everflow towards the Troll's End Bridge.

'So Ralph, what's the tally?'

'As I remember it, the New Iron Town Delvers got taken to the cleaners by the Citadel Eagles and lost 6–2.'

'Ballgames aside?'

'Well.' He took a contemplative draw. 'Let us say it's not so much what is happening, but rather what is not.'

'How do you mean?'

'Remember Scout Telfine?'

'How could I forget, such an unalloyed addition to the Citadel Guard. I forgot to mention, I bumped into him at Guard Central, about to lay a dragon's egg, from the look of him.'

'Yes, indeed. It has been remarked upon before. A man with a pike so far up his own fundament he has trouble putting his hat on. And if he has a nice word to say about any of the Citadel's folk, apart from men, I have yet to hear it. He is right about one thing, though: even more so than in your day, when we have an incident involving an elf you really have to watch which way the dragon is flying, and when you hear leather wings flapping you keep your head well covered!' He poked absent-mindedly at the embers in his briar with a pipenail. 'Or otherwise you are going to get dumped on from high up.'

'So, the heat came down?'

'No, that's just it, Nicely. The opposite, if anything, happened. Let's just say that the investigation so far has been characterised by a period of untypical cool and clement weather.'

'Josh said folks were getting rattled, though.'

'Displacement twitching from those that mistake activity for action.'

'Always the way, Ralph. Some people have got to be seen to be doing something, even if it's thrashing around like a swimmer well out of his depth being tickled by a kelpie.'

'But we didn't get grief from the folk that really mattered.'

I pulled on my pipe.

'Which should tell us something?'

'I don't know what though, Nicely.'

'How about background on the dead elf? I just hope he wasn't some well-connected lordling slumming it.'

'I don't think so,' said Ralph, looking genuinely perplexed. 'We've run our own trace on this Truetouch character, of course, and come up with a big fat pixie's breakfast. No real close friends, no address, nothing.'

'Did you talk to a young lord by the name of Highbury, by any chance?'

'Oh yes!' Ralph raised his eyebrows and looked to the roof, as if for release. 'And what a charmer he was as well, a delight to waste an hour of my life with him.'

'Had you heard the rumour that he might be running for political office?'

Ralph gave this some consideration before he answered. 'I hadn't, Nicely, but somehow I'm not surprised, judging by what else has been crawling out of the woodwork this year. It's enough to make you consider taking up whittling wooden teeth for Wulvers.'

'But Truetouch ...?'

'He might just as well have stepped straight out of the Hidden Lands.'

'Elves tend to be more tight with each other than that.'

'Sure, I guess when you've been round the mountain as often as they have, you tend to get a pretty full address ledger.'

'So how about his other Surf Elf buddies?'

'Another blank. Everybody seemed to be vaguely aware of him, but that was all.'

I thought of the figure on the beach, holding the towel. A hero in nobody's story, probably not even his own, but with a nice line of threads and a smile that surely must have opened a few doors somewhere?

'What is Widergard coming to?' I asked Ralph. 'Folk minding their own business, whatever next: men not overcompensating?'

'And dwarfs not carrying grudges?'

'That really will be the day!'

Ralph stretched his long legs and they clicked like so many breaking twigs.

'And then finally, some time during the small hours last night, the elves turned up and took the body.'

'Was it the dune huggers?'

'No, that's another thing. Top-of-the-tree, real Higher Elves. Then, when I get in this morning we get the word, a lot of new boys are being drafted into the team; all from off the Hill. And a couple of elfin "advisors" suddenly turn up, doing interviews. All completely unconnected, or so they say.

'Next I get the whisper that they are asking rather a lot of questions, including quite a few about you, Nicely. And every time you pick up the horn those elfin ears are sent a'twitching in your direction.' He broke off and by the pipe light I could see him considering. 'Anything else you can tell me yet, Nicely?'

'Nothing that makes any sense, Ralph. I'm not even sure

who I'm dealing with. I've two, maybe three cases on the go, and try as I might to keep them separate, they all seem to be getting mixed up.'

Ralph got up to leave. 'Well, just as long as you are aware that there are probably some very important people now watching from the shadows.'

'I appreciate the warning.' We made for the door before I remembered the reason for my call. 'Tell me, Ralph. Who would you go to ask for information about elves?'

'The elves?' he replied helpfully.

'Let's say, if one didn't want any more involvement of the pointed-ear persuasion.'

Ralph paused at the door. 'How about Arito Cardinollo?'

'What, the gnome scribe?'

'The same. Lives out in Little Hundred. He wrote a best-selling scroll on that very subject last year.'

'Oh yes, of course, it got up a lot of perfect noses.'

'Elves have been his life work, and he's been very, shall we say, discreet, in the past – when awkward questions needed some answers.'

I laughed as I imagined what some of those questions might have been. 'Thanks Ralph, I owe you.'

'For what, Nicely? Nothing happened. I haven't even seen you.'

I let him go down the staircase first and caught up with him waiting by the parked wagons. He looked the Helmington up and down with a mixture of distaste and curiosity. 'If this is what you end up driving, I'm glad I never went private.'

'The offer is still there Ralph,' I said with a laugh. 'Strongoak and Fieldfull has a nice ring to it.'

'Fieldfull and Strongoak sounds better.'

I laughed again and then got serious. 'Ralph, I have just been thinking – it would be very useful to get a tail on lord Highbury. Whatever is going on here, my grandfather's bones tell me that Highbury is up to his pointy ears in it.'

'I'm not going to argue with you there, Nicely. And certainly not with your grand-da's remains either.' He paused and gave the matter some thought before continuing, 'But if I'm found putting the tail on any elf at the moment, without a reason more solid than an ancestor's anatomy, I'm going to kicked round all five levels and back again.'

'Oh, well – worth a try.'

'I'll give it some thought. By the way, the old bird told me you might be after these.' Ralph threw me a set of wagon keys. 'I cleared your Dragonette with the top brass and sent it down to your grease goblin Sceech for an overhaul. I think you're going to be needing a fast set of wheels to keep ahead of this particular game.'

We both took a moment to consider what exactly the game might be, and if we were winning, before we waved our goodbyes. Ralph's parting shot seemed particularly apt.

'Don't go spitting in the eye of any dragons, Nicely; especially the big pointy-eared ones.'

As I gave the Helmington some steam and reversed out from under the bridge I thought, just for a minute that I saw something move in the shadow of one of the bridge supports. I looked again and it seemed to be clear. I took this as a sign though, if Petal wanted to jump me again the shooter under my jacket was not going to be there just for show.

13

THE HOMELY HOUSE BAR AND GRILL

The Wizards' Quarter was a strange place even by Hill standards. It was in an untidy part of Old Town and seemed out of phase with the rest of Widergard. It was still furnished with the trappings of a bygone era. I swear the lamplighters conspired in this, by keeping the place permanently under-lit, or maybe the wizards just don't pay their bills. A few years back a terrific stink had been kicked up when there had been some talk of turning the whole Wizards' Quarter into a theme park. The wizards, even in these days of reduced influence, had so far managed to resist this move.

The Wizards' Quarter also provided cheap accommodation for any number of purveyors of other occupations which, like wizardry, now also do not command the respect they once had; poets and scribes and such-like. And in the cheapest of the cheap I found Renfield Crew, the scribe who had written *The Green Book*'s account of the political dealings of Mr

Hardwood that I had read in the Citadel library.

If cellars can have subcellars, I'm not sure what subcellars can have by way of lower floors. Renfield Crew lived in such a place though, in a chamber that the poor unfortunates in the dungeons of old would have looked down on. I only stumbled upon his new abode by accident in the end. I'd almost given up, when I leant on a fence for support, in order to remove something from my boot that I really didn't want on my boot. The fence turned out to be an unlocked gate, and that led to a staircase that I then floundered down in a very inelegant fashion until I hit the first turn. From there it was another two flights to the particular hole in the ground that Renfield inhabited. By the time I had carefully reached the bottom of the other staircases, and taken in this hovel, I was able to conclude that Renfield's literary career was not on the up and up. 'It's all because of Hardwood!' insisted the disgruntled scribe, when the sight of a bright shiny crown finally got me past the impressive display of padlocks, bolts, fasteners and clasps which protected his few miserable possessions. It transpired that it wasn't his possessions that he sought to protect though, but his equally miserable personage.

'He is out to kill me, you see? I dared write the things that nobody else would! Oh yes! The power of the quill, you see! Yes, I made him fear me. Me, Renfield Crew! I made him fear the quill of Renfield Crew! That is the power of the word!'

Renfield Crew, the feared scribe, was obviously still swinging his axe with no handle and I couldn't help but feel sorry for him. If wretch ever became a sought-after commodity then Renfield was going to be a millionaire. He was thin to the point of famishment, with interesting skin conditions usually found in sailors who have been shipwrecked on deserted atolls for many years, living only on whelks. He had an odd number of teeth, or maybe it was an even number of teeth. Whatever, every other one seemed to be missing.

His room was in an even greater state of disrepair: a few crates pretending to be furniture, a stove and a sleeping palette. Writing must really be its own reward because it certainly didn't seem to provide anything else.

'I'd won awards, you know?' He pointed to a few framed bits of parchment hung on the walls of the sub-subcellar, which were the only items breaking up the otherwise uniform coating of mould. 'Oh yes, awards! For "most promising reportage" and "investigative insight" and "naked ambition".' He blinked a few times behind spectacles that seemed to be cultivating their own special coating of mildew. 'I'm not so sure about that last one.'

It seemed Renfield was determined to prove his grievances had some grounding in reality even if his life no longer did. The loss of his job and the closing down of *The Green Book* were both the result of the press owner being bought out shortly after the Hardwood piece was pressed. Renfield was still tracing this sale and had come up, via a chain with more kinks than a chain-mail corkscrew, with a company that may, or may not, once have had a connection with Mr Hardwood. It seemed pretty scant evidence to me.

Renfield did still write; from what I could see he wrote lots, on just about anything that would hold ink: waste board, packaging, the backs of posters liberated from outside of Citadel entertainment establishments of every ilk – here low and high art definitely rubbed naked and well-dressed shoulders.

'Soon, I'll have it all! Soon, I will be vindicated! The

whole of Widergard will see I was right about Alderman Hardwood! And they'll learn about how he victimised me, ensured no press would hire me, made my life the black pit it has become!'

'So, you've got fresh evidence as well, have you?' I tried to see what he was currently writing, but the little pixie of distrust had lit a candle of anxiety behind his eyes.

'No, no! Get away! Not yet, not yet!' Renfield gabbled, grabbing at his damp and decaying writings. 'Not until it's finished! Who are you anyway? He sent you, didn't he? Get back, get back!'

Renfield Crew's few remaining faculties had gone west for a holiday. I gave him my card, which I think he saw as an opportunity for an interesting new expansion in his writings, and asked him to get into contact if he found anything solid for me to chip at. I climbed sadly up the three flights of stairs and went to find myself a wizard.

The cold-light sign outside *The Homely House Bar and Grill* flashed half-heartedly in the still cloying air. I opened the bar door and smoky air slipped round me like an old familiar overcoat. The wizard had arranged the time and place for the meet. I asked how I would recognise him, and he laughed mysteriously, and said I would know. I expected to find him, a mysterious figure lurking in some dark nook. What I did not expect was to find a place full of dark nooks (a nookery?) and sat in each one, a hooded and shadow-wrapped, staff-hugging mysterious figure.

I was feeling a little edgy after my conversation with Renfield and not in a mood for playing nice as I made my way to the servery. The keeper was seated behind it with his evening scroll. He glanced up and spoke in my general direction from behind some truly appalling dental work.

'Can't you read?'

'Sure,' I replied. 'Five different languages in four different scripts.'

'Well.' He pointed to a badly penned sign on the servery top. 'As this doesn't seem to be one of them, this here sign says, "No Gnomes", that's G-N-O-M-E-S.'

'And I am a dwarf, D-W-A-R-F, and this is an axe, do I need to spell it out any clearer?' I watched the little gears turn over in his brain box.

'Bog no, master. It's a bit difficult to make you out in this gloom.'

'Try turning a few more lamps on,' I suggested.

'I would do, but this is the way the wizards like it. They say it gives the place atmosphere.' He got up off his stool and reached for a crock. 'We don't get many dwarfs up here in the Wizards' Quarter. What can I get you? A goodly flagon of foaming ale, is it?'

I cannot stand stereotyping, and I didn't think he had anything to match Mother Crook's brew, so I replied tartly: 'Juniper sling, very dry.'

'You what?'

'I said, a juniper sling. You having problems with your hearing as well as your eyesight? Perhaps both could be improved by moving your head nearer the floor.'

'Bog no, master, I'm going bowling tonight.' He started on the cocktail. 'Olive and a twist?'

'Yes,' I replied, turning round and surveying the darkened bar.

'I'm sorry but I'm all out of those little cheesy biscuits.'

I let him have that one, took my drink and made for a likely-looking candidate, hiding in one corner. It was a process of elimination. As far as I could tell in the gloom and smoke, he was the only person in the place sitting by himself.

'What's the matter with the Citadel suddenly,' I said, taking a seat. 'Has there been a mass outbreak of hives, or has the council brought out a sconce tax suddenly?'

'It's what the punters expect,' replied the shrouded figure. 'The mysterious image, all runes and pointed hats. Personally,' he said, putting a flint to a large lamp on the table, 'I feel it is all rather outdated. Still, we have to go with market forces, and as we seem to do most of our business in these places, we have to give the punters what they want. Anyway,' he adjusted the wick to a more reasonable level, 'perhaps we can dispense with that now.'

'And what's with the anti-gnome policy?'

The wizard blinked a couple of times as he played with the lighting.

'I had never noticed that,' he admitted.

'Yes, powers of observation make a wizard, I'm told.' I looked around by the improved illumination. 'So, how is business? It doesn't seem to be too bad.'

My drinking companion gave a shrug. 'You would be well advised not to believe quite everything you see when dealing with the concerns of wizards.' When I looked blank, he carried on. 'For example, it has not been unknown for some wizards to employ people to sit with them, to make commerce appear a tad more busy.'

'Which is not something you approve of, I take it.'

'I think, Master Dwarf, that it is bad enough that we have to ply our art like a half-crown camp follower, without colluding in the charade.' He said this with all the dignity one would expect of a wizard.

Not that I am much of a judge, to be honest. I have not had a lot of dealings with the mystical services. To be completely honest, I am not too sure what to make of them. They look like men, they talk like men, but treat them like men and you are liable to wake up with the head of a horse next to you, or worse, just with the head of a horse. If they are not men, then where do little wizards come from, you may ask? If anyone has ever found a lady wizard, I have yet to hear of it.

I guess it is just one of those mysteries of life, like how they get those ships in bottles, and how they make bottles that big anyway. And yes, I know all about witch queens and sorceresses, but they are pretty thin on the ground and would have to be remarkably fecund to keep the Citadel wizard supply topped up. There are rather a lot of wizards, considering that 'wizarding' might now be considered an endangered trade.

I broached the matter at hand. 'Given the current employment situation then, I take it you might be open to some negotiations concerning a problem that is currently needing my attention.'

'Master Dwarf, you have the floor.'

I flashed the shield. 'Nicely Strongoak, Master Detective. Please call me Nicely.'

'Nicely, an interesting name.'

I smiled thinly. 'A bit of a long story.'

'Well, no matter. I am Tollingstaff.'

'Also an interesting name.'

'Also a long story. However, as I was saying, Tollingstaff, Wizard, as certified by the White Cartel and the Citadel Licensing Authority. Fortunately, we have been able to escape so far without a need for some form of identity card, so you will just have to take my word for it. I usually have my clients call me Tollingstaff the Expedient. I dropped the rainbow-based coding scheme, as I found people were getting confused between myself and Vermilion & Co., interior decorators. I use the "Expedient" appellation instead, as the punters seem to like it, and it establishes a proper working relationship. In your case, Master Detective, as one professional to another I am willing to make an exception; friends call me Tolly.'

Yes, I liked this wizard. We spat, shook hands and I plunged into the tale. 'You know Alderman Hardwood, the industrialist?' The wizard supped his ale.

'I know the individual, by reputation. Given his prominence in the affairs of the Citadel, I do not think that there can be a single individual, even the humblest of gnomes, who can claim ignorance on that score. I am also aware that many refer to him as a financial wizard. A term I have always found more than a little galling.'

I thought about this. 'I can see how this might put a kink in your pointy hat, but from the way I read the runes, in all these old stories, wizards never really used to do that much, well, wizarding. Certainly not of the spells, magic and staff-waving kind. Oh, they lit the odd fire and set off fireworks as required, but most of the time they seemed to be dealing with nothing more esoteric than facts and information.' I could see the wizard shift rather uncomfortably as I warmed to the subject. 'It seems to me that by virtue of their positions – after all, they had the trust and confidentiality of kings and other high folk – and, with their own enviable intelligence-gathering network, this put them in ideal positions for being power-brokers. Now if these modern industrialists, with their connections in the markets, on the exchanges and council rooms, have achieved a similar pre-eminence, then surely they deserve the title of "Wizard" just as much.'

Tollingstaff inspected his ale before he replied, as if searching therein for inspiration. 'A neat speech, Master Detective, and I fear there is more than an element of truth to it. We wizards became too introspective. We spent far too long poring over old manuscripts, and forgot that the world outside was changing apace. Somewhere along the way, we missed the last boat back to the Hidden Lands, and have been left feeling stranded ever since. However, our arcane knowledge can still be put to some use, I judge, or else you would not be here.'

I took the clipping from my purse. 'This you will probably have heard of, but may not recognise; it's the Hardwood Emerald.' The wizard took out a pair of half-moon glasses, surveyed the picture and nodded. I continued: 'From what I've been reading about this stone, and from what I have learnt, and from my own gut feeling, I believe that there may be some doubts concerning the authenticity of this ring. To be more exact, about its exact provenance and place of manufacture, which at the moment seems to indicate "manmade".'

The wizard began to look interested for the first time. 'You think that perhaps this is not as described, and hence perhaps did not arrive into the Hardwood hands, in, shall we say, the appropriate manner?'

'What is more, I was wondering if this could be rather more than just an expensive piece of family jewellery. Specifically, I have been wondering if this may be a magic ring, and that is why I have come to you.'

Tollingstaff stroked his beard – a nicely clipped goatee affair – very thoughtfully. He took out a pipe, a long-stemmed handyman, with some fine engraving, and he began to fill

151

it in a workman-like fashion. He companionably passed his pouch and I took out my knotwood briar.

'You know,' he said, after the pipe was lit satisfactorily, 'there were not really that many magic rings. It's rather like magic swords; if they don't perform the job at the appropriate moment the owner is not likely to find himself or herself in a position to ask for a refund.'

I had to laugh at this.

'Oh, they did exist all right,' he continued, 'magic rings, and the power they embodied – but folk, and by that I really mean all folk, tend to think that because magic rings feature in so many of the legends, the fields of Widergard must have been strewn with them. Their number, although I cannot give it to you exactly, was actually very small. The histories of many are reasonably well known, although what happened to them finally is less clear. Most of the rings – if you ignore their mystical powers – were quite unremarkable, particularly undistinguished looking, and they will probably turn up in a Fifth-Level flea market sometime when their magic runs out. Along with magic swords best used for ploughshares and enchanted spears that wouldn't even make good clothes props.'

This was all news to me. 'Their magic can run out?' I said with some surprise. Whatever next – virgins on unicorns don't always stay that way and heroes can have body odour problems? Just goes to show you that you can't trust anything or anyone these days. I bet that some well-meaning body will soon announce that politicians don't always have our best interests at heart, either.

'Of course, magic can run out, my dear dwarf! continued the wizard. There is a power in this universe far, far greater than mundane magic!'

'Black Sorcery?' I ventured.

'Entropy!' he replied. 'The whole universe, Widergard included, is running down – magic rings and swords aren't excluded.' He took a deep draw on his pipe. 'Bane of wizardry, entropy.'

'Makes it harder?'

'No, it means we can't give guarantees. Everybody wants a guarantee these days. How can you give a lifetime guarantee when the world is full of immortals and entropy won't let up?'

'I suppose that's one of the reasons there were so many phoney magic rings?'

'Exactly! As for the ones with real power, that is an appreciable amount of commercial clout, so their movements are more closely curtailed. So, bearing all of this in mind, I must say a humble origin is more likely for this particular piece of finery. There have been many other fine man-made pieces. Still ...'

I interrupted his musings: 'Just look at it, closely.'

This he did, going to the trouble of taking an enlarging glass from his cloak.

I thought about reporting such a flagrant breach of traditional tool use to the Detectives Guild. I mean, you don't catch me walking around with a wizard's staff, do you? Mind you, you don't catch me walking around with an enlarging glass either.

'Have you really seen work like that on anything else made by men, Tolly? Look at the faceting on that emerald and the cunning design of the setting. I'm not buying it.'

'Yes, I take your point, but a magic ring is, after all, more than just a pretty bauble. There were other distinguishing attributes.' He held the picture up to the inadequate lamp and scanned it again with his glass. 'I must admit, though,

I had not considered this before, despite having heard of the emerald, of course. What is your opinion on the manufacture, then? Dwarfish?'

'No,' I shook my head firmly. 'Too little weight to the whole thing, the stone is cut all wrong and they would have used dwarf silver, not gold, for the mounting. Elvish, I would think.'

The wizard's finely trimmed eyebrows shot up. 'Now that would be interesting. If our esteemed Alderman Hardwood, a leader of the community, was in possession of an elfin ring ...' He looked at me keenly. 'You have not explained your role in these proceedings. Who exactly is your client?'

I had a poke in my briar with a match. 'The ring has gone missing, and I have been hired to bring it back. Let us just say, that I would like it to go back to the rightful owner.'

The wizard gave me a calculating look. 'I think, Master Detective, that there may be more to it than that.'

'Perhaps,' I conceded. 'It seems that all of a sudden a lot of different people have been taking more than a passing interest in my affairs. And there have been casualties.'

'Oh yes, a dead elf.' It was my turn to raise an eyebrow. 'Yes, Master Dwarf, just because wizards do not have the pre-eminence of old, it does not mean we have completely lost use of our senses. We still keep an ear to the ground to keep in touch with what is happening in the place we helped create.'

This was interesting, somebody was finally willing to break cover and admit to knowing something about Truetouch. This wizard had sources, that much was for sure, but exactly how far could I trust him? Well, you have to speculate to accumulate as my great uncle Sanzaza 'Grinder' Strongoak used to say. But then again, he was killed in a mine cave-in while speculating for gold.

'There is also another matter that I am attending to,' I confided finally. 'A missing person job that I have undertaken that seems to be having unexpected ... ramifications.'

'It appears that business has been brisk in the detective trade; perhaps I am in the wrong trade? Tell me, Nicely, if I may indeed call you that, have you always been in this line of work?'

I was surprised by the change of tack. 'I started off with the Public Defender's Office in New Iron Town, then moved into the CIA and then the Guards here in the Citadels, before I went private. I find a dwarf can go to places and do things where someone else might be a bit more conspicuous. For some reason we seem to be able to mix with the highest and the lowest, with equal ease. It must be our generous natures and open manner.'

'Quite. Only that is not what I was thinking. I was more concerned with whether you had any skills in the traditional dwarf crafts.'

'Well, I was a reasonable scholar, if that's what you mean; mathematics, engineering, construction, mining, delving, excavating, quarrying. I just had a feeling that there might be more to life than a hole in the ground.'

I still feel this, even if the holes I now tend to find myself in are all of my own making.

'But can you find your way around underground without confusion?' Tolly said, twisting his goatee in an unbecoming fashion.

'Can a demon barber dance the split-end hop?

'I have absolutely no idea as to the meaning of what you just spoke,' Tollingstaff shook his head sadly.

'Yes, wizard. I mean yes!'

'Good! First, though, I think I would like to get another opinion concerning the origin of this ring.'

'We haven't discussed pay rates yet.'

'No, we haven't.'

He pocketed the picture and got up, ready to leave. Apparently that was the end of the discussion. I'd heard that wizards weren't exactly verbose, but Tollingstaff the Expedient could give lip-buttoning lessons to a clam. Finally, noticing my frustration, he relented slightly: 'I will take care of this for a while if I may, and we will go track down someone in my enviable intelligence-gathering network who is admirably qualified to help us.'

We drank up and made our way to the Helmington. Parking had been easy in this part of town. Tolly said that not many wizards could afford to run their own transport. I got my first real good look at the wizard as we got into the wagon. The courtesy-light showed a cloak of a serviceable gabardine. Under it he wore a blue worsted three-piece that looked uncomfortably warm for this weather (mind you, they always do say that wizards are notoriously thin-blooded). He was younger than I had assumed, the goatee beard barely knotted. He had a small nose-ring, the sort that most younger wizards favour, and enough gold in his ears to buy a good set of wheels, if he should ever require them. I am quite content to wear one large gold hoop; it should be enough to buy me my ride back to New Iron Town, if needs be.

We were heading downhill to find Tolly's contact. I needed some fuel and pulled in at an empty stall. The pump boy shouted across as I opened the door, 'Hey, can't you read?!' I looked up, to where he was pointing: 'Elf Service Station'. This was getting beyond a joke, so I just sharpened the old axe on the forecourt and watched the sparks fly up into the night air – the pump boy soon came round to my way of thinking. What a way to run a business!

We dwarfs have a fairly ambivalent attitude to the petrochemical industry. Although our subterranean interests have always leaned towards the unearthing of precious metals and stones, when times have been hard, and to do our bit for the industrial revolution, we have of course mined coal. Most of the largest open-cast works in the north, I am now rather ashamed to admit, were made by dwarfs. And, as with the construction industry, we soon had a very nice number going, thank you. When it came to drilling for oil and gas we must have had our heads stuck somewhere other than in a hole in the ground! Maybe it was just complacency; whatever, we blew it completely. Men had drilled, tapped and barrelled before we had even woken up to the possibilities of this new fuel, and it stung. There is one thing that the Dwarf Brotherhood loathes above all else, and that is seeing the opportunity for a quick return go out of the palace door. The coal and oil industries have since then co-existed in a state of some unease. I related this story to Tolly as we headed down the Hill. He wondered if this tended to colour my attitude to my client. I wondered too.

We finally pulled up in front of what was once a Temple of the Knights of the Outer Circle, and was now a major art gallery. I was about to meet a Citadel luminary, name of Slant (artists, like elves apparently, can manage with only the single designation). It was a good thing that Tolly had told me that the artist was a man. This would not have been my first impression. He had a voice like a troll, he was as broad as a troll and he was as grey as a troll (though this, he later informed me, was caused by his largely nocturnal, celebrity lifestyle). His large skull, with its closely cropped bristles of hair, had as many bumps as a troll's and his spade-sized hands – if they had not been engaged in gesticulating excitedly – would surely have been dragging on the ground in a troll-like manner. Fortunately, when you caught a glimpse of the eyes, they were as lively, deep and brown as a pint of newly pulled ale, and all thoughts of direct troll kinship vanished immediately. Slant, Tolly had told me, was a very skilled and gifted artisan, a great worker of metal, producing everything from the most intricate pieces of jewellery to room-size sculptures requiring under-floor reinforcement. This was his first one-man exhibition, and tonight was the reception.

Upon entering the temple I'd immediately made out the artist. It would have been impossible to miss him. Slant dominated the room, built like a bastion projecting from the gallery backwall and seeing off admirers from all sides. His more than ample frame was draped in an outfit that seemed part artist's smock and part war pavilion. When he caught sight of Tollingstaff he leapt across the room, picked him up, and playfully threw him in the air, just making the catch before the wizard hit the flagstones. So much for the dignity of wizards.

'Slant, will you put me down, man, before you drop me!' Slant just threw him higher. 'Glad to see you were able to make it, Tolly. You should get out more. Too much time spent in small dark rooms. All those scripts and stinks can't be healthy. You should take up a hobby; bird spotting's very therapeutic, I'm told. Lots of fresh air and nature stuff. Mind you, you do a fair turn in the flight department yourself. Look everyone, it's the famous Pied Wizard.'

'Slant!' shouted Tollingstaff, who was turning distinctly pale, offsetting his dark garb. 'And who's this with you?' said Slant, after he had finally finished ruffling the wizard's feathers.

'This,' said Tolly, with some trace of formality as he straightened his attire and regained some trace of colour. 'This is Master Detective Nicely Strongoak, and it is on his behalf that I am here, not to be used as a beanbag by some grunt with more muscles than brain cells.'

Slant gave me a sly look. 'Would you like a game of beanbag too?' he asked.

'Only if it's my go first,' I replied, tensing and mentally preparing myself for any quick moves on his part.

He gave it a moment's consideration, then said: 'And I bet you would.' He laughed, a roar like one of those big cats from down south.

'All right!' he clapped his outsized hands and I think I felt an eardrum perforate. 'I will be back with you later, got a few potential purchasers here that I have to impress. Just get stuck into the goodies. There's a whole mess of food and drink, and we have some major artistic types here, so have some fun, and do enjoy the show.' He leapt off again.

We were still in the entrance hall of the former temple, an impressive structure with a vaulted roof and wide glass windows, although as I felt forced to comment, the plaster beams did not add much. Tolly was of the opinion that much of the progress made in the development of the industrial basis of Widergard was due to the search for an effective cure for woodworm. This, of course, was not a problem that dwarf homes had. We moved through to the main exhibition rooms, where Slant's pieces were displayed. To my great surprise, I did enjoy the show. Even though my aesthetic sensibilities are somewhat atrophied, my dwarfish instincts could tell that this man had a natural affinity with metal. His small pieces were incredibly intricate and his silverwork showed that he was capable of great delicacy and feeling. I particularly enjoyed the larger pieces: sheets of steel and copper welded together at fantastic angles. He also had a sense of humour, albeit in dubious taste. One work entitled *Man's inhumanity to pixie* resembled the front window of a wagon with a thankfully unrecognisable organic blob caught in the wiper. Also the food and drink were excellent and available in copious quantities, the way dwarfs like it. Actually there aren't many things you can do to a dish of food that a dwarf will not approve of, if the dish is large enough.

Slant caught up with us at the finger stall. 'So, what did you think? Can I put you down for a couple of the big ones?'

'I suppose it depends how much a piece is going to set me back,' I replied. He named a figure. 'I like it lots,' I said with admiration and not a little envy, remembering youthful days in New Iron Town with an old power torch.

'Slant,' said Tolly, when we had finally managed to steer him to a quiet table with enough spare seats to accommodate his frame. 'What do you think of this?' He took out the clipping and handed it over.

'Nice, very nice, and old, very old. Should know this, can't quite place it.'

'Origin?' I queried.

'Why, it's elvish of course.'

'Are you sure?' said Tolly.

'No doubt, stake my reputation. What's the deal, anyway?'

'That,' I said, 'is the Hardwood Emerald.'

Slant gave a long, low, whistle. 'I've heard of it, but never seen it. Mrs Hardwood doesn't wear it very much and I am not surprised; it must be obvious to anyone with any knowledge of the craft that this was not man-made.'

'Nicely,' began the wizard, 'would you mind getting us all fresh drinks?'

I can take a hint like a blotter takes up ink, so I left them to their discussion and made my way through the press of people to the hospitality stall. Fortunately I caught a steward with a tray and took whatever was on offer. This gave me some time valuable thinking time too. So, it was possible that Mrs Hardwood was in possession of an elfin ring, as I had suspected, and if my guess about the nature of the conversation I had just left was correct, probably a magic ring too. How did the Hardwood family get possession of such an item? The elves were not renowned for handing them out as party favours. And what would be the Alderman's reaction if he found it missing? What lengths would he go to in order to recover it and what punishment would he hand out to whomever was foolish enough to liberate it?

I was not at all surprised Mrs Hardwood did not want to go to the City Guards.

14

WALLS AROUND THE CITADEL

By the time I was back with the drinks some decisions had been made. Slant emptied his glass in one swallow, made his excuses, and returned to the throng. Tolly and I took our time while the wizard did some explaining, or what passed for explaining in wizard speak: a language that I was beginning to realise was not designed for the imparting of information, but for the hiding of it. He finally said that he might be able to do something to help: we had to wait until late, though. I was beginning to realise why wizards had such a reputation for secrecy. However, as we had yet to strike an actual deal, and money had not been agreed upon, so I had no real grounds for complaint.

Coming on close to midwatch we left the reception, which with Slant's encouragement was showing all the signs of developing into a full-scale party. I drove back up the hill and with Tolly giving directions we made our way back to a quiet part of Old Town. We parked behind a ramshackle building close up to the Citadel Wall. I got out of the wagon and was making for the road when I realised Tolly was heading straight for the wall, the one separating the Second and Third Levels. I followed him along a small path with well-worn stones, through a small overgrown garden, and past an ancient-looking statue. The path appeared to peter out as it reached the wall, but Tolly was not deterred. In fact the wall appeared to be completely engrossing and I soon realised why.

'A secret door!' I said, a trifle too loud, earning myself a reproachful glance. 'That's it, Master Detective, let the whole Hill know.'

'Sorry, Tolly, it's just that I've heard that there are tunnels built into the walls, but I have never come across one. Who would have thought it, in Old Town of all places!'

'Sometimes, Nicely, the best place to hide something is out in the open.'

'Good point. What have you there, a magic key?'

'Lock picks, if you must know, and I could do with a bit of peace to use them. Why don't you go keep a lookout, before some surprised passer-by spots us and notifies the Cits.'

It may not have been magic, but it worked, and I soon found myself staring into a very black and very inviting hole. 'This is not just a tunnel in the wall, is it? This goes right into the very Hill itself.'

'That's right. The whole of the Citadel is riddled with tunnels; a labyrinth in fact.' Tolly took out two old-fashioned torches and lit them with a pocket flint. He handed one to me and I looked into the tunnel mouth. 'This is dwarf-made or I'm a goblin's grandmother! I had no idea, how do they keep this hidden?'

'Mostly, by not telling extremely loud dwarfs!' I was pleased that the average wizard's reputation for grouchiness was not altogether ill founded.

I stored that up for future usage. I was beginning to understand all the right marks for winding up Wizard Tollingstaff. My business demands a great array of skills and many a useful thing has been let slip by an angry man, dwarf or, indeed, wizard, if you can get on their goat, or goatee for that matter. See, detecting has lots of seldom-advertised bonuses, in addition to allowing you to mix with women with bad intentions and undergarments that you can read the news through.

Tolly took a deep, and to my mind rather theatrical breath. 'This whole complex is mind-numbingly old, the tunnels were obviously built before almost everything else on the Hill. The dwarfs who delved them returned home and, gradually, as the rest of the Citadel was constructed, they were just sort of forgotten, except by people who needed a more private manner of getting from A to B.'

'Wizards?'

'And others. This section is said to be one of the oldest. I was not really sure of its existence until now.'

I turned to face Tolly. 'This is very exciting. However, how does it concern us?'

'That, Master Detective, we shall see in good time. For the moment, though, I ask for your patience and your assistance. We need to get to the centre of this maze and that is a task beyond my skill. Are you equal to it?'

I stepped inside. The air, although hardly sweet, lacked the rank smell that told of poor circulation and possible cave-ins. The tunnel wall at my side felt as smooth as it must have when it had originally been hewn, and was clearly a work of great skill. Whatever the wizard's plan, this was too good an opportunity to miss. 'Do you have any chalk?' I asked, and Tolly replied that he had it in abundance. There was nothing else for it. 'Let's go see what this is all about, then.'

Before we began, the wizard pulled the door to, but left it open a crack, with a good strong doorstop to prevent it closing completely. These sorts of doors had a nasty habit of only having a keyhole on one side. I had a quick scout to begin with; looking for signs of wear on the floor and sides that might have pointed to the most commonly used path. I went a short distance up some of the side branches, trying to get a feel of the place. When I was confident that I had the main feed, we set off. It was hard to believe that somewhere above us were the roads and buildings of the Citadel. The rock had swallowed all the sound of the late-night inns with their drunks and good-time boys and girls. Here, we had been transported back to a simpler time and place. Dour and doughty dwarfs had cut this path. They had come a half-year's march from their native Northlands and constructed a network that would not have disgraced many a fine dwarf hall.

'A dead end,' said Tolly.

'Don't worry. We will have a few of them,' I said as we retraced our steps. 'It's no problem. The method of cracking a dwarf maze, you see, is largely one of trial and error. By eliminating the dead ends we begin to construct a sequence of correct turns, and – here is the part not generally known to outsiders – we arrive at a strict arithmetical progression. Each dwarf family in the business has a series of closely guarded path codes; hopefully this is one that I know. Then, once we have that figured out, the way should become apparent. They can be difficult, but as long as we mark the way clearly with the chalk we should not have too much trouble.'

Tolly looked considerably more at ease. So, just in case

the wizard thought this was getting too simple, I added: 'Of course, each family also had a reputation for adding a few specialised tricks of their own devising.'

'Such as?' asked Tolly, suspiciously.

'You know, the normal sort of thing: false dead ends, turning rocks, sudden pits, spears coming out of the walls and, naturally, a hideous guardian or two.'

'Guardians?' said Tolly, now quite pleasantly worried.

'Yes, but don't worry about that. There isn't much that could survive down here over all these ages, is there?'

We made steady progress. I was beginning to work it out. My head was spinning slightly; it was a seventh-level progression and I had not worked one of these out since night school – that interesting period in a dwarf's education when he is left by himself in the dark, in the middle of a mountain with no food and minimal water. It is no surprise that all the best mathematicians in Widergard are dwarfs.

Some time later I smelt a change in the air quality.

'There's a large chamber ahead,' I told Tolly confidently. We turned a couple more corners and there it was. We placed the torches in convenient holders by the entrance and took in the sight. 'Well, Tolly, feast your eyes on this. You will not see better work this side of the Iron Ore Mountains.'

And indeed it was impressive. Our puny torches could hardly do it credit: a huge vaulted dome cut into the living rock with winged arches and great buttresses of carved stone. Expert drainage and effective use of damp courses had kept it free from any seeping water or wayward stream. It was a monument to dwarfish engineering. Even the wizard was momentarily lost for words.

'You know Tolly, this reminds me of the Citadel Central Archive. I wonder if this was dug at the same time as the building was constructed? It could explain a lot.' We walked around, heads back, eyes vainly seeking to accommodate the grandeur. 'This really should be open for all to view. It would be one of the wonders of the Citadel. What it could do for the tourist trade doesn't bear thinking about. Why, half of New Iron Town would pay good gold for a glimpse of this. I can't believe it's been hidden for all this time.'

'The reason, I believe, Master Dwarf, lies in front of us.' He pointed to a raised dais in the centre of the hall. I had been so busy looking up I had missed it. We approached the platform. On it was a marvellously wrought model of the Citadel as it must have been before the urban planners and the road engineers had got at it. I made out the Archive and Citadel Hall, all perfect in every detail. What caught the eye, though, was the walls. A ring fastened each of the beautifully executed gates.

'Walls of the Citadel,' I started, almost involuntarily, 'One to ten!'

'Yes,' said Tolly, 'I see you know the old rhyme.' He finished it:

'One for the elves,
And one for the men,
One for the wizards,
And the Keeper of the Trees,
One for the dwarfs,
But none for the pixie.

'Many a truth is hidden in a children's rhyme.'

'You are right, Tolly. It's been running through my mind a lot recently, but it never seemed to make much sense – until now, that is.'

167

'Of course, it's changed in the telling over the years. The original verse actually read: "One from the elves, and one from the men" and so on. It tells of the time of the founding of the Citadel, when the gates themselves were constructed. Each of the Free Peoples of Widergard donated a magic ring and used the power therein to fortify one of the walls of the Citadel. This is why the walls are named as they are – the Elf's Gate, the Dwarf's Gate and so on.'

'The ten walls, then, are the five around the Citadel and the five here on the model with the magic rings.'

'Yes, and any foe would have to conquer the combined might of all the peoples of Widergard if he sought to conquer the Citadel. It is in the magical construction that you see here, as much as in the actual stonework, that the real strength and unity of the Citadel rests. Or did once.'

'Why didn't you tell me?'

'To be honest, Nicely, I was not sure I could trust you. Things are hardly as they were when these gates were built, after all. And as I am sure you would be the first to admit, many less than scrupulous individuals would be more than happy to have in their collections what you are now privy to. Plus, to come clean again, I was not sure of my facts. I had heard of this place's supposed existence, but I have never been here. It could have been a rumour. It is not always wise to place too much credence in old tales or even old rhymes. Very few, I would wager, are the number now alive in Widergard who know for certain of this room's whereabouts.'

'But surely this should all be under lock and key in a museum.'

'Look at the model more closely, examine the gates; you have not yet understood the full import.' I got up close and saw what I had missed the first time. A ring with a mouth-wateringly enormous dragon's eye – the red diamond so beloved by us dwarfs – fastened the lowest gate, the Dwarf's Gate. The ring on the fourth gate, the Tree-friend's Gate, had a form of brown ruby which even I could not identify, but in the torchlight it shone warmly like one of Grove's eyes. The Wizard's Gate, which partitioned off the Third Level, and which closed the largest and most fortified of the Citadel walls, was a stunning multifaceted diamond. A sky-blue sapphire fastened the Gate of Men, and on the uppermost gate, still known to all and sundry as the Elf's Gate, there was nothing.

I had not realised I was holding my breath until I let it out in a low whistle. 'Indeed,' said Tolly. 'I would not like to comment on what we might call the theoretical, magical implications of removing the model from this place. Whatever, I do not think it would be ideal for either the morale of the Citadel folk, or the well-being of their representatives, to exhibit it with the most important ring missing.'

'The Hardwood Emerald.'

'I am afraid so. There were not many candidates for such a gem, if, as you suspected, the Hardwood Emerald was indeed an elfin ring. At the moment I have no idea how it might have come into the Hardwood estate. It would not have been by legitimate means, though.'

'Power and influence can open many doors, Tolly, even hidden ones.' I stared at the model, the old rhyme still playing through my head. I was suddenly aware of a move-ment out of the corner of my eye. Tolly caught it at the same time – a shadow cast on the cavern wall by the torches at the entrance. A shadow, large and menacing; a shadow with curved spines and a swinging tail, and with

169

it the sound of claws being dragged across rock and the leathery flap of wings.

'Tolly, if I didn't know for a fact that they had been extinct for ages—' I left the question hanging.

'Yes, if I didn't know better I would say—' Tolly began. Whatever else the wizard was about to mention was lost in a loud roar. Flame shot into the cavern, illuminating the roof in all its glory. Flame scorched our hair and singed our eyebrows. Flame seared our suits: the flame of a dragon!

15

OF DRAGONS AND NATURAL SELECTION

'I always thought dragons would be bigger,' said Tollingstaff the Wise.

'What, bigger than a malnourished porker?' I added.

'Yes.'

We watched as the little dragon waddled, rather endearingly, into the cavern. It spoke:

'Hang on, just got to get me breff back, getting a flame up like that ain't too easy. Phew! Sorry about the trick with the shadows, couldn't resist it. Hope I din't make you pother your pants.'

Tolly and I looked at each other and silently agreed to keep quiet on that score.

'Excuse me,' Tolly said. 'I hope you don't mind me asking, but you are a dragon, aren't you?'

'Well yes, obviously! I sure ain't no spring chicken.'

'It's only that my colleague and I were just thinking,' I went on, 'that dragons, by reputation at least, are usually mentioned as being somewhat bulkier. Have you perhaps been ill?'

'No, mate. Fine fettle, me. Had a cold at the end of the Blue Age, or was it the Green? Nearly burnt me nostrils out, all that sneezing. But uvverwise, mustn't grumble.' The little reptile executed a neat quick-step to emphasise his point and finished with a flourish. "Aven't you heard of evolution?'

'Pardon?' Tolly and I said in unison.

'Evolution, mates. It's your evolution!'

'Oh yes,' I grunted, 'evolution.' Evolution, as I understood it then, was what scholars had come up with to account for what happened when we all decided to invent a need for boots. It was all to do with swinging around in trees, and how some people fell out – or were evicted – and went hiking; whereas the rest decided that this travel business was all very well, but not for them. The climate was nice here, there was plenty of food, so why don't we just get on with it and evolve right here? I liked the story, as it explained why the goblins appeared to be hedging their bets, just in case they need to get back up the trees in a hurry. I know there were a lot of people, particularly in the Citadel Alliance Party, who were less impressed. They were not happy about having possible kinship with gnomes, let alone goblins and trolls. What all this had to do with dragons, I did not know and I said as much.

'It's natural selection, mates, natural selection,' the dragon said, resting his rump on the platform's edge. 'All those bi'logical forces that led to you dwarfs and Men—'

'Wizards,' interrupted Tolly, with just a trace of annoyance.

'Begging Your Mage's pardon, dwarfs and wizards. Anyway, all those forces that was busy wiv all the uvver people of Widergard was also doing their business on us

172

dragons.' When Tolly and I still looked blank, he tried again, small flames playing sweetly around his snout. 'Look, mates. Imagine you are a full-blown dragon, breaving fire, laying waste to the countryside and consuming your fair share of maidens. What are you?'

'Unpopular?' suggested Tolly.

'No; well, maybe in some quarters,' said the dragon, who had taken to circumnavigating the dais, 'but what you undoubtably are is conspicuous, right! A ripe target for every hero with a magic sword, or burglar climbing down your chimbley, who may want to give you a quick jab in the soft underparts, whilst you are trying to catch up on a few moons' kip. Eat one and another half-dozen pop up, until one day you don't wake up quick enough, and what's the result? The result is evolution's big elbow, the big trip down the Black Pit, and no more big dragons. The big heave-ho. Whereas, us, their somewhat smaller brevren, who once had our arses burnt just trying to live off the scraps of the big boys' barbecues, we showed them a thing or two about survival. And they called us "Worms" – I ask you. Stay small and nimble, watch the stodgy food, that's the secret, and keep the Bog away from anyone carrying anything larger than a toothpick.'

Tolly looked at me and we both looked blank and then shrugged in unison. This was getting to be a double act. I wasn't sure if I could lose my detective's license for such synchronised tomfoolery, but I didn't think I should make a habit of it and risk losing my hard-earned dwarf-of-the-world image. 'So, correct me if I'm wrong here,' I said to the ambulating lizard, 'but did I not just detect a slight trace of wistfulness in your voice?'

The dragon stopped, took his tail in his hands and

thoughtfully proceeded to use it to comb his scales. 'Yes, you're right. It must have really been something, flying through the night sky, wind in your scales and the smell of burning village in your nostrils.' He sighed deeply and hiccupped a flame. 'That oil, you know, makes a terrific flame, but what it does to the digestion!'

'So, little dragon,' Tolly asked, 'how do you come to be here in the bowels of the Citadel?'

'Well, it's one fing 'scaping being skewered, it's another getting the pot roast on the table every day. So, get smart, that's the answer. Find yourself some steady employment. Why not? Brains outdo brawn any day. Which reminds me, I can't sit here all day gassing wiv you good folks. I've a job to do.'

'Which is what, exactly?' I asked.

'Sorry. Din't I make it hobvious? How hextremely remiss of me.' The dragon executed a tricky bow, tricky if you lack a waist, that is. 'I am your friendly – well, as friendly as circumstance will allow – Guardian of the Citadel Labyrinth.'

Tolly and I could not help a snigger. 'Look,' I began, 'we don't want to hurt your feelings, and the trick with the shadow and the flame was really impressive; it's just that one disadvantage of your size is that you do tend to lose out somewhat in the intimidation stakes.'

'I thought you knew me better than that, mates. I don't go in for all that mauling and mayhem stuff.'

'What do you do, then?' We felt obliged to ask.

'Me? I just burn off chalk marks.'

I thought about it for just half an instant, about the same time it took Tolly to also work out the implications. 'Quick, Tolly, grab the runt.' We both flung ourselves forward and collided as the dragon slipped through our fingers. There was a sudden spurt of flame and we saw one of our torches burn up in a twinkling.

'Oh no!'

The dragon gave us a cheery wave, and before we knew it there was another spurt of flame, another dead torch, and then blackness. This was the real-article black – the 'wave your hand in front of your nose and see nothing but your retina doing a random light show' sort of black. Pitch-black, jet-black; a blackness of the darkest achromatic visual value. I have been in mines ten leagues underground and never found darkness of this quality.

'Nicely,' said the wizard, somewhere to my left. 'Is this serious?'

'It could be,' I replied. 'Can you magic a light at the end of your staff?'

'Nice idea, Master Detective. Only, it appears to have escaped your finely honed senses that I do not have a staff.'

'Oh, yes, I did wonder. Trolling*staff*. What's the matter, have you not collected enough coupons or something?'

'Very droll. Dwarf. If you actually are interested, there happens to be a bit of a shortage at the moment.'

'A shortage?'

'Yes, staffs don't grow on trees, you know. Well, they do, naturally. But it's all rather involved, and let's just say there are rather a lot of wizards at the moment and not enough staffs to go round.' Tolly did not sound too happy about this state of affairs.

'No need to get ratty. Don't you like being in the dark, wizard?'

'It's not my favourite way to be. I am just trying to think, how are we going to manage to do anything at all without the torches?'

'I don't know about you, but I'm going to use my flash-light.' I took the aforementioned item from my pocket and lit up the forlorn wizard with it.

'Very funny, dwarf. Tollingstaff the Expedient, and Nicely the Indispensable. A pretty pair we make indeed.'

We returned to the dais to make plans. When in doubt, light a pipe, so we sat on the edge of the platform and filled up with pipeleaf. To save the flashlight I turned it off, and we talked, illuminated only by the pipe embers. 'No chance of working our way out of the maze without the chalk marks, I suppose,' asked Tolly, already knowing the answer.

'Unlikely,' I had to say. 'Even if I could remember the sequence, everything is numbered with reference to the first turn we made at the beginning of the maze. I would be unlikely to remember it backwards. I mean, I could give it a try, but the chances are slim.' This only got me a mutter from the wizard by way of reply, so I carried on. 'Then again, we still have the pocket dragon to consider as well, burning off all our new marks. It's pretty hopeless.' Again, all I got was the mutter as the wizard sucked energetically on his pipe. 'I'm glad to see you are taking this better now.'

'Yes, sorry about that. Back when the torches went out, I just panicked for a moment there.'

'That's all right, I shouldn't have tugged your beard. Still, we do seem to find ourselves stuck up in the giant's castle without a beanpole. Any ideas?'

'Finish our pipes, and have a think about insurance.'

'Insurance?'

'Yes, insurance.'

Tollingstaff the Wise did not seem to be willing to add to this cryptic comment, and that left me none the wiser, so

I thought about rings and mazes and what the world was like when this complex had been constructed. The dwarfs had done a fine job when the cavern was built; such craft-work didn't come cheap. I somehow could not see them going to all that trouble, simply to lock it up and forget about it. It was built to be admired, and if it was meant to be viewed by the kings and queens and whoever else was in charge of the Citadel at that time, then I could not see them all tripping down the maze from a secret door in the wall of the Third Level. My knowledge of the White and Wise was not exhaustive, but I knew they were not big on 'tripping', not when they could do 'parading' and 'flaunting'. And if ever there was a good reason to flaunt it, this was surely it.

This meant one thing: 'Tolly, there must be another door!' This startled the wizard out of his cogitations.

'What's that you say?'

'It makes sense. This chamber and the model, they were a focal point of the community, a symbol of the co-operation that built the Citadel. All this is meant to be seen, and by the High Folk as well. All the White and Wise! That means another door. There must be another door!'

'I take your point. However, finding such an entrance is another matter. After all, the secret door we used was all but forgotten.'

'But that was an emergency entrance, probably required in the planning laws. The other entrance would be more noticeable, dramatic even. Let's try to find it. It must be worth a go.'

So we made our way round the walls of the cavern, walking in opposite directions, looking for any clue to an entrance. I used the flashlight and Tolly did his best with his pocket flint. No joy; as far as I could tell it was all solid rock. I asked Tolly how he was managing. When I received no reply I looked round and searched for him with my flashlight. He was standing still, head to one side, listening.

'Come on Tolly, put some effort into it or we are soon going to be one dried-up dwarf and one wizen wizard.'

'I am just waiting for something.'

'What for?' I asked, only to be answered by a distant roar, cut off with a choke and a gagging noise.

'For that, I think, Master Detective. Come on; let us take a seat again. I don't think we need to bother looking for an entrance now.'

'But what was it?' I asked, as we made our way back to the centre.

'That was the sound of insurance, oh Strongoak the Indispensable,' he said smugly. I could tell I wasn't going to get any further explanation out of him for the moment so I joined him and we lit another pipe. Within a short while I heard heavy footsteps and saw a light approaching from around the bend in the tunnel. I shone my flash at the entrance and, into the chamber, dragon held round the neck by one huge hand, strode Slant.

'Sorry to keep you waiting. This little chap took some catching, and then some persuading, before he would take me to you.' The dragon gurgled something that did not quite make it past Slant's fist. Slant translated for us. 'The little chap says it was not fair to go hiding in the dark; which I think coming from him is pretty rich.'

I turned to the wizard. 'So this is your insurance policy?'

'And a fine one it is too.' Tolly strode down and thumped Slant on the shoulder. 'There are not many in the Citadel who can intimidate Slant, and he can move very quietly when he wishes.'

'Not quiet enough it seems,' said Slant. 'While following the two of you to the hidden door, I noticed that you already had a tail on you. A man, or somebody reasonably tall at least. I must have spooked him, though, as he made off.'

'News to you?' the wizard asked me.

'News,' I confirmed, considering the ramifications.

'Well, Master Detective, I am sorry I could not trust you completely, at least not straight away, even with your pretty shield.'

'Don't even consider apologising, Tolly. If I had an insurance policy like Slant, I must admit I would sleep safer at night.'

'And Slant, when you see what is on this platform, I am sure you will agree your trip was worthwhile.' The wizard beckoned the big man forward and he gazed, gob-smacked, at the Rings of the Citadel, as we told him the story of the missing stone.

'I suppose you're going to make off with the others,' the dragon managed to say.

'Not at all,' said the wizard, 'have no fear on that account.'

'I knew you was top-of-the-tree geezers,' said the relieved reptile. 'Only when the Elf Ring disappeared, it fair ripped out me granddaddy's pump. He never lived it down, took to lying with his head in a bucket of water. Said he'd shamed the whole family. We couldn't kindle a spark from him. I'm the last of the line now, and I would hate to fink that I'd managed to lose the rest of the rings.'

'No,' said the wizard, 'if anything we shall endeavour to see that the missing ring is returned to its rightful place, or at least its rightful owner.' The wizard and I exchanged looks.

'Now,' said Slant, 'much as I hate to tear myself away from

such a visual treat, it has been a long night, and I for one am ready for my bed. If our little friend will just direct us out, the maze is still going to take some time to negotiate.'

I looked at the dragon. 'I don't think that will be necessary Slant, will it, Dragon?' We stared at each other for a while, then he conceded. 'Ah, why not then? Let's use the front door. All right mates, you all get on the platform, then just press on the chimbleys on those lit'l models, as and when I tell you.'

We followed his directions and as he shouted out the names of some of the more famous Citadel buildings, so we pressed each chimney stack, which gave like a small button. Finally, I pushed down on the top of the Citadel Archive, and we felt the platform move below us. Gradually, we were aware that the whole dais was moving, and upwards! We were on an open lift heading for the cavern roof. I managed to get a look, over the edge of the dais, at the huge pillar on which we rode.

'Look at this engineering, will you? Outstanding, and all done with pig-iron and no steam hammers.'

The others were too concerned about the approaching ceiling. They need not have worried. As I expected, a section of the ceiling moved to one side to make room for the ascending platform. What I did not expect was what came hurtling down from the ceiling to greet us: a large amount of solid oak, followed by a cascade of scripts and scrolls. If it had not been for Slant we would have been hurt, at best, or even knocked off the dais. He managed to knock the structure to one side and we watched it plummet to the chamber floor, where it was blanketed by a fall of parchment.

'Axes and blood, Dragon! What was that! Some last trick?'

The dragon, looking very uncomfortable as Slant's fist tightened around his neck, protested his innocence, saying he had no idea. It soon became clear, when, much to our surprise, we found ourselves in the middle of the Citadel Central Archive, in front of the Widergard Frieze. The information booth had bombarded us.

'They should have known better than to put anyfing there!' said the dragon, flapping angrily in Slant's knuckle embrace. The dais had now come to a halt, fitting snugly into the floor, without so much as a gap.

'Things get forgotten,' said Tolly. 'Even wizards can forget. All right?!'

'But this is important,' said the dragon indignantly.

I was still too busy admiring the engineering to pay much attention. 'Tolly, didn't I say the chamber looked like the architecture in the Archive! And here we are in the Second Level.' I stepped off the impressive piece of dwarfish ingenuity.

Don't get me wrong, detecting is in my blood now and I'd rather be looking for clues at a crime scene than gold in an ore seam any day, but sometimes I just have to hand it to my forefathers: when dwarfs are hot they are steaming!

'Yes, we were climbing upwards back in the tunnels, even before this lift,' explained Tolly, also stepping off. When Slant unburdened the platform of his considerable bulk, there was a noise of gears moving and the dais began to sink.

'Hey, what about me?' cried the dragon, as the dais disappeared from sight. Slant let him go and he flew over to perch on the very top of the peak of the Citadel. 'Right mates, don't you folks forget, if you can find that ring it would make me granddaddy's skelington positively rattle wiv pleasure.'

'Sure, little lizard,' said Slant, 'and if you get bored down there, I could always find a job for you doubling as my power torch.'

What the dragon's thoughts on that possibility might have been we were never to know, as the platform disappeared before he could share them. We looked closely at the floor. There was no trace of a join.

'Now, that's what you call engineering,' I muttered to nobody in particular.

The private guards that patrol the Archive were a bit surprised to find us there in one of the most secure places in the Citadel. The wizard's natural authority, my shield and, most of all, Slant's size got us through. As Tolly had said, there weren't many people in the Citadel who Slant could not intimidate. We took the first street-train of the morning down the Hill. What the driver made of us I neither knew nor cared – just another bunch of happy Hill fellows after a very long night, maybe. I checked for any sign of a tail, but if Slant had been right, we had certainly lost him. We swapped numbers before I got off the train and went and picked up my wagon. I made it back to my rooms, and the welcoming bedroll, just before the first blast from the Day Watch. I fell into a deep sleep as the Citadel stirred around me.

16

HERE THERE BE DEMONS

I still had one other vein to tap before I contacted Mr Arito Cardinollo, the source of all (non-elf) wisdom on elves. I needed to follow up the lead that Mother Crock had handed to me concerning Leo Courtkey – the royal lead. It was going to necessitate me being out of town for a few days. Ralph wasn't going to be happy about that but Ralph wasn't going to know.

I drove into the Two Fingers to call round my various scouts. The light was on in my reception room. I entered wondering about who was visiting, but my nose, as normal, was ahead of me. It whispered about expensive perfume, it murmured about a mane of hair misted with water from an enchanted pool and it spoke quietly about sin. My nose was one very happy protuberance.

'Mrs Hardwood. If you are going to make a habit of this I really must redecorate.'

'Don't worry. I do a lot for charity.' She got out of the chair with a dancer's grace. 'After missing lunch, I thought I had better come round. See if there were still any … hard feelings.'

'Let's go through into the office and check.' I unlocked the door and picked up some mail, throwing it onto the desk and then sitting down next to it. This unfortunately put me at the wrong height for talking to Mrs Hardwood, bearing in mind what she was wearing. The dress was of a demure grey, but it had a neckline that plunged further than the Great Troll in the Everflow Chasm. A dead animal kept her shoulders warm. I tried to keep my eyes on her face, which was no hardship either.

'So, Master Detective. Any news on my missing property?'

'Business talk already? And just for a moment there I thought you might be missing my big brown eyes and snappy dress sense.' She came up closer.

'My pardon, Master Strongoak. Your raiment is most becoming. I particularly like your tie.' She pulled it from my vest. 'Big and fat. So much more preferable to those small thin ones you see around these days.' She wound me in and was about to land her catch when the office door burst open.

'Nicely, my mother just told me— oh, I'm sorry.' Liza stood there surprised, mouth open, her hand still on the doorknob.

'What's the matter, child?' drawled Mrs Hardwood, in a voice that dripped with depravity. 'Never seen a dwarf getting his tie cleaned before?'

'Not with a tongue, no,' she replied.

'Liza! Don't run off!' I began, but it was too late. She turned on her heels and was out of the office quicker than a mermaid on a bow wave.

'Sorry, Master Detective. Did I spoil a little something there?' The amusement was evident on Mrs Hardwood's face.

'That's all right; just business.'

'Oh yes, business, of course. Well, I just hope she didn't get the wrong idea about our business.'

'Oh no, Mrs Hardwood. I'm sure she got exactly the right idea.'

'Good.' Mrs Hardwood pulled her dead animal closer and backed off to a distance that didn't qualify as an invasion of my personal space. She played with her hair in a manner straight out of *The Naughty Girl's Guide to Bad Behaviour* and casually added: 'Only my need to recover my missing item is becoming rather more urgent and I'd hate to think that I wasn't right at the top of your priority list.'

'Mrs Hardwood,' I assured her, 'you are the first thing I think about in the morning and the last thing at night. Especially the last thing at night.'

With a small laugh and a little-girl smile (Chapter 2 of *The Naughty Girl's Guide to Bad Behaviour*: 'Smiles, Flirts and Teases'), Mrs Hardwood left the office. Suddenly the place felt like a theatre after the audience had gone home.

I followed after her down the corridor, a few strides behind, and watched the lift descend. I wasn't sure that the office fire insurance could handle a more prolonged visit. I carried on round the building but Liza was not in her office. I kicked the corridor waste bin on the way back just because I could. Looking out of a window I saw her waiting for a hire wagon and I took the stairs down to street level two at a time. Out of breath, I caught up with Liza just as the hire wagon pulled up and realised, a bit too late, that I didn't have a clue what to say.

'Ah, Liza ...' I managed at last. 'Back there, it wasn't what it looked like.'

'I'm sure your social life isn't any of my business, Master

185

Strongoak.'

'My social life doesn't get that exciting!'

'Well, in that case I'm sorry you've not had the chance for anything agreeable, like a pleasant roof-top picnic, recently.'

I was wondering whether I should dig myself deeper into the hole I was already in when the wagon driver made up my mind for me.

'Would you two lovebirds mind getting on with it? I'm losing steam here!' he shouted, with all the tact his profession is renowned for.

'Look Liza, I have to go away for a couple of days.'

'Fine,' she replied, getting into the wagon.

'I'm following a lead – to the Fortress of the Desolate Wastes.'

'I hope you have yourself a very nice time, then. You seem to be good at that.'

And before I could get another word in, the wagon had pulled out.

To make matters worse, who should come strolling along but Scout Telfine, having overheard everything. He wore a smile like the wolf that caught the cat that ate the cream and his trouser creases cut the air like one of those whips they call a Lugburg Lick.

'That's what happens when you go fishing outside your own waters,' he said, with a particularly nasty tone.

'I'm sure I don't know what you mean, Scout.'

'Citadel folk – they're not meant to mix. It never works.'

Social comment from a minor officer of the law was not on my list of 'must have' for the day.

'Does Sergeant Fieldfull know you are out on your own?'

'Of course.'

'Then how about your mother?' I added, somewhat

unnecessarily.

I left Telfine to his scouting, took the lift back upstairs and gave the waste bin another good kicking. I finally pulled myself together enough to attend to the calls I needed to make before I headed out. 'Missing Persons' could give me nothing new on Perry Goodfellow, though, and none of the staffing agencies had him freshly signed onto their books. Doroty was busy and Josh was out. So, in the end I resorted to going home and counting my suits. I do this when I am too keyed-up for anything else useful. It is a form of therapy, I guess. The answer was still thirty-four. It was no good: I needed more cupboard space.

I put a couple of the lightweight numbers into a travel trunk along with a few other things a well-dressed dwarf detective needs to retain his image and I took the trunk down to the Helmington. I considered picking up my Dragonette; it certainly was a better ride, but the Helmington probably provided a little more of the cover I sorely needed.

The route east took me near to the stud farm where Rosebud was housed. I thought about the horse and his connection to the dead elf Truetouch. I still had less than nothing to tie them together. All that thinking was giving me a headache, so for light relief I reviewed what I already knew about the King of the Desolate Wastes, Leo Courtkey's one-time employer.

As the histories tell the story, when the elves returned, bringing with them that good old democratic principle and all the trappings of power politics, royalty was made to look rather redundant. Although it is not the official version, as far as I can gather, reading between the lines, the Crowns and Coronets (who were at this stage somewhat past their dragon-slaying best) were given a choice. The choice was this: either you throw in your lot with the rest of the Citadel or we cart you all off somewhere where you can do very little damage. A large number (a very large number) took the latter option, and they were rewarded with the Desolate Wastes. This is, of course, that famous area in the Uttermost East, where nothing of interest could ever be found and hence no one of interest ever went. Generally flat, boring, and, well, desolate; that part of Widergard that used to be distinguished on the maps by the classic line: 'Here there be demons', just in case.

As the usurped were royalty, the democratically elected new regime could not just dump them in the middle of nowhere with a few packing trunks. Kings are used to living in palaces built on towering summits or craggy peaks. Nothing in the geology of the Desolate Wastes could quite fit the bill, so they built one – a mountain, that is. And because of conservation laws and height restriction they put it in a hole in the ground.

It was legendary in construction circles. The greatest triumph of the dwarfish construction business: The Fortress of the Forbidden Wastes. Massive walls and soaring towers, all out-competing each other to reach the sky, but still outdone by spires and steeples that threatened to pierce it – well, if they hadn't all been stuck at the bottom of a canyon, of course.

I had yet to see it in the stony flesh, though, and I was not about to see it tonight. The surroundings were getting distinctly desolate and the long summer dusk was darkening imperceptibly into a brief daylight hiatus as grey as a pilgrim's nightgown when I decided to lay the axe down for the evening. I found a halfway decent-looking lay-by inn and parked the Helmington where it would get the most of any morning shade.

The heat out here was a dry heat. It dried your eyeballs between blinks, it dried the sweat on your back before it even had a chance to cool you; it dried the very tongue in your mouth as you went to speak. I was grateful to be out of the wagon. I stretched and looked on down the Great East Road as it disappeared into the gathering dark, the heat haze still playing above the black stuff that spread into the distance like a child's greatest fantasy liquorice.

The inn was surprisingly comfortable considering that I did not imagine they got much custom. In my room the asthmatic air-conditioning worked overtime but brought some relief. I bought a cooled flagon from the plywood bar then went back to the room, filled my pipe and watched the stars come out.

Some time during the night I had a dream. I was back on the Gnada Peninsula. It was hot, but for some reason I was wearing formal attire. As I looked over the sea, I could see a line of elves surfing. They caught a wave and were carried towards the shore. As the wave began to break the white tips began to turn into elfin horses. Now the elves were truly riding the waves. I saw Highbury draw a sword as the waves grew higher and higher. I realised I was in danger of being swamped, but I was rooted to the spot. Behind Highbury I spotted the dead elf Truetouch, not riding, but being carried as a lifeless burden, his eyes staring blankly. His horse, though white, had a Rosebud on its muzzle. To my surprise I saw the corpse's mouth open. He was trying to tell me something. The lips formed words; I strained to hear them above the sound of the pounding surf, but no sound came out. I could feel the spray now and shouted to the dead elf, willing him to speak. Then the waves were upon me and I woke up bathed with sweat. At some point during the night, the ailing air-conditioning unit had gone to the great Appliance Paradise out west, where all white goods finally find eternal rest from their life's labours.

I staggered out to the small bathroom, and stuck my head under the water pump. Through bleary eyes, I looked at my reflection in the vanity mirror. I needed a shave, but otherwise, as faces go, it all seemed to be in order – no ghosts lurking. I went back into the bedroom and opened the balcony door, then staggered back to bed and slept undisturbed until morning.

I paid gold and did not bother with the tally. I had no idea who might be paying for this journey – it's hard to inventory a hunch. I had put a fair number of leagues behind me, before I began to notice that the old Desolate Wastes did not look quite so desolate any more. A few road signs began to spring up and the occasional small hamlet. All the signs pointed in one direction: This way to the Fortress of the Desolate Wastes. I guessed that the place must have become a bit of a tourist site. My suspicions were confirmed a short while later when I passed a large stagecoach carrying Citadel plates. Musing on the vagaries of fate, I nearly missed my first glimpse of what has frequently been referred to as one of the wonders of the New Age. The chasm opened up beneath me like, well, like a hole in the ground. And what a hole! The far side was almost lost in the heat haze; I could just make out the distant canyon cliff. Even by itself it would have been some sight, but put an artificial fortress in the middle and you have something quite breath-taking. The Citadel has sometimes been likened to a wedding cake, gift-wrapped with five stone walls. The Fortress of the Desolate Wastes was something else completely. If the moon had splintered and a large section had fallen and wounded the heart of Widergard, it would have looked just like this: awesome. Sometimes I missed the construction business.

Well, I had found my fortress. The road down the canyon wound like a dragon's tail and was not much smoother. Halfway down I got myself stuck behind another stagecoach and sat grinding my teeth as it wormed laboriously down. It was one hot, tired dwarf who finally pulled up in front of the massive ironclad gate that marked the front entrance to the Fortress of the Desolate Wastes. The stagecoach had disappeared around the back some place – presumably to find the visitors – but I try to do my business through the front door; it keeps things on the right level. I picked up a brass knocker that had done time as the head of a battering ram. I used both hands.

After what seemed like an age, the door was finally opened. Another one of those old retainer types opened it. He could have been the twin of the old boy Goodenough who worked for Mrs Hardwood. Maybe there was a school somewhere that turned them out by the dozen.

'Nicely Strongoak,' I began.

'Their Royal Highnesses maintain a charitable trust for the underprivileged and are not in the habit of giving at the door.'

I found myself standing slack-jawed as the door closed in my face. I gave it another try: 'Nicely Strongo—'

'Sorry, we never give at the door.' I took timber in the face from him. So, I knocked one last time.

This effort got more of a reaction. I pulled the axe free from the door, noting that it was laminated, built with cheap workmanship and must have been of recent origin. The old retainer blanched a more reflective tint of alabaster and beckoned me in. Goodenough would have been less accommodating, I'm sure. Goodenough would probably have complained that axes today weren't what they used to be.

I asked to see whoever was in charge, and the lackey led me through a small maze of reception rooms to a large hall where various folk were milling around trunks and handbags. I realised that this must be the coach party I had followed down the canyon. The jolly old retainer backed nervously away, saying he would fetch my bag. He had obviously decided that I must have been a lost sightseer. This was probably as good a cover as I was likely to find. Although I was not on any list, word of my pleasant face, winning manner and facility with the axe must have preceded me, because I soon found myself in a pleasant, and private, guestroom. Unfortunately, it was only on the ground level, but it had its own plumbing and a good view down the canyon; maybe tourism was not so bad after all. I had time to make use of the facilities, and after the best part of a day spent driving, it was gratifying to wash away those bits of the wastes notably attached to dwarf-hide. I felt good when I got out of the shower, and even better when I put on a fresh suit (seersucker – so called because the prophets just love that material, easy to wash and no ironing). Another lackey appeared with the good news that drinks were about to be served in The Great Hall.

The Great Hall was just great. Drinks were not so wonderful; too sweet, and very weak. I do not think my fellow guests were overly worried, though. Quite a few of the local nobility were about, and the sightseers seemed to lap it all up. Considering the amount of trouble the Citadel had gone to so that the folk all had equal representation, this struck me as a tad ungrateful. Here were the Citadel men and women, and even a few well-heeled gnomes (no dwarfs, I was pleased to note), all bending the knee as if they had been born to it. I circulated a bit and managed to get some of the top boys and girls to one side. I learnt a lot. I was told all about Baron Goodfew's designs on the laundry room, and about how Princess Littlelight was likely to make a serious bid for the total control of the ballroom and how Prince Idleless was certainly not to be trusted as he had been seen in conversation with the Guardian of the Well. Yes, I learnt a lot. By the end of it I needed a real drink. I caught the eye of a lackey. 'Hey, any chance of something with a bit more of a bite to it?'

The lackey was tall and thin with a very, very, long nose. Mind you, that description seemed to fit most of them. He looked all the way down this nose and said: 'The correct form of address to someone of my rank is "your high lord".'

Fine. 'Hey, any chance of something with a bit more of a bite to it, your high lordship?'

'Certainly, Sir. I will see if we have anything to offer the more discriminating pallet.' He returned with a couple of small glasses containing a green liquid. I took one. Maybe it was just my imagination, but I think it smoked slightly. I took a bite and it bit back. After I finished coughing I thanked his high lordship and congratulated him on the brew.

'Thank you, Sir. How about a cheesy biscuit?'

'I must say, you just don't know how long I've been waiting for a cheesy biscuit.' I helped myself to a few and washed them down with the contents of the other glass. 'Sure packs a punch, that.'

'I will pass on your congratulations to the gardener. He calls it Green Death, an interesting mixture of distillates of aniseed and spearmint. I am glad you like it. The Baron

Guardfield will be most pleased, I am sure.'

'Baron Guardfield being the gardener, I suppose.'

'Correct, Sir.'

I scratched the stubble a bit. 'I suppose everyone round here carries a fancy title, even a gardener who dabbles in making illicit gravy?'

'Oh, most certainly! If you consider, with the number of royalty around and the limited space, even in a mountain of this size, it was inevitable that the number of servants would run out, and the lowest of the ranks would have to be conscripted.'

'I had better watch myself then; don't wish to give offence to some nobility. I might even forget to curtsy for the king.'

'And which king would that be, Sir?'

I was somewhat taken aback by this. 'Well, I meant the King. As in the King of the Desolate Wastes.'

'That could be one of a number, I'm afraid, Sir.'

'How come?'

The high lord scratched his nose in a most unlordly manner. 'As I recall, there are at present something over fifty who go by the title.'

'Even bearing in mind the current trend towards job sharing, it sounds a little crowded at the top. I thought in general that one was usually the appropriate number for such a position.'

'The problem is which one.' The nose got itself a thoroughly good going over. I watched in fascination as it reverberated gently to a halt. 'Unfortunately,' continued the owner of the proud proboscis, 'when it was decided that we should take up residence in the Fortress, there were rather a lot of kings. The King of the High Mountains, for example. The King of the Lost Mountain, the King Under the Mountain,

194

the King Over the Mountain, The King by the Side of the Mountain, the King ...'

'I get the idea,' I interrupted.

'And that is just the beginning of the mountain set. We then have Witch Kings ...'

'Which kings?'

'Yes, very droll, Sir. I believe that one went down big in the Blue Age, and the Green Age and even some of the Red.'

'Sorry I brought it up. So, little chance of finding the real King of the Desolate Wastes?'

'Oh, every chance. As to whether he's the king you are after, well, that's another matter.'

'Who said I was after a king?'

'My mistake, Sir. I do not know what put it in my mind. Of course we have lots of dwarfs visiting at this time of year, especially carrying a battle-axe in their luggage. Just look, there's one now. Oh, no, my mistake, it's the hat-stand. Strange, not another one in sight at all; how peculiar.'

'All right. Let's just say that I wanted to meet a king with an interest in horseflesh. Hypothetically.'

'Well, hypothetically, of course. Let me think.'

'By the way, is it permissible to tip nobility?'

'Certainly not! Waiters, however, I am given to understand, look at things very differently.' I dropped two crowns in his tray.

'And what a delightful sound they do make. If rather a hollow noise.'

I added a couple of friends to keep the others on the tray from getting too lonely. They disappeared with an ease a magician would envy. 'Well, hypothetically, I suggest kings 1418, 1427, 1434S and 1434N.'

'The kings are numbered?'

'Oh no, those are their room numbers: floor 141, room 8, floor 142, room 7, floor 143 …'

'I get the idea,' I interrupted.

'Well, we have to keep track of them somehow.'

'And S and N?'

'South-facing and north-facing.'

'I promise I'll be on my best behaviour.'

'Oh, do not be concerned about that, Sir. You have something much greater than nobility.'

'Oh yes: and what's that then?'

'Gold, Sir, gold.'

Bearing this in mind, I went into dinner. And what a merry affair it was. Mead was sloshed, chicken legs gnawed and thrown to the waiting dogs (Earl and Lady Rotfang and family, in cheap skin jobs). Just like the good old days. Many a merry chorus was raised: songs of great valour and songs of impossible quests, songs of lost princesses and songs of the slaying of giants. For a short while we were all back there, except of course we weren't. Because the songs were all written long after the events. Valour really has little place on a battlefield, where one's only preoccupation tends to be splitting the enemy's head before he splits you. Impossible quests tended to be impossible because they could not be done, and consequently they did not get done. Lost princesses were generally lost because someone very important did not want them found. And the last thing I heard from the boys who know these sorts of things, the most recent theory about giants was that they all died out due to a particularly nasty little bug that went round. And that is irony, folks. Still, for a while there we were all heroes, and why not? Just do not get to believe your own press.

The whole thing wound up very quickly, the top boys and girls seemed very keen on getting their shut-eye, and I was soon back in my room. I checked my luggage. The trusty axe was gone. A small token was left in its place, stating that the axe was redeemable from the weapons rooms (Axe Annex) on departure. I lit a pipe and waited.

17

THE KING OF THE DESOLATE WASTES

Taking a flashlight and my handy Get-to-Know-the-Fortress Tourist Guide, I left the room. The guest quarters were on the bottom floor. Kings apparently warranted something a bit more lofty. I needed to climb the mountain. Without too much trouble I found what I was looking for: The Endless Staircase. Another marvel of dwarfish engineering; a stone spiral that wound from the lowest dungeon to the very pinnacle. The guide said the exact number of steps had been long forgotten, although each Winter Solstice there was a charity event open to anyone tempted to try to count them. Me, I took the lift.

The plan was for a bit of simple breaking and entering; nothing would be taken, just a quick look around while Their Majesties slumbered. I had just drawn a blank on floor 141 when I heard voices – and not just any voices. I immediately knew them to be goblins, and even more surprising, sounding somewhat refined as well. I ducked behind a pillar, just in time. Two sets of footsteps approached. I held my breath.

'Stop dragging your feet, Cribbage. We've only got all night.'

'I know, I know. Give a goblin a break, won't you, Gabbage? And me with my terrible bunions.'

'I said you should have had them seen to, Cribbage. It's those heavy boots you wear.'

'They were handed down to me, you know, Gabbage.'

'Of course. I handed them down to you. Straight after we removed them from the poor sod stuck in the tree. So, is this the right room?'

'Does it really matter, I ask myself?'

I heard a door creak, then a shout, a new voice: 'Assassins, assassins, in the dark!' I tensed, but unarmed against the two large grunts, I did not fancy my chances. The goblin named Cribbage spoke: 'No, we're not.'

'Pardon?'

'We're not assassins.'

'Really?'

'Really.'

'We're here to take you to a place of safety.'

'Oh right, I'll just pack a few things then.' The voice was cut off by a gurgling noise followed by a thud.

'Enjoy that, did you, Cribbage?'

'Yes, I believe I did, Gabbage.'

'Leading the poor lad on like that. You should be ashamed of yourself.'

I watched them drag the body away. They wore tabards with a strange insignia: a white rose held in a white hand, with blood trickling down from the clenched fist. Below it were the letters BRA. Shaking my head, I made my way to floor 142 and the next king on my list. I hoped I had seen the last of this unpleasant pair, but our paths were not to be separated that easily. I had no joy on floor 142 either. The king obviously had an interest in horses, but I'm not sure it was strictly legal. Certainly immoral. I blame it on the inbreeding.

On 143 I heard voices again:

'So Cribbage, he was in league with the duke's brother to remove the countess and thus put their niece once-removed first in line for complete world domination of the sewing room. So, he had to go. Now do you see?'

'Sorry Gabbage, I still don't get it. You just tell me who to throttle.'

Hidden behind a chest, I heard another door creak and another shout: 'So, you butchers, creeping up on me in the dead of night to do your deed.'

'Nope, not us.'

'Excuse me?'

'You have us all wrong. We're the shiny heroes, come to take you to sanctuary.'

'Honest?'

'Honest.'

'No joking?'

'Cross my heart.'

'No little white lies?'

'Do we look the sort?'

'Well, yes.'

'Trust us.'

'I'll just grab a few things … urgh.'

'It's quite good fun, Cribbage. This leading them on.'

'I thought you would like it, Gabbage, if you gave it a try.'

'I like the look of relief that floods over their faces, just before your hands get on their throats.'

I managed to slip further down the corridor, to 1434S. This king's interest in horses seemed to revolve principally around their ability to jump particularly large fences. Not Rosebud's speciality at all. So I made my way round to the north of the mountain, hoping that the goblins would have left. No such luck.

'And naturally, Cribbage, a position of influence in the potting sheds would be a big step forward for the baron and could even lead eventually to a toe-hold in the summerhouse, but first he had to get rid of Viscount Brig.'

'No, it's no good, Gabbage. I'll have to sit down sometime when we are quiet and work it out with a bit of paper and a pencil.'

'Here we are then, Cribbage.'

'Villainous scum! Come to slit my throat, have you?'

'Nope, we are here to escort you to a place of safety.'

'Don't give me that. I have heard all about how you lull your victims into a false sense of security with your smooth talking.'

'No, straight up. We really are here to help you.'

'Do not come a step nearer. Back, I say. One step nearer and I will jump. I will not give you the satisfaction. If die I must, let it be by my own hand.'

I heard a distant cry, which faded into the distance.

'That's torn it, Cribbage.'

'One hundred and forty-three floors has done more than torn it, Gabbage.'

'No, I mean it's put the cat among the pigeons.'

'They look a bit too large and vulture-like to be pigeons, Gabbage.'

'No, Cribbage. We cocked up. We really had come to

save him.'

'Oh yes, I forgot.'

While they were busy at the window, I made it past the open door to room 1434N. I slipped the lock and tippy-toed in. Finally, I had hit pay dirt. At first it seemed like any other suite, slightly larger perhaps. The unlit corridor had a number of rooms leading off it. Two rooms were characterless and uninteresting; my torch illuminated precious little beyond the fact that royalty accumulated as much junk as everyone else. The third was different. On a large chest by the door was a photograph of a woman with long black hair standing by a black horse, a horse with a white mark on its nuzzle. The torch barely wavered as I picked up the photograph, but waver it did. She was younger, quite a lot younger, but there was no mistaking the cheekbones of the woman I now knew as Mrs Hardwood.

'I suggest you turn on the light, Sir. It will save on your batteries, which, I am given to understand, are quite an expense these days.' The voice was old and tired, but had a certain quality, one that I can only describe as 'majesty'. I found the light switch, and turned to find the voice's owner.

He was seated in a large armchair that all but swallowed him. He was short for a man, and his clothes had seen better days, but he sat in that chair as if it was a throne and his gaze did not leave my face for an instant.

'My wife, you know.'

'Your wife?'

'In the photograph that you are so interested in. My wife.'

'Your wife, a queen?'

'Yes, a queen. That's the nub of it, I suppose: a queen. If she had been *the* queen, it might have all been different. She might still have been here, if she had been *the* queen. But all

202

the other queens, it was just too much for her, I suppose.'

'May I ask your queen's name?'

'Queen Celembine. King Lustafor and Queen Celembine; I thought it had a good solid ring to it, obviously not good enough.'

'And Her Majesty is no longer in residence then?'

'Oh no, long gone, long, long gone. Or at least it seems like it now.'

'No divorce, I suppose?'

'Damn right, Sir. We may be little more than a footnote in history now, but we do not behave like commoners.'

'And the horse?'

'The horse? Oh, Rosebud, I bought it for her as a wedding present. Amazing turn of speed. Doted on him they did, her and that little rider.'

'Rider?' I said excitedly.

'Yes, strange little chap; very winning manner, though, in every way. Cannot for the life of me think of his name.'

'Courtkey?'

'Perhaps. Honestly don't recall. He loved that horse, though, more than any person around here. He never seemed to get on with the other men in the stables much. Doted on the horse though, just like my queen. Or did I just say that? He left when she did. Damn horse was the only thing she took with her. Didn't even bother with the jewels and all the other presents I'd bought her. Just took the horse, and the rider, I suppose. Never saw any of them again anyway. Might as well have disappeared up the Great Crack of the Lord of the Stone Giants.'

'I don't suppose you have a picture of him, do you? The rider?'

'Now why would I have something like that?'

I felt like saying, maybe to help a suspicious dwarf detective, but I let it pass. 'Your queen, by any chance was her maiden name Merrymead?'

'Why yes, Celembine Merrymead! My, but you ask a lot of questions for a common thief. If that is indeed what you are. I took you at first for one of the court assassins.'

'Court assassins?'

'Yes. Can't miss them. Unpleasant chaps, wear the Insignia and BRA: By Royal Appointment.'

'You have goblins on the payroll?'

'Yes, unfortunate necessity, I am afraid. As you may have noticed, royalty is rather thick on the ground here. In fact rather thick everywhere as it happens and, given the rate at which some of them breed, and their instinctive desire to achieve positions of influence, I am afraid assassination seems to be the simplest solution.'

'Oh yes, of course.'

'Well, we can hardly manage to hold a war, all living under the same pointed roof, as it were. Not like the good old days. Well, that is our story, or mine at least. Now, how about yours?'

'I think for this I had better sit down as well, your majesty. We may be some time.'

18

A DARK HORSE.

I sat in the wagon, watching the sun go down over the stud farm, chewing on the information that I had obtained from the King of the Desolate Wastes, and tallying it with what I had already learnt from Clubbin and Mother Crock.

I was not exactly sure what it was that had brought me back to Rosebud. All I know is when I had woken up in the Fortress of the Desolate Wastes, I had felt a touch uneasy, and it was not just the thought of the court assassins still wandering around. This unease was still with me after I had broken my fast with something solid, and satisfied my coffee urge. Well, as much as my coffee urge can ever be satisfied without a permanent drip-feed being attached. And that's not possible yet, I checked. It makes you wonder what these scholars do all day instead of inventing something useful.

On the way back from the Fortress I made better time. Around midwatch I stopped off at a lay-by. I wasn't very hungry, so I just bought some fruit for the journey, but I did take the opportunity to find a horn and get in touch with my answering service. Messages were picked up and messages were left. Mrs Hardwood's scribe had called to arrange a lunch date. Josh Corncrack had been on several times, threatening blood and bones if he didn't get an exclusive for *The Citadel Press* concerning 'whatever it was I was up to that was driving everybody crazy'. More importantly, there was a message from Grove. It turned out that the barkeeper at *The Old Inn* had not seen Perry collect his goods in person. Some friends, unspecified, had picked them up on his behalf. I wanted to get back to Grove, but unfortunately, as his message made clear, the extraction of this information from the barkeeper had involved dangling him, by his ankles, over an open barrel of his own beer. Grove was thus seeking further employment, and lodgings, and would get back to me when he had a number. The last message I had was from Renfield Crew, the scribe. He sounded excited and said he had some information on Mr Hardwood that I would find exciting too. Fortunately he also sounded as if he was now back shooting with a full quiver of arrows. I put him top of my 'to do' list.

When I finally made it back to the outskirts of civilisation proper the sun was dropping behind the Citadel, casting a long shadow over the plain of Rhavona. Now, as I have admitted, I can just about tell one end of a horse from the other, but it is a close thing. All I had to go on was an old picture on a kid's trading card, the words of an outmoded noble, and that little thing that resembled a detective's hunch. Maybe my detective instincts weren't completely atrophied after all. Oh yes, and I now also had a copy of a photograph of a queen who was now married to a very different sort of high-powered leader. I found a hardgoods store still open and bought what I needed there, then I picked up some provisions; it was going to be a long evening, but I had an itch that needed scratching before I visited Renfield Crew.

I parked the wagon where I could get a view of the stable, without being seen myself. Taking out a fresh new bottle from my pack, I unscrewed the top and took a sample, then wished that I had thought to bring a skin of water instead. It was still far too hot for hard gravy. I screwed the top back up tight, got out my pipe and waited.

As soon as it was dark enough to cover my movements I made my way around the back to Rosebud's stall. I found it with no trouble – good old dwarf night vision. He was jolly pleased to see me and nuzzled for the sugar I had picked up along with the provisions. The job didn't take long. I stepped back to admire my handiwork, and fell into the black pit that is always ready to swallow up a dwarf detective who doesn't pay enough attention.

I came to, lying on a bed of straw. I knew it was straw because that is where the horses crap and my nose was confident that this was what it was poking into. There was another smell as well: the paint thinner which had spilt as I fell. I was still clutching the rag I had used on Rosebud. A lantern was swinging from the rafters. I then realised that the lantern was stationary and it was me that was not so steady. The rafters then turned out to be the arms of the tall stable man I had met the day before.

'Thought you'd be back, I've a feeling for these things.' He placed the lantern on a convenient hook. 'I've been keeping watch at the Lancer's stall, though; nose steered me wrong there.'

He sat on a large stool and rested his hands and chin on the long staff that had dealt me the blow. 'Remember me?

Clubbin?'

I nodded. Some detective I was. Big clue in the name there.

'I generally like to introduce myself to those I've maced. Mind you, you've a fine skull there, they don't usually come round this quick, unless I'm losing my touch. I was just fixing myself a pipe.' He threw his pouch over and I caught it. 'Good,' he said. 'Co-ordination is fine, no concussion.' He lit a long-stem with a match, which he struck on a boot that must have taken the best part of a heifer's hide.

'Mind the sparks,' I said, pointing to the paint thinner, and carefully filling my own briar.

'Oh yes. The thinner. Don't expect no apology from me, though. Even if you were right, no call to be creeping round a stable at night.' I could not think of a reply worth the effort. 'I've finished your work for you. Best come take a look.'

He led, lantern in hand. I got up and followed. We left the animal in Rosebud's stall happily clearing up the sugar spilt as I had fallen. Clubbin outpaced me, but no way was I going to run to catch up, so I followed his guide-light as quickly as I was capable. He took me to the Dark Lancer's stall. The horse was pleased to see us. He seemed docile now, he seemed positively friendly, he seemed everything he should be, except for the distinctive white mark on his muzzle, in contrast to the all-black horse I had left happily eating in what I could no longer really call Rosebud's stall.

'Maybe I do owe you something after all,' said Clubbin, pulling a bottle from behind a hay bale and throwing it in my direction. I pulled the bottle cork with my teeth. The contents smelt like horse liniment, and might well have tasted like it – I've never been that desperate – but at least my eyes leapt back into focus. I threw the bottle back to Clubbin and it was effortlessly plucked out of the air. He took a drink and then asked: 'What do you reckon we have here then?'

I eased myself up onto a convenient crate, a respectful distance from the unmasked horse. 'As I read the runes, I think we have a winning horse with a lucrative pedigree, but no desire to do what a stud should do. We also have another stallion, a winner without the parentage, who is the same general size and colour as the first horse, but for a distinctive marking. He, at least, has the, how shall we put it, the enthusiasm for the job?'

'Sounds good so far,' agreed Clubbin, taking a long draw of his pipe.

'So with a bit of black dye, Rosebud becomes the Dark Lancer and with a bit of white bleach the Dark Lancer becomes Rosebud. The problem is thereby solved and everybody is happy, and very much richer. Especially the stud owners.' I eyed Clubbin carefully to see how this went down.

'Yup, that's about how I read the runes too. And it wouldn't take much for that very rich stud owner to keep up the pretence when the horses are out of my sight either.'

'Does it sound like the sort of stunt he might pull?'

'This is horse racing, Master Dwarf; I'd be surprised if he didn't. I'm thinking there might be more too it as well.'

'Such as?'

'Remember that last race, the one I told you that Rosebud did so poorly in?'

'Oh yes, when he ran out of legs?'

'Maybe he never did.'

'Meaning what?'

'Come on, you've not just come down from the mountain. Big money bet on an outsider, that's the normal reason for a sudden loss of form by a favourite. But perhaps it was the Dark Lancer that was going off his form and so they did the switch. They clear up on the betting and the Dark Lancer's value is assured, for winning the race and for later stud payments.'

I thought about this. 'That could also explain why the so-called Rosebud was pulled out of racing at the same time that the Lancer was supposed to be going out to stud.'

'Indeed,' said Clubbin. 'You know, as I recollect now, I do believe that Leo Courtkey didn't ride Rosebud in that last race. It was the Dark Lancer's normal rider.'

'That would make sense. Maybe he was asked to take a dip, but refused. They certainly couldn't have fooled him with a dye job.' We both pulled on our pipes, contemplating. Finally Clubbin broke the silence. 'Or perhaps he took their gold and hightailed it out of there as speedily as his own two legs could take him.'

'It's possible, especially if he had been supporting expensive habits.'

'True. Some riders take a lot of different things to kill their appetites to stop them putting on weight.'

'Like Moondust, for example?'

'It has been known, if they can find the money. It's not a cheap way of slimming.'

'So where does that leave us?' I asked.

'Well,' said Clubbin, 'it leaves me out of here, that's for sure. All of this went on before I started work here, but I should have suspected something and I want nothing to do with it now. Still one last thing to do, though.'

It did not take us long to swap the two horses and put them back in their rightful stalls. Rosebud did not seem too impressed with his reduced circumstances. The Dark Lancer seemed overjoyed with his surroundings, especially his winning rosettes. 'Well lad, you earned them,' said Clubbin, patting him reassuringly. 'I wish I could be here tomorrow, when all the rich Citadel folk come out to see their mares covered by the great Dark Lancer. I don't really think I should be hanging about, though.' He gave the horse one last pat.

'He'll be all right, will he? The Dark Lancer, I mean,' I said some time later, as we drove back to the Hill.

'They're not about to put him down, if that's what you mean. Don't worry; word will get around very quick, and they won't be able to pull that stunt again. Most likely it will be put down to something contagious, but Dark Lancer, he's a personality, and he'll probably end up opening summer shows and parties. He'd like that, lots of sugar and fuss, but thanks for asking. As for the real Rosebud, well, you've probably heard the saying: you can't keep a good horse down. He'll probably be siring a few champions now under his own name!'

Clubbin fell quiet again for the rest of the journey. Just before he got out on Lower Fifth he said, 'That book of pictures you were after, it seems it's only gone missing. Somebody has been covering their tracks. Thought you might want to know that.'

I dropped him on a corner, just by the gate, and he disappeared. One more dark shadow lost in the night. He never did say sorry for the macing, and I never did hold it against him.

I sat in the wagon for a moment joining up a few of the dots. Leo Courtkey certainly looked like the number-one candidate for the role of Hardwood Emerald thief. Even if he were no longer working there, he would know the security arrangements and it sounded like he had a habit to support. Was he, even now, sitting on a beach somewhere in the far south sipping cocktails?

It wasn't very far to the Wizards' Quarter and Renfield Crew's deepmost dwelling. I found it easier to find this time; it was probably the flashing lights on the roofs of all the Citadel Guard wagons parked outside that helped.

I knew the tabard-wearing Cit guarding the top of the staircase: Caff Twoson. He had been a new boy when I was fresh off the mountain too. He had a strong back and a quick smile, a combination that had made him popular wherever he patrolled. His singular lack of ambition was the sole reason for his lack of advancement and did not reflect on either his wit or ability. He gave me a quick heads-up: 'The shiny gold badges want to send you back to New Iron Town by instalment plan.'

'That good, eh?'

'The word is that the only reason they're not carrying out that particular option is because the White and Wise are busy thinking up something even nastier to do with you.'

'Great! How's Ralph?'

'Sergeant Credible Ignorance is currently downstairs and I'm sure will be delighted to be updated as to your current misadventures. As for myself, I'm going to walk over yonder and advise that member of the local community to "move on" … unfortunately leaving this entrance momentarily unguarded.'

'Thanks, Caff.'

'For what? I've not seen you.'

'Who has?'

'And Nicely … I hope you've not just eaten, because this one's not pretty.'

I walked carefully down the staircase, not looking forward to what I knew I must find. The hovel was better lit than before, thanks to the presence of a number of Citadel Guard mobile lights. What they illuminated was not pretty – not in any way.

Ralph was standing by the stove staring at the surprised expression on Renfield's face. It was a very natural, lifelike expression. The fact that Renfield's body was propped up against the sleeping pallet some five feet away told a different story.

They say that the quill is mightier than the sword, but the sword is a whole lot messier.

For a seriously skinny guy Renfield sure had his full quota of blood. It hadn't helped towards the embellishment of his quarters any.

'Nice trip?' said Ralph, after we had retired to the bottom of the staircase and leant against the wall to take a pipe.

'Now what makes you think I've been anywhere?'

'Probably because I asked you to not leave the Citadel for a while. So from past experience I would expect you to have headed out for a week in Tall Trees at least.'

'The Fortress of the Desolate Wastes, actually.'

Ralph registered real surprise. 'Now that's an interesting destination – my in-laws went there last year. I'm assuming it was tat?'

'Oh, yes – it was the pinnacle of tat.'

'But advantageous?'

'It depends really how you might classify advantageous, Sergeant Credible Ignorance.'

Ralph drew long on his pipe and sighed the sigh of a much put-upon public guardian. 'I suppose you know what was in the very late Renfield Crew's pocket?'

'I imagine it was the business card of an increasingly unpopular dwarf detective.'

'And how long do you think it will take me to find this card?'

'Twenty-four hours?'

'Twenty-four hours it is.' Ralph looked back into the scene of the slaughter. ''What aren't I seeing, Nicely?'

'He was a writer. Where's his writing? There should be papers, parchments, fragments of old posters even, which he might have used when he didn't have money to buy anything else to scribble on.'

'Got you.'

'All gone, all conveniently disappeared.'

'And what might they have said?'

'That's the one-thousand-crown question, isn't it?'

'So what are you going to do, Nicely?'

'I'm going to see a gnome about an elf.'

'And then we nail whoever is responsible for this butchery?'

'We certainly do, Ralph. We certainly do that.'

19

LITTLE HUNDRED

Historians do not, as a rule, have an easy time in the Citadel. I mean, what is the point of spending years poring over old manuscripts, trying to figure out what went on in some age-old war, when, for the price of a stamp, you can find out from someone who was actually there. It must be quite galling to have your latest work put down by a near-immortal: 'Actually Gedred the half-dead could not have killed Slut, the Goblin King, because he was round at my place for cocktails at the time.' Still, that does not stop them scribbling, and as historians go, the scribe Arito Cardinollo was one of the better known.

I'd had a poor night's sleep thanks to all the questions rattling around my noggin. Could Mr Hardwood really be implicated in the killing of a disadvantaged scribe who happened to write a largely forgotten piece of speculation some years before? Or had Renfield really turned up something new? As for finding Perry, I felt further away than ever from solving that particular problem. I just couldn't see him sipping cocktails on the beach with Leo; Liza couldn't have chosen that badly, surely?

I was surprised the Cits weren't camped out on my door-step as I finally headed on out. I now owed Ralph a very large drink or three. My twenty-four hours were ticking down quickly.

I took a street-train out to Little Hundred. It's not the place to take your wagon, as one is liable to come back from a visit and find a market has been opened in it; this year you were more liable to find it had been trashed. Some of the summer's worst violence had been centred on this ghetto area. The quarter had come into being when land reforms led to the reorganisation of the gnomes' traditional homelands in the Hundreds. With the resulting over-farming and the Dust Basin Disaster, many thousands of gnomes headed for the urban areas. As the Citadel did not have the kind of conditions they were accustomed to living in, ever resourceful, they created their own. Corrugated iron, old packaging, dead wagons; you name it, everything was put to use to create a maze of tunnels and small buildings. The effect is rather like an ants' nest opened for public viewing and can make you feel a touch uneasy. Not that I have anything against gnomes, it's nothing to do with their colour, or their noses or anything stupid like curly hair on their feet, but I do get an occasional twinge of good, old-fashioned liberal guilt. I know that of all the races in Widergard, they have got probably the worst deal, and I also know that solving the problem is certainly beyond my capabilities. Whatever, the trip to Arito Cardinollo was likely to be the highlight of my day.

It was still hotter than a dragon's tonsils and running for the street-train did not help my demeanour or disposition. I handed the boy a quarter-crown and pushed my way on. The train was fit to bursting, full of homeward-bound workers, at the end of their split shifts. No seats inside, so I stood on the platform, which was no problem as I was glad to get away from the heat of the boiler.

Folk do tend to romanticise about the good old steam street-trains, how they are so much part of the Citadel's magic, but they probably never had to sit next to the boiler on a hot summer's day. With the bellows wheezing like an asthmatic ogre, the pistons hissing like incensed serpents and the wheels squealing against the tracks on the bends, it feels uncomfortably like being banged-up in a necromancer's dungeon. Mind you, it's the best place in Widergard on a winter's morning. And if our learned Councillors and Aldermen are really interested in learning what the people they represent think, they could do a lot worse than travel, at least once a week, on a Citadel street-train. All of life, as they say, is there. Well, nearly all of life. In all the years I have been domiciled in the Citadel, I have yet to see an elf on a street-train, and that about says it all.

A group of gnome girls got on, red scarves and spotted skirts giving the train a sudden carnival atmosphere. They would be heading down the Hill as well, after an exhausting shift in the sweatshops of the lower Third Level. You would not think it to look and listen to them. Hands that had been working the looms for hours, now clapped along to their happy sing-song voices; eyes that had been straining at the finest stitching were now gleaming brightly at the possibilities of an evening spent dancing and singing. Make the most of it, girls. It would not be long before home time meant just more work. Cook the meal, wash the children, put them to bed, then get them up and still the same demanding grind in the sweatshops facing them the next day.

It was a sobering fact that while unemployment amongst the male adult gnome population was a staggering seventy-five per cent, the textile industry was still crying out for the skills at which their women excelled. Unfortunately, the vast influx of gnomes into the Citadel following the increased mechanisation of agriculture had meant there was no shortage of workers and the textile industry could still offer minimal wages. This was not an ideal situation and trouble was bubbling away like a simmering gnome bean stew. The husbands, resentful and frustrated, smoked too much pipeleaf, whilst the overworked mothers lost control of their youngsters, who too easily got involved in petty crime and gang street-life. It was a sad situation for a once proud and independent people with their own culture and roots.

Not that you would have thought that anything was amiss listening to the group of youngsters as they rode the street-train, laughing and singing their way down the Hill. A group of men came down the stairs, shooting filthy looks at the party of gnomes. I snarled in their general direction and they left the train in a hurry. Sometimes I despair for all hopes of proper integration.

I made my way up to the top deck and found the space that the men had vacated. I got the nod from two Brothers travelling on the back seat. I didn't know them and I just gave the signal that said I needed some thinking time, then found a seat near the front of the train – just like an excited kid.

The street-train smoked at another hold-up – two wagons had collided and the citizens were settling the dispute in the time-honoured fashion – by taking turns to see who could hit the other the hardest. The Citadel Guards were on the way, but their wagon was stuck in the same queue we all were. I understand there was a move being mooted to get the Cits on horseback. It couldn't happen too soon.

Building a city on a mountain may be aesthetically pleasing, and the huge encircling walls and spiralling roads were just fine for keeping out the goblin armies, but they do not encourage an efficient urban transport system. The planners say that it is all the fault of the conservationists. The conservationists say that if the planners pull down one more treasured building, they will find themselves up to the knees in their own hardcore surveying the bottom of the Bay. I personally tend to go with the conservationists; the last chance the road builders had to improve things, the best they could come up with was a ring road.

The bickering wagon drivers soon apportioned blame, by one fall and a submission. The crumpled wagons were swept into a side alley and all the monies were paid out on the bets taken on the combatants. The Cits finally arrived, and waved us on.

The street-train turned through a narrow arch, narrowly missing a gnome market that had sprung up, mushroom-like, the minute a crowd had gathered. I could see stalls laden with armies of fruits and vegetables, thrown into relief by the strings of lights. Huge polished squashes squatting like Eastern Mages, a carnival of fat peppers in red, green, yellow and orange, and tiny dragons' teeth no bigger than your finger, but hot enough to have you crying for mercy and more ale. Carefully we navigated this throwback to the gnomes' more pastoral heritage. We almost made it without mishap, and then I heard a large crunch. Oh, well!

The crunch turned out to be some poor gnome's livelihood, and not the transportation, and I therefore breathed a great sigh of relief when the train passed through the last of the Citadel gates and we began to make up some time.

Soon we were in the cauldron of activity; laughs, loves and despair, that is Little Hundred.

Little Hundred is a maze and I'm good in them, but unfortunately it lacks the logic of the one under the Citadel Central Archive. I only got lost four times. Gnomes feel friendlier towards dwarfs than other races, but the spare axe was a comfort. Much of Little Hundred is daubed with slogans of the 'Gnomes go home!' variety and although many had been painted over, unrest is still evident in the broken windows and burnt-out homes. In the middle of the maze, where Arito lived, things were better.

The gnome lived in a hole. Boy, was it a hole. His front door was made from the fender of a '42 Dragonette, the model before mine, and would be a collector's piece in a few more years. I had knocked. Entering when I heard the faint 'Come-in', I then paused to survey the devastation. Dirty dishes were piled up next to mounds of grey underwear, and everywhere was the smell of heavy-duty pipeleaf, the gnome special variety. What was a respected scribe doing in such conditions?

'Look at him will you, Wilmer. Knocks, as if we could run to a lock.'

Through the wall of crockery and clothes and many twinkling lamps, I spotted the gnome. Although obviously old, the hair on his feet and head were both as brown as a new conker and his eyes twinkled like the lamps. 'So, you got a name, or you some sort of sheriff? If so, the wagon's been stolen and the music maker's under that pile of togs! If you can find it, take it, you've earned it for finding me.'

I would not have touched the togs for all the gold in Iron Town. Instead I pushed a card in his direction. 'The name is Nicely Strongoak, Master Detective, and I've come about elves.'

'Elves, he says, you hear that, Wilmer?' The old gnome sat himself down on a rocker with no rock left in it. 'Well, if it's elves you're interested in, I suppose you already know that I am Arito Cardinollo, and this, this is Wilmer.'

He pointed vaguely to his right and I looked around for his companion. At first I saw no trace of anyone, but then I noticed a parrot's pen. Instead of the expected bird, I saw, sitting on a small perch and reading a tiny scroll, something that made my jaw drop: a fat, sweating, unshaven pix. He was not as the funny papers usually paint them; the pointed boots were down-at-heel and the trousers of his bright green suit had certainly seen better days; instead of a jacket he wore a stained vest, over which red braces sought to keep at bay a spreading gut. He was probably the most degenerate example of any of the Races of Widergard I had ever come across; and I've seen a troll in a pink trouser suit, and met goblins who mixed stripes with checks and topped it off with flares and platform shoes.

'Wasa matter, musclebound, dropped yer axe on yer foot?'

The pixie had a surprisingly deep voice, for someone at home in a birdcage. Not that I had any experience with the pix. Some experts considered that they were amongst the very first, if not the first, of the races to settle in Widergard. Others thought that they were all a figment of the earliest elves' imaginations – come magically to life. They were certainly now very elusive, seldom seen in public life, even by the elves. This led to all sorts of stories about them. Some people thought they had wings, some people said they lived off nectar and dew, but no people I had ever met had ever mentioned that they had a body odour problem.

'Pix are lucky you know,' the gnome commented, by way

of some kind of an explanation. 'It's just that Wilmer here, his luck is kinda messy.'

Wilmer seemed to take exception to that. He donned a ridiculous pointed hat, at least two sizes too small, threw down his scroll, stuck out his tongue and said, 'Nice to meet you, fat boy,' and then disappeared.

'Neat trick,' I said, with a grin.

'Yes,' said the gnome. 'Apart from the elves, the pix are the only race that can claim to have what are normally considered magical powers. They aren't really of course, but the pix's extra abilities, like their incredible sense of smell, are very useful. For example, Wilmer has already given you the once over and said that you are not carrying any concealed weapons.'

'He missed the axe,' I said, coughing and pointedly raising the shaft at my side.

'Not at all. Do you think, given the arrangement of the room, that it would do you much good?'

He was right. All the piles of rubbish and clutter made it just about impossible to attempt even a half-hearted lunge, let alone get up a good swing. Also, all the rubbish provided numerous hiding places for a gnome of his stature.

'You're cautious,' I said.

'Given the atmosphere in the Citadel this summer, and some of the attacks being made on gnome property, I think it pays. You should know, Master Dwarf, you look like you have been around.'

'I've done places and been things.'

'That is the trouble with travel.' The gnome let out a sigh. 'It does broaden the mind.'

'Trouble?'

'Yes.' He found himself a stool and waved me in the

direction of an old settle. I cleared myself a space with the axe, and perched warily at one end. 'Trouble. Now, take me,' he continued after re-lighting his pipe, the heavy leaf making my eyes smart in the enclosed space. 'I've never travelled. Lived all my life here in Little Hundred and so, thankfully, my mind has remained focused, concentrated – unbroadened – and thus able to think in depth upon a single subject.'

'Which is?'

'Why, elves, Master Dwarf, as you well know. Why else would you be here?'

He offered his pipe, but I stayed on the side of caution and filled my own. 'So, Arito, how did you get interested in elves?'

'Always been interested. It's in the family. We have records dating back to the very first Shire. Priceless they are. I was weaned on stories from these books, and many were the tales about elves, and I just became hooked. Fascinated I was, as a youth; I longed to see them, travel with them, be around them. I never did. Somehow the scrolls and parchments always seemed more interesting than the real thing.'

'So, you became an expert on elf history instead?'

'Yes, and it is not an easy subject. You would think, given their longevity, that it would be a simple matter. The question is, not what the elves know, but what they are willing to tell you. I think it is better to say that I have become an expert on elf history for the rest of Widergard. I am sure nothing I have to say would be of the slightest interest to any of the High Folk. But come, tell me, what aspect of elfdom interests you?'

'Genealogy.'

'Yes, a fascinating subject. But be specific. What in

particular? Come on, come on, out with it!' The gnome was getting interested, I could tell.

'Well, for a start, what would you call a typical elf?'

He drew on his pipe. 'Now that's an interesting question. Interesting, interesting. Elves really are as alike as, or rather, as unlike as a ...' He held a lungful of smoke while searching to find his simile.

'As beans in a gnome stew?' I added helpfully for him.

His laughter set him coughing, with tears rolling down his rosy red cheeks. 'Very good, Master Dwarf, as beans in a gnome stew. I can see you must be an expert on good cooking.'

Indeed, I had to admit that I had eaten my way halfway around Widergard. I was also a patron of and had shares in *The Burrowers*. I mentioned this to Arito.

'Ah, yes,' he said. 'Many the happy evening I have spent over a bowl of broth and ale at *The Burrowers*.' This surprised me. *The Burrowers* was the Hill's only dwarf restaurant, and was kept pretty much secret from the rest of the population. The reason for this is simply that, contrary to popular belief, dwarfs are excellent cooks. Most people tend to think we must munch on anthracite with lignite desserts. The truth is that our rich meat dishes with numerous pungent and dark spices make dwarf cooking one of the greatest in Widergard, and *The Burrowers* was certainly the best restaurant this side of New Iron Town. The reason we do not tell everyone about it, is simply so we can keep the best seats for ourselves. For Arito to know, it showed a great degree of acceptance on the part of the dwarf community and some taste on the part of Arito. Not too surprising; gnomes are also very good cooks on the whole, doing excellent things with vegetables, as befits their agricultural origins. They can make potatoes so light they seem to fairly float off the plate and their bean stews are legendary.

'I must admit,' sighed Arito, 'it seems an age since I have been to *The Burrowers*.'

'Maybe I'll stand you a meal there then.'

'Now that's an incentive! So, it's beans we were talking about. Beans in a stew. Ah, the humble bean, each so different, yet each so alike.'

'And how to pick one out of the stew?'

'Well, Master Dwarf, first describe your bean.'

'He was short, for an elf, I mean.'

'Good.' Arito adopted a serious air. Gone were the affectations; this was an expert speaking about his specialisation. 'We can probably rule out the Higher Elves then; as you are indubitably aware, they are tall; although many of the Sea Elves are short, and yet, because they never settled in Widergard, they are considered High. Complexion?'

'Fair.'

'Come, Master Detective. Next you will be telling me his eyes were blue.'

'No, what I meant was, he was fair, even though he spent a lot of time on the beach, and a lot of the other elves had really golden tans.'

'I see. How about his hands?'

I thought hard, trying to picture the dead elf. I remembered Truetouch carrying the drinks, his hands holding the tray. 'I think his fingers were quite short.'

'We are building an interesting profile here. With the height and fair skin, which is usually a melanin adaptation to the weak sunlight of the far north, I would have thought one of the Woodland Elves of the Long Pines. But they are very nimble and they have slender hands and very long fingers.

Perhaps what we have here is a Stone Elf from the Eastern Hold.'

'Oh yes, I've heard tell of them from my childhood.'

'I'm sure you would have, for of all the elves they have had the closest dealings with dwarfs. They are said to have loved the tall mountains of the east and built many fine halls there. Did your elf have particularly pointed ears?'

'Yes, I think they were!'

'Sorry, that was by nature of a trick question. The Stone Elves had very small, almost rounded ears, better for the higher altitudes at which they lived.' He pondered for a while and then we got into very fine detail: shape of eyes, arch of brow, fullness of lips. I tried to magic up the dead elf's face, but all I could get was the image of Truetouch sitting in the front seat of my wagon and the horror of the axe work. Working hard, I dragged back a less gruesome memory.

'He had what you might call a winning smile.'

'Good, good, interesting – very interesting. Anything else that comes to your mind, please? Every detail helps, no matter how trivial it might seem.'

After addressing what seemed to be every permutation of body shape, speech and mannerism, Arito asked if there was anything else I could add about his general bearing. I thought for a while and said, rather weakly: 'He seemed to sweat a lot.'

That one had the expert chewing at his pipe. Nothing he could think of seemed to quite fit the bill. Arito said he needed some time to look up some references and check some scrolls. We could, however, be looking at some mixture which, given the elves' conservatism when it came to marrying out of their clans, would be unusual, but not unheard of – except amongst the Wise and White of course.

The lamps were coming on all over Little Hundred as I left Arito – one IOU for a top 'blow-out' safely in his pocket. The bric-a-brac that lined the alleyways and tunnels took on a different identity in this light. Garish packaging became colourful street decorations and polished chrome reflected a thousand different colours, so that an instant party atmosphere was created. I could hear one or two early songs coming out of the inns that had popped up, almost out of nowhere, along what passed for a thoroughfare. These were drinking songs, but not the songs of drunks, sung just for the pleasure of having lungs and the energy to fill them, even if it was with the Citadel's steamy, polluted atmosphere.

Old fathers sat on improvised doorsteps, passing the time with whoever wandered by. And other gnomes did stop and time was passed, and generally what a good time it was. Other busy gnomes were still making their way home, to family and friends; but even they had time for a quick word or pleasantry. Cooking smells were in the warm summer air and all seemed right with this bit of Widergard. I did not know how wrong I was.

20

A FIRE DOWN BELOW

The talk and smell of food had made me hungry. I wanted something a bit more substantial than the 'new style' cooking of the elves. First though, I needed to collect the Helmington from the Two Fingers. Whilst there I decided to check my answering service. I took the lift up to my floor; it was still too warm to consider scaling the stairs. As I made my way down the corridor, I could see the light shining in my reception room. Although this was not the obvious action of a would-be assassin or more burglars, I played it careful and crept down the corridor, axe at the ready.

The sign writer who had written, 'Nicely Strongoak, Master Detective', on the reception door had very cleverly left the centre of the 'o' as a spy hole. It is a little high for me, but by standing on tiptoe, with my hands on the door, I can just see through. I was just putting my weight on the door when it was opened by a surprised Liza Springwater. Caught off guard and off balance, I tumbled forward, knocking her to the floor and ending up on top of her in a compromising position.

'Is this the way you treat all your clients now?'

'Only those bigger than me.'

'I don't think that's strictly true. In fact, I would say you are probably the only dwarf I have ever seen eye-to-eye with.'

We both laughed and I helped her up. The lucky accident had helped defuse what could have been an awkward situation.

'I'm sorry about bursting in on you like that the other day,' she said. 'And I was probably rather huffy on the street.'

'That's all right, honestly.'

'I mean, your personal life really is none of my business.'

'That was business,' I reassured her.

'It did look a bit like funny business, you have to admit.'

'Liza,' I said looking at her straight, 'sometimes my business is a very funny business.' She blushed slightly.

'My best outfit as well,' she replied, changing the subject and brushing off the dust from her raiment. I said it looked splendid. It did. I had never seen her dressed like this. A brown leather tunic top and skirt were hung with heavy metal ornaments. They were not gold, but they were well crafted. Knee-length boots were turned over, dwarf fashion, and small beads were braided into her hair. I wondered if she also knew that this was the way dwarf maids wore their hair.

'How was your trip?' asked Liza, as we made our way through the connecting door into the office.

'Informative.'

'Mixing with royalty now. You'll be spoilt.' Liza sat on the desk as I checked my mail. 'Don't worry,' I replied. 'Dwarfs are guaranteed unspoilable, or your money back.'

'Well, I suppose it never did Perry any harm.'

'Pardon?'

'Working for royalty, I mean.'

'You never mentioned this before.'

'No, but wasn't that why you went?'

I pointed her to a chair. 'I think you had better tell me all about this.'

'It was just something he mentioned in passing one time,' she said, pulling out a chair and perching at the edge. 'Somebody he worked for, before he was at *The Old Inn*, they had something to do with royalty. He thought it was a bit of a joke.'

'Do you know any details?'

'No, sorry. He never said any more about it. Is it important?'

'It just might be.' I stared out the window, trying to fit this new piece of the jigsaw into the picture, then went to my file trunk. I soon found the list of employees that Mrs Hardwood had prepared for me, and I looked at the neglected part, the names of those who had moved on. Yes, sure enough, there was the name 'Perry Goodfellow', right along with 'Leo Courtkey'. Should have done your home-work properly, detective. I mentally kicked myself half way round the Citadel.

Liza spotted the look on my face.

'What is it, Nicely?'

'I don't know, Liza,' I said, truthfully enough – because I was certainly not about to tell her my true suspicions. Could Perry be sitting on that beach alongside Leo sipping cocktails after checking out the surf?

Liza continued: 'When I came to see you before, it was to say that the Gnada Trophy had turned up again, just in case you had not heard. Do you think it might be Perry that brought it back?'

She looked disappointed when I said I had already heard.

She looked even sadder when I told her that it did not look like it was Perry who had brought it back.

'But don't despair, he might have had a friend drop it off.' Liza did not look convinced and I wasn't either.

We stood for a minute, and then I broke what was threatening to be an awkward silence. 'Look, I've still to check my calls, but then, if you've not eaten, how about we both go get ourselves something solid inside. I could eat the back end of a dragon.'

'Yes, thank you, Nicely, that would be nice. Some friends were taking me for a meal, trying to cheer me, but I thought you might be back, so I wanted to give you the news about Perry. I must admit, I'm pretty hungry too now – but I'll pass on the dragon.'

I took my messages from Doroty and Josh Corncrack first. Together they painted an interesting picture of our absent rider. It seems that young Leo Courtkey had form over and beyond his athletic ability; nothing major, but it looked like he may have developed one or two habits as a racer that his subsequent salary could not support. He had even made two lines in the news scrolls when his employer, Mrs Hardwood, had been forced to post bail for him. Doroty also added that the sheriffs would be grateful for information concerning his whereabouts, as he had skipped from his bondsman. I left a message with Josh asking him to scour the picture archives at the Citadel Press for anything to do with Leo Courtkey.

'Is that to do with Perry?' asked Liza.

'I only wish I knew,' I sighed. 'Does that name, Leo Courtkey, mean anything to you?' She shook her head.

'Should it?' Liza asked, quite reasonably, but I didn't have a clue on that score either.

It was time for some food that was going to stick to the ribs and some ale that was as black as the pit, and there was only one place that provided this. So, swearing Liza to secrecy, I set the Helmington in the right direction. The conversation with Arito had got my juices flowing. *The Burrowers* was going to be busy, it always was, but being a secret shareholder, and thus on very good terms with the proprietor, had its advantages.

'Ginger' Oliver Groundstroke was everybody's idea of a dwarf. His red beard was long, tucked into his belt, and he wore his plait coiled. We were both of the same height, which as I have said, was not very short, even by man's measure. His wide shoulders tapered down elegantly to the slim hips and legs of a natural dancer, and feet made for standing on. As you will gather, this is of course a very attractive combination, which explains the great attraction of dwarfs to the more discerning sections of the community. This was not lost on Master Groundstroke and I had to admit that Ginger Oliver was a bit of a rogue. Two large gold earrings added to his bandit appearance, and the fact that he spoke only an obscure dwarf dialect in the restaurant stoked the fire of his reputation. I was one of the few people in the Citadel who knew that by training 'Ginger' was in fact a linguist; I have lost count of the languages he can speak, but they must cover most of Widergard. He had spent most of his time on the Hill at the Citadel College – until his other appetites got the better of him. This academic connection was still celebrated at *The Burrowers* by the annual meal of the Citadel Conservation Group, the infamous Endangered Species Barbecue.

'A fine-looking maid that, Nicely,' said Ginger Oliver, from the bar, as I fetched the ale. 'She must be new in from Iron

Town for me to have missed her.'

'Oliver, either it's the heat in here, or age has finally dimmed your lights, but that lady is not a dwarf.'

'Well, hack me off at the knees and use me as a doorstop, if you're not right. Maybe it's me age. I must come and join you both later for a better gander.'

'Much later,' I said, carrying the crocks back to the corner table. I had managed to get a relatively quiet table away from the stage. The noise, though, was still great. The heat seemed to be making everyone just that little bit more on edge, the music a little louder and the drink a little stronger. It was well into suppertime and the atmosphere was, shall we say, lively.

'I like it here,' said Liza, and indeed, she certainly seemed to. She tucked into the 'four day beef' with a gusto I have rarely seen in a woman. Hog Roll went the way of all flesh and the cinnamon spice cakes and port barely touched the sides. I think it was what she needed, given her current worries, and I too found myself relaxing for the first time in days. I ordered a couple of 'Cave-Specials' and we sat with Flaming Dragons, and watched the floor show, the main attraction being a drunk juggler, which was really wild, but you really had to be there.

Ginger Oliver did come over for a few words. Liza thought he was swell, but his beard was a bit too long. I scratched reflectively at the stubble that had grown since this morning. It was well after midwatch when we both stumbled, slightly the worse for wear, into the wagon. I made it back to her place without any mishap, and was helping her with the seat belt when, with no malice aforethought, she was in my arms. For a minute that went on for an age, all was right with the world; then we suddenly found ourselves back on

Widergard and opposite sides of the wagon. She was as flustered as I was.

'Nicely, I'm sorry, it's just that with all this business about Perry, at the moment I don't think I can – you know.'

'Hey, don't even mention it. I've got policies about this sort of thing too. Still, we had ourselves a fine evening, right?'

'It was just about perfect, Nicely. I really want to thank you.'

'Come on. Get yourself inside will you, before the guard gets us for vagrancy.'

We said our goodnights and I watched her go lightly up the steps to her rooms. I then drove slowly back home. Peat, the night watchman, gave me a wink on my way upstairs. This did not really register until I saw a faint light from my rooms shining under the main door. Slowly I eased it open, wishing I had thought to bring my axe. Peat was not in the habit of letting would-be assailants in, but things had been getting strange recently. I was not sure who was wearing white these days. The hall was empty and unlit, what light there was was coming from the bedroom. I made my way to the open door; a supine figure was sprawled upon the bed, back to me, unnaturally still. I walked round to get a better look at the occupant.

'Mrs Hardwood.'

At the sound of her name she stirred, and a voice thick with drink or powders said: 'You're late, I must have fallen asleep.' Her pupils were too dilated even for this half-light. I threw her a wrap from the storage chest and then let it take my weight.

'Mind telling me how you got up here?'

She fluttered her lashes. 'That was easy, your watchman didn't even need bribing.'

'I'm not exactly in the book.'

'Ways and means, Nicely. Ways and means.' She stretched like some large cat. She was wearing a dinner dress that was cut by a master. It must have been magic that held it together, because there was little enough material. She filled it to perfection, more curves than a dragon's tail. I just sat and filled my pipe.

'Well Nicely, you don't seem very pleased to see me.'

I made fire and drew heavily. 'How about you tell me what you are doing here?' She propped herself up against the headboard. It was a family heirloom, carved by Woodland Elves in some half-forgotten age; it would never look the same again. Long fingers traced the engraved design.

'I got lonely. Don't you ever get lonely, Nicely?'

'Go tell it to the gnomes, lady.'

'I would, but I didn't have their number.' I was too tired for these games. 'So how come we missed out on cocktails?'

'It's not my fault you turned up late; we had people for dinner, important people.'

'And lunch?'

A look of petulance crossed her face. 'That was my husband's fault; he doesn't let me have any fun.' She punched a pillow with imperious arms, then coyly looked up. 'I'm here now though, so come on.' She could almost carry it off; if it hadn't been for the slur in her speech and the way her hair had gone after she had passed out. She pumped the pillow; I ignored it.

'I have a couple of questions for you. Why didn't you tell me that Leo Courtkey had a record?'

'Leo who?'

'Leo Courtkey. On your staff list. Ex-staff list.'

She was still playing the spoilt kid. 'You can't expect me

to remember everyone who has worked for me. A lot of people work for me, Master Detective.'

'Yes, but you don't play bondsman for everyone.'

'Oh, I don't remember.'

'And how about Moondust?'

'Moondust. I don't know anything about Moondust.' She tried indifference, but her eyes betrayed her. 'Look, why all these questions? This isn't going to get my ring back. Anyway, I can think of better things we could be doing.' Her fingers did some magic and the dress fell apart. I caught the front of it before it hit the bed. Up close, behind her expensive perfume, I could just make out that smell of Winter Ice.

'So, you don't know anything about Moondust, eh? Well, I wonder who supplies your little habit.' She took off like a dragon. I just caught both her hands before she had a chance to take my eyes out, but she still struggled. 'And these friendly suppliers of yours, I don't suppose they ever ask for any favours, do they? Just set up this dwarf, will you? Should be easy, cook up some story, flutter those long lashes, we all know what dwarfs are like.' This got me a knee in the chest and then she came up close again. 'You want me,' she hissed. 'I could tell that the moment I met you in the office.'

'Well, I've got news for you, I do not make a habit of sleeping with my clients.'

She relaxed for a moment, then spat out: 'Not even little secretaries?' before continuing her futile struggle.

'Naughty, naughty, my lady. And when did we see her then? Have we been playing detective too?'

'I don't need to be a detective to work out what's on your mind, the way you look at her.'

'But that's young Perry's girl. Or didn't you know that?'

'Perry who?'

'Why, Perry Goodfellow, late of your employ.' She went suddenly limp. 'Well, well,' I said, 'perhaps you didn't know after all.'

'I know all about you, Master Detective. I know people who could cut you down so small even other dwarfs would miss you.'

'Now that is fighting dirty, my lady.' I finally managed to get her pinned. 'How about Leo Courtkey, I suppose you knew everything about him. Or, more importantly, he knew everything about you. Was that it? Was he fingering you?'

She laughed at this, a sound with a slight manic overtone. She calmed down enough to look me straight in the eye. 'Him, give me the white finger! Some Detective you are.'

This puzzled me. Obviously I was missing something.

'So, did Leo scoot with the emerald, or was it young Master Perry who relieved you of the burden – or perhaps it's not even missing at all?'

This spurred her on to another bout of struggling. 'I don't know what you are talking about. It is missing, it is missing – now let me go!'

I pinned her harder to the bed. 'Not until I get the truth from you.' All the fight seemed suddenly to go out of her and she slumped back, her face hidden by hair. In a small voice she said, 'If you like this, Nicely, I don't mind, you can tie me down if you want to. I know lots of games like that.'

Up close. 'My, you do have problems.' She turned her head and deliberately sank her teeth into my shoulder. Letting go of one arm, I managed to lift her head. The long black hair parted and framed her face; her lips were wet. In amongst the craziness of her eyes there was a look, of what, triumph?

237

A moment of stillness, then her eyes closed and she reached forward for me.

The horn rung like an alarm clarion in the next room and I dropped her to the bed and got up. She punched the bed, snarling curses. 'I had you there, I had you!'

I answered the horn. 'Nicely Strongoak.'

'This is Hardwood, I believe you have my wife there.' The voice on the other end was old, but still firm. It sounded as if it came from a long way away – not leagues but ages.

'Maybe, I have – do you want her back?'

'Yes, it is past her bedtime.'

'Shall I drop her off?'

'No, a wagon is on the way.' He hung up. Not even a good night. Some people, eh?

By the time I got back she had disappeared into the bathroom. The sound of running water, and a few moments later she stepped out. She was ready for the ball again, the magic dress back on, and the hair was piled impossibly high. Without a word, she let herself out. I followed her down to the lobby. Peat the watchman had popped off for a smoke. I was glad, as it saved explanations. In a little while, a long black wagon appeared. It was a Battledore '83. Goodenough got out, as straight-backed as ever; he didn't seem pleased to see me.

I opened the door to the back seats. She got in without a word.

'Good bye, Queen Celembine,' I said, as I held the door. 'Do have a pleasant trip, your majesty.' There was a sharp intake of breath. The message had found a home.

'Not that bad a detective, eh?'

I closed the door. Goodenough seemed on the verge of speaking, but swapped words for a stare that would have extinguished a dark lord's furnace.

He got back in the driver's side and the wagon drove off with a spume of steam that I think probably came from the engine and not Mrs Hardwood. I could not see if she looked back. Somehow, I do not think so. A black Battledore '83, they were common enough in certain circles, weren't they?

I went back into my rooms and kicked the chest a few times, but this did not make me feel any better. I dragged the sheets off the bed and threw them in the laundry chest, but her perfume still filled the room. I was too keyed up for sleep anyway and it was too hot there.

I took the Helmington down to the Two Fingers and let myself in. The lift was turned off for the night, so I had to walk the sixteen floors; finally the Endless Staircase. The exercise did me some good, and I felt better when I took the office bottle to the window seat and caught some breeze. I thought about men and dwarfs, and dwarfs and elves, and elves and men, hoping for some great insight, but all I got was a headache.

Sometime around dawn, I put down the bottle, wiped the back of my neck and stretched. The window seat was hard on the back-lap. I saw a trace of colour creeping over the Greater Citadel; Nicely got to touch the rosy fingers of dawn yet again, and then, suddenly realising it was way the wrong direction to be the rising sun, I found my spyglass and trained it to the west. Down below, off towards the Bay, Little Hundred was burning.

21

A MATTER OF BUSINESS

Stopping only to pick up my cap, I ran to the lift. It had just arrived, the daytime doorman must have cranked up the juice. As the doors opened onto the lobby a figure fell out. I only just managed to save him hitting the floor. He was very badly burnt and bruised and out of uniform, so it took a while for recognition to sink in.

'Scout Telfine! Axes and blood, man, what's happened to you?'

His eyes flickered and in a voice only a shade above a whisper he replied, 'Got your address from Ralph Fieldfull's ledger. Needed to tell you ... you may not be the useless trip hazard I first thought you was.' The eyes closed again and although I shook him, Telfine was not adding any more for the moment. His battered countenance looked grim. I was afraid he had gone west, but the pulse, though weak, was regular.

I carried him back into the lift. In the lobby, Jakes had just came back from switching on the power and he helped me getting Telfine down to my wagon. I set off round the Hill. There was a strong smell of smoke coming from Telfine and I didn't think it was from an outdoor spit roast. What was going on, Telfine? The scout wasn't saying, he just coughed up more foul-smelling fumes. I took him to a private healer's nearby: The King's Hands' Hospice, which I have used so much I run a tally. If the fire was half as bad as it looked from this distance, the physics at Citadel Central were going to be busy for some time. The healers took one look at the ailing man and wheeled him into emergency. The others took one look at me and decided I'd probably make it through the rest of the day. I left my details and hurried on out.

By the time I reached Little Hundred the real sun was beginning to shed some proper light, although the great pall of smoke was doing its best to blot it out. Gnomes were pouring down the streets and roads, carrying their few belongings in whatever was available, wheelbarrows, carts, stockshop trolleys. Most headed towards the Hill, and an uncertain reception. The Citadel Guard and the fire-sheriffs were doing their best to contain the blaze. The omens were not very good. It had been too dry for too long and Little Hundred was a tinderbox ready for a spark. There was no way I was going to get anywhere near Arito's place. There did not seem to be anything else I could do to help, and I was about to make my way back to the healers to check on Telfine when I saw Ralph, in the thick of things as normal.

He spotted me at the same time and came running through the smoke, shouting: 'Nicely, am I pleased to see you! I feared for a moment that you were in the middle of this!'

'Why?'

'The fire, from what we hear, it started at Arito Cardinollo's

241

place.'

'Have they found him?'

'No sign.'

I felt a cold lump grow in my gut. 'Just how bad is it?'

'Well, it's not good. We have it contained south and east, but it's still spreading west, and north towards the Citadel. Most of the building that way is good stone, so that should help slow it down. Small recompense, but no listed buildings seem to be in its path.'

'You've moved quick, Ralph.'

He gave me a rueful smile. 'You are not the only detective around, you know. There are other ears still functioning in the Citadel. We've been expecting a stunt like this for some time. I've had double watches, cancelled all leave, with the services on stand-by.'

'That must have made you popular.'

'It's paid dividends, though.' We walked together and found a clear area on a bit of higher ground. 'The main problem is to the west, heading down towards the Bay; too much wood and too many small businesses with combustibles. We don't seem to be able to stop it, and if it gets to the main industrial sites and the chemical works, well, I don't need to tell you, it's goodnight Citadel.'

'I don't suppose there's any chance that it wasn't deliberate?'

'Come on, Nicely, does a goblin have warts? No, this little fire came out of nothing and spread too quickly. Fortunately the alarm was sounded very quickly, which cut down on the casualties.'

'Are there many?'

He looked grim. 'Enough. We're not going to know until we can get the gnomes settled and do a head count. But I'll tell you, either someone underestimated the way this would spread, or else they just didn't care.'

'Any sign of anyone else around, other than gnomes?'

Ralph looked at me strangely. 'No, but we did have one report that a dwarf was seen hereabouts earlier.'

'And I can tell you when he left and what he was doing.'

'It wasn't an accusation, friend. I don't see you torching people in their beds, Nicely.'

'Sorry, Ralph. Been that sort of a day already – and you should know, I just delivered Scout Telfine to the healers.' Ralph was stunned at the news. Telfine hadn't turned up for his last shift and was facing a dressing down, but the panic over the fire had put it out of everybody's minds. 'Blood and bones, Nicely, how bad was he?'

'They're not sure yet. A lot of smoke inhalation and some nasty burns.'

This gave him a lot of food for thought; a real feast for the noggin and no mistake.

'He was out of uniform as well, Ralph. He said he'd found my home address in your ledger, before stupor cut his strings.'

'Curse him for a fool,' spat Ralph angrily. 'I'll rip the hide off him! I wondered if he was poking around places where he shouldn't be!'

'You think he might have been trying some undercover work on his own?'

'He's so keen I wouldn't put it past him.'

'But what exactly?'

It was a good question but neither of us had an answer to it.

We had no more time for discussion. Ralph got called off at that point, and I left quickly before some other eager scout got me tied up with different questions I had no answers to. I needed to reach the Bay area before the fire. It was not easy to find the place I wanted. I had, after all, been blindfolded before. I made my way carefully round the emergency vehicles. The Wars of old must have been like this: the flames, the men shouting and running, and the innocents with their bundles of goods trying to salvage something from the wreckage.

This looked like one battle the Citadel was losing. The thought did not make me happy. I needed to find me the right sort of goblin to be nasty to. I knew the very party.

The dock area was quiet, though. Most of the ships had hastily cast off and were safely out at sea and the rats were finding other accommodation. There were still a few workers around, packing and moving out important documents. I stopped someone and described what little I could remember about Petal's office. He shrugged; it did not look too hopeful. Fortunately the smoke from Little Hundred was flushing a lot of interesting things out of the wen, other than the rats. I spotted the grunt with the shooter, the one who had nabbed me after the Citadel concert, as he ran down a back street. I left the wagon and followed him at pace.

Goblins can move swiftly, especially the large kind, and I was weighed down with an axe, but he didn't go far. The location tallied with what my nose could recall; this was the place. He ran up the metal steps. I needed another entrance. There was a fire ladder at the back of the building. By my calculation, this would take me up to Petal's office. I used my axe and belt as a makeshift grapple, and managed to pull the ladder down to a height suitable for climbing.

The fire escape led right up to the office window, and the office was empty. The window was also unlocked; shame on them, don't they read the posters? 'Watch out, there's a goblin about.' In a trice I was in. I searched the scarred desktop for incriminating evidence. As usual there was nothing to give me the slightest help. The chest did not want to give up its contents easily and I didn't have time for any tricky stuff, so I used the tardy dwarf's lock-pick and the handaxe made short work of the drawers. However, again I drew a blank. I really didn't need this. I had coffee that needed drinking, pipes that needed smoking and pretty damsels that surely, even now, were a pixy's spit away from distress.

I looked around the room one last time. There had to be a coffer. Petal would have a really big and strong coffer. Folk like Petal always did, they were just so untrusting. Sign of the times it may be, but even I would have a coffer, if I ever managed to accumulate anything valuable enough to put into one. I hadn't been scanning many sales handbills recently.

I found it built into the wall behind the Certificate of Racial Purity; good solid steel that would withstand a full-on belch from a dyspeptic dragon. As strongboxes go it had one of the best locks made by goblin or man; but then again, I am a dwarf. It took me about five minutes to break it – I'm getting out of practice.

There is an argument in some quarters about who first invented the lock – dwarfs, elves goblins or men – or whether, perhaps, it was invented independently more than once. Dwarfs don't get involved in this debate because they are convinced of their primacy. We're also slightly ashamed to admit that we invented the lock before we managed fire or the wheel, just in case it reinforces unwelcome stereotypes.

The coffer swung open on well-oiled hinges – my, but those goblins take care of the details well. There was a lot of parchment and the folding money that us dwarfs do not like dealing with, but that wasn't what was getting my nose twitching.

It was sitting in a small box made from cheap board and it was as beautiful an example of gem work as I had ever seen. It was the green of every forest on every vibrant spring morning since the world first started turning. It was the Hardwood Emerald: the Elf Gate ring. It was stunning.

The sound of goblin voices coming up the stairs brought me back to the here and now. I barely had time to pocket the gem, close the coffer and hide behind the door before it opened. Petal came in by himself and went straight to the desk. His jaw dropped as he sat down, exposing those oh-so-perfect teeth, and he looked up, about to shout, when he noticed me. I put one finger to my lips; the other hand held the axe in throwing position. I gestured for him to raise his hands. Somewhat to my surprise, he smiled, or what passed for smiling, and took one of those foul-smelling leaf sticks that goblins smoke from a silvered box on the desk. I walked slowly towards the desk, and just as slowly he finally raised his hands. I reached into my pocket; one single bead of sweat glistened on his brow, one tiny drop of saliva formed at the corner of his mouth. He thought he knew what was in that pocket. He edged back as I quickly withdrew my pocket lighter. I watched him relax back in his seat and I lit his stick. Mother Strongoak taught her little boy good manners, which is why I keep my spare axe sharp. I'd hate to inconvenience anybody with a raggedy wound.

'So, Dwarf, what can I do for you?'

I ignored the question and walked round to the certificate on the wall, all the time watching from the corner of one eye. His right hand was twitchy. There was something under the desktop I should look out for.

'Is this for real?' I said, pointing to the framed deposition.

'Course it's real, best I could buy.'

I checked the names at the bottom; half the members of the Citadel Heredity School seemed to be on there. It was sad what some academics had to do these days to earn a crust. I paced round to the other side of the desk and sat in the same seat I had occupied only a few nights before.

'I'd like some information, Man.'

'Well, why didn't yer give us a call?'

'You're not in the book.'

'Now ain't that just right. Fancy me forgetting.'

I put the axe on the desk, close enough so he might just be tempted. 'What I need to know, Man, is who you are working for?'

This only made him smile wider, more saliva collecting on his new pearly whites. 'Well, Master Detective, I thought that was the sort of thing that you were paid to find out.'

It's funny, nobody tells a potter how to 'pot', or a black-smith how to 'smith', but there's always some joker who thinks he knows all about being a detective. If it was as easy as they make out there'd be a lot more successful detectives and fewer dead ones.

'That's just what I'm doing now, finding out.'

'It'll take more than that axe, Dwarf.'

I took out a spectacularly sharp needle-dagger from the sheath on my leg. It's known as an eyeball burster and I guessed that Petal knew the name by the way sweat began to accumulate on his deeply furrowed brow.

'Come on Petal, old fellow, me lad. Half of Little Hundred is up in flames. I'm not the only one that is going to be wanting the answers to a few questions. If it's not me it will be the Cits.'

'What they got to link me with that?'

'Me, for a start.'

'Now don't you go trying to pin that one on us, Dwarf,' he said, losing his smile.

'What's with this "us" now, Petal?'

'On the goblins, I mean. What have goblins got to gain by doing something like that? Firing Little Hundred, where's the profit?'

'It depends who is paying you and why.'

'We don't want to go rocking the boat. Bad for business.' He relaxed again. 'And you gotta remember, we're all businessmen now. It's all getting organised: racketeering, powders, the ladies. It's all profits and loss. Got to show a margin on the books – not that we keep any books, you understand. No point in rocking the boat, no point at all.'

He had a point.

However, I had one too and I prodded him with it, drawing a bead of blood alongside the brow sweat. 'That depends, doesn't it, Petal? Maybe it might be convenient to rock one boat if you are in with the new captain of a bigger, better ship.'

Petal shrugged. 'Don't know what you mean.'

I reached back for the axe, swung it and buried it in the desk, almost giving him a new parting at the same time. He reached under the desk, but I had seen that coming. The hand not holding the dagger pulled out the shooter I had removed from the body of Truetouch.

'Now, look what we've gone and made me do to that lovely desk, Petal, and I liked it as well.'

'No shooters, Dwarf!'

'Ok, so why don't you just put those hands on the desk

there where I can see them.'

He complied, bringing out a knife that could pass as a sword in some circles. 'I thought you dwarfs didn't hold with firearms?'

It was my turn to smile. 'It just shows you that you can't trust anyone these days. I always thought you goblins had bigger teeth.' He didn't say a word, but his eyes looked like two bullet holes, his smile a scar in his face.

'Now Petal, let's try again: who are you working for?'

He aired the new teeth again. 'What's the magic word?'

'Bang.'

I could see a thought flicker across his brow like an advertisement in cold-light. 'Look, Dwarf, I'm going to give it to you straight.' He relaxed again. 'There's a really old saying, you've probably heard it before: why should I sign up to fight all your battles when you're not signing up to fight any of mine? So that's me. I hustle a bit here, and I do an odd job there. Sure, I play all the sides, but like I said, I would not fire Little Hundred, there ain't no percentage in it.'

'Come on Petal, I've no time for riddles in the dark. This ain't no fairy story. Give it to me straight or I start chopping off a few bits the surgeons didn't attend to.'

'Master *Detective*, like I said, think a bit. Who do you know who might be wanting you to keep your pointy cap out of their business, and not just in the Bay area either?'

I waved the shooter in his direction. 'What about a dead elf that's lying somewhere on a cold table in the Citadel? A dead elf with dress sense and a winning smile that everybody seems strangely reluctant to get excited about?' Did you get paid for that one as well?'

Petal smiled even wider, like a snake contemplating swallowing a pony. He sat back and looked me straight in the eye. 'I would not waste an elf for all the gold corn in Widergard, my arse would be elf fodder. I'd swear to that on my mother's bones.'

I didn't know why but I believed him. I thought of mentioning the Hardwood Emerald, now snuggled in my pocket, which I had presumed he'd lifted prior to giving Truetouch a new parting, but I decided to keep that knowledge to myself for the moment.

Petal, perhaps sensing my uncertainty, continued. 'You know, Master Detective, I would not be surprised if we did not have a little bit of free enterprise going on here. I think someone is bringing in boys from off the Hill to do some of their dirty work.'

'Like decapitating a scribe with a hard-luck story and a grudge against a very senior political sponsor?'

Petal grinned again. 'Now we can't be having that, not more "outsourcing". Maybe I should hire myself a detective to find out who's doing it? How about that, eh? Yeah, how about it, Master Detective? You look like you could do with the work.'

'I'd rather start a business cauterising piles for ogres, thanks.'

Petal stopped grinning, which should have warned me. I thought he just found my sense of humour too scholarly.

I had Petal and the door covered with my shooter but I had forgotten about the fire ladder that had provided my own way in.

I span, ducking and firing in one motion. The runt coming in through the window fired at the same time but with one leg over the sill, he wasn't exactly balanced. My shot hit home and his missed, just the result I look for in this sort of encounter. The added ventilation to his skull ruined his poise still further and he slumped awkwardly forward. A cry from Petal told me where the runt's bullet had ended up. I can take good luck like that any day of the week.

By then tickler-wielding grunts were rushing through the office door in numbers that made me think twice about the effectiveness of the shooter, but I emptied the chamber anyway, just because I could, and who wants to make a quiet escape when you can do it in style? The collapsed runt had left enough room at the window for a lithe slim dwarf detective to easily slip through; not so easy for a large grunt with a knife clenched in his teeth. Mind you, he soon dropped this when I pinned his hand to the windowsill with the needle-dagger. By the time they had freed the screaming grunt and cleared away the runt's body I was back at street level and making tracks. My last sight of Petal was of him holding a blood-soaked rag to what remained of an ear.

Smoke from Little Hundred still seemed to be heading in this direction, but I managed to find an inn open. I ordered a quick pick-me-up and asked to use their speech-horn. I got through to the healers; Telfine was alive, conscious and asking for me. That was going to please his chief, Ralph. Telfine was fighting the healers, who were trying to give him a sleep draught. He was winning for the moment, but could not hold out indefinitely. I found my wagon quickly enough but the journey back up the Hill was a nightmare. The flow of gnome refugees made driving almost impossible. I needed to hear whatever Telfine had to say, though, and I was concerned that I would not get there before the sleep draft took effect.

The healers ushered me straight through to intensive care the instant I had my head through the door, not even waiting to tie me into a gown. The reason for this was apparent as soon as I was ushered into Telfine's room. He had tubes sticking out of every orifice, he was heavily swathed in bandages and he was also sitting on the edge of the bed holding two physics back with what looked like a particularly wicked form of scalpel that could have given my needle-dagger a run for its money. When they had said he was fighting the healers I didn't think they were being quite this literal.

'Good, finally, the Master Detective himself,' he coughed, as I burst in.

'Telfine, axes and blood, get yourself back into that bed, you were almost burnt to a crisp.'

He coughed up more foul-smelling fumes, and in a hoarse voice said: 'I didn't know you cared.'

I moved slowly forward and took the scalpel from him, to the relief of the physics, and then helped him lie down again.

'I didn't say I did, but you've got one very angry Sergeant to explain things to after he finishes saving the Citadel. And he is a friend of mine.'

'Yes, I guess I have at that. They rumbled me, Master Detective. I got too close to him. Those pointy ears must have heard something that made them suspicious. He nearly did for me, the tree poker!' Another racking cough doubled him up.

'You're not making sense, Telfine. Save your strength.'

'No, you've got a right to know, and the chief. I've been tailing him, you see.'

Now I was surprised. 'You tailed your chief?'

'It was all that rubbish about dental work and the act in your rooms. I thought you were involved in some sort of cover-up, see? He's got a set of gnashers that could chew through dragon hide. So I trailed him down to the Dwarfholm Bridge.'

'You did?'

'Yes, wasn't too bad, was I? You never saw me,' he coughed again. 'You never saw me when I followed you with that wizard either.'

'No, you took us both,' I admitted.

'I overheard you and the chief talking about that elf – Highbury, and I thought I'd tail him too and try to see what it was all about.' Telfine lay back exhausted. 'He was a different matter. I didn't know about those cursed pointy ears … not just how good they are.'

'No, most other folk don't,' I agreed. 'Now just relax, I think I'd better get a physic.' Before I could leave, though, Telfine grabbed at my arm.

'No, it's important. That tree prodder, he was arguing with this elfess … gorgeous, she was. Seemed to know you, at least your name was mentioned. I could understand that much.'

I suddenly went very, very cold.

'I was trying to hear better, but one of his pretty boys must have seen me. I was maced. Just like a junior scout! When I came round I was in a house in Little Hundred, fire everywhere. They tried to set me up! Think of it. Me!'

'I know the feeling,' I said with real sympathy.

'Yes, I guess you do. Well, there I was: lamp oil all around and flint in my pocket. Just because I've been heard to say a few harsh words about gnomes in the shiftroom, doesn't mean I'd try to set fire to the little ground huggers, does it?' He coughed again. 'I don't know what happened to her. The elfess, that is. Don't know at all.'

'Take it easy.'

'It's all right, I'll manage for a bit longer. They weren't

clever enough, see? They forgot what a warren that Little Hundred place is. The room was built on old tunnels and when the floor gave in I was able to crawl out through them. Seems I was wrong about you … you did have it right … had to tell you.'

'Come on, Telfine, you've got to get some rest.' I motioned to the physics, but Telfine struggled on.

'No, must finish my report first. Before they maced me, I managed to hear a few more words. He said her name, the gorgeous elfess, that is. Thel, Thela, I think it was.'

'Thelen!'

'Yes, that's the name. You'd better find her. She wasn't in the Little Hundred with me, but I don't rate her chances much; that Highbury tree prodder, he did not look happy.' Another fit of coughing proved too much for him – the physics moved in and I moved out. Telfine must have walked all the way from Little Hundred to my place; some achievement for a man in his condition. As I left the room, I turned back for a moment. I had forgotten to ask the scout where he had heard all this! The sleeping draught must have finally taken effect, as his body suddenly relaxed. The last words he managed were: 'Tell the chief, I'm sorry.'

Axes and blood, how could I have been so stupid! Where had they been? Then Telfine's clenched right hand opened and a small trickle of sand fell to the floor. I knew that clue.

I still didn't understand everything though, but there was only one place for me to work it all out: I had to go back to where it all had started.

254

22

RESCUED

The ride to the Gnada Peninsula was not as pleasant as on my last visit. Smoke blowing from the south filled the sky, giving it an unnatural hue. I then noticed that there were also clouds blocking the sun for the first time in weeks, although they did nothing to lessen the heat. I missed my Dragonette convertible; the Helmington was handling like a troll. I found a bearer's office open and addressing a pouch to myself, then slipped the Hardwood Emerald inside. The bearers proudly boast that they bond your goods to a value of 100,000 crowns. I didn't like to tell them just how much more the contents of this pouch were worth.

Once I finally made it off the Hill I was able to put my hand round its throttle and give the wagon a good shaking. It seemed to appreciate it and almost before I knew it, I found myself on the beach where I had first seen Highbury surfing – could it only have been scant days before?

This time the beach was deserted. The giant rollers crashing in from the Big Sea looked too rough even for enchanted boards. The Surf Elves' beach huts looked empty as well. I was not about to take a chance on that, though. I parked well away and, axe in hand, made my way round the back of the largest hut. As I thought, the wooden walling soon gave way to a bit of gentle leverage with the trusty steel. I soon had a large enough hole made and I eased myself through. I was in some kind of storeroom, windowless but with enough light coming through the cracks for my dwarf eyes. Paint, lamp oil and various leaflets, not exactly extolling racial harmony, filled the space. Everything you needed for a bit of urban mayhem. In one corner I found piles and piles of clothing, and not elvish, but gnome togs. Now that was interesting. I made my way carefully to the door and listened – no sounds of conversation.

I opened the door slowly. It was a large room with shutters over picture windows. In the middle of it was Thelen, tied to a chair. She had her back to me, facing the door and was bound and gagged. She was in one of those elf trances that pass for sleep, and did not appear to see me as I walked in front. Her lovely face was a mess. One eye was nearly closed, swollen with a bruise, livid green against her fair skin. Some blood was dried in the corner of her mouth and her bottom lip was split. Somebody was going to pay for this. Somebody was going to pay and pay, and after they had paid all they could pay, they were going to find brand-new ways to pay. And I was going to help them and, yes, I was going to enjoy it.

Thelen started as I gently shook her. I put my finger to my lips as I ungagged her. She nodded agreement, and to be honest I don't think that there was any voice left in her. The knots had been tied by a master, but were no match for the axe. We almost made it. I just hope that isn't what they get to put on my tombstone when the time comes: 'Nicely

Strongoak – he almost made it'.

Elves move so quietly; the first thing I heard was the hut door opening. I turned: it was Highbury.

'So, Son of Stone, it appears you have taken a liking to our beach.'

'Just thought you might want another swimming lesson, Goldy.'

'The name to you is Lord Highbury, Dwarf, and you may come to regret that remark.' He smiled without warmth and entered the room, followed by a group of Surf Elves. I shifted from foot to foot, axe in hand. 'I do not think axe-work will be required, Son of Stone,' said Highbury, pulling out a shooter. I cursed not reloading mine. I was disappointed in the elf though, but tried not to let it show too much. 'Well, Lord Highbury, I thought the "better-than-you" nobility had some swollen-headed rules about not carrying firearms?'

'Oh, we do a lot of things that elves are not supposed to do.'

'Including setting fire to Little Hundred, I suppose.'

Again the smile. 'Very good. I would say prove it, not that it matters and not that it is going to help you now.'

'I suppose you've been behind all of the trouble in the Citadel this summer.'

'You pay us too large a compliment, Son of Stone. You do not think my small band could manage that, do you? The different races are not meant to live together. The hostility is natural, we have just helped it along.'

'So that's your angle, is it? You want everyone to pack up their things and toddle off to their mines and halls; that separate development business. What about the gnomes, where are they supposed to go back to now that their homes are gone to dust? And how about the goblins, or are you one of those who believes the only good goblin is a dead one?'

The elves edged closer. Highbury continued: 'That's the problem with so many mortals, even ones as long-lived as you dwarfs. Your insight is so limited. It's nothing compared to our viewpoint. Of course, the inferior races have their role as well; we are not actively against them, although they do tend to breed rather, shall we say, profusely, which will have to be stopped. We can see the larger picture – given our long-term perspective – and quite frankly the Citadel, and all of Widergard, is going to the pits unless something is done to stop it.'

'And you young lords are just the ticket, are you?' I couldn't hide my derision. 'What about that democratic process you elves are so fond of saying you brought back for us all? Where does that fit in?'

Highbury just smiled and something clicked.

'Of course,' I said, 'the elections. Well, you're not going to win it with the Citadel Alliance Party, so which other candidates have you in your pockets?' Highbury still looked far too smug for my liking.

'Come on, you can't really believe you can win it. You aren't going to get the gnome vote with this separatist argument, and the gnomes are going to have a lot of sympathy from the rest of the Citadel after the burning of Little Hundred.'

'Really, Master Detective. So you think the gnomes are going to just sit back and take it, after their hovels have been fired? I'm sure they are likely to be quite upset, and probably retaliate, and where will all the sympathy be then?' I had a bad feeling about what he was telling me. It was just a bit too much like a possibility.

Thelen spoke hoarsely for the first time: 'That's the plan, Nicely. After the firing of Little Hundred, they are planning a series of "gnome retaliations", which will provoke real bloodshed and split the Citadel right down the middle.'

'Citadel splitting' was not an option that appealed to me. The Citadel was where I lived and where I made my living. The Hill was messy and frequently bad tempered and often made you want to spit, but it was also full of life and energy and rude vitality. Somehow, out of all the places in Widergard, it had achieved a balance of all the different folk that sort of worked. Yes, it was not perfect and some folk certainly had more than their fair share of the pie, but I'd be cast into a pit of boiling pitch before I let some group of spoilt bush fanciers with superiority complexes start running things.

I was about to throw another question Highbury's way when there was a start from Thelen. Someone was behind me – they must have come through the hole I had made in the storeroom. Fool me twice – shame on me! I turned, but this was no goblin lightweight and I was far, far too late. Cold metal punched my ticket to dream time.

I came round, groaning, trussed up like a spider's lunch box. I was lying on rough wood; Thelen was facing me, similarly trussed up. They had not bothered to gag us. They must have been confident. I became aware of a noise that wasn't just a return performance by the *All-Star Syncopated Gnome Home Jump Band*.

'What sort of accommodation is this?' I muttered. 'How do they expect anyone to sleep with all that racket going on?'

'That, Nicely, is thunder and rain and the sea as well. The weather has finally broken.'

'Terrific,' I muttered, aware of a steady drip of water

falling from the roof. 'Just what I need. This suit is going to be ruined; wool hates water more than dwarfs do.'

This managed to raise a smile from Thelen. 'Does nothing dampen your spirits, detective?'

'Yes, stripes worn with spots. That and hogget pudding without enough gravy.'

She laughed, wincing slightly, and licking her split lips. 'Nicely *irrepressible* Strongoak.'

'It use to be my middle name,' I admitted, 'but I changed it officially to "Nicely *vengeful with a war-mallet* Strongoak."'

'I hope to meet him soon.'

'Don't worry,' I said, pulling at my ropes, 'I hope he'll soon be with us.' The ropes refused to budge, though. The elf that tied these bonds had even put twine around my thumbs and that was the mark of a professional. 'Oh well,' I continued, 'at least there's little chance of us being overheard with all that going on out there.'

'It also seems to be holding up their plans. They are still next door, not instigating carnage, so we must be grateful for that, I suppose.'

'Yeah, this is my grateful face. You should see my beaten-up-and-bound face. It's a stinker.'

'Your grateful face is bleeding, Nicely.'

'Which means my heart is still pumping and for that I am very grateful.'

Thelen had herself another rueful little laugh.

The situation certainly wasn't looking promising. Ralph would be far too busy to wonder what I was about and Telfine would be lucky to recover this side of the New Year. It seemed that survival was in our own hands and they were securely trussed.

'Not much of a rescue,' I finally admitted.

'I don't suppose there's any chance that the Citadel Guard are waiting around the corner, ready to pounce?'

'Sorry, I didn't have time to tell them.' I gave it a few seconds before I admitted: 'I didn't actually think of it, to be honest.'

'Oh well, I deserve this, it will teach me to play detective.'

'You didn't deserve this, Thelen, the gnomes in Little Hundred didn't deserve to have their homes burnt down and Truetouch didn't deserve to die.'

'I should have let you in on all I suspected.'

Which is true. It's never easy to work properly as a detective if you're not kept fully informed. And along with total co-operation, I'd like to have an end to famine, peace among all the folk of Widergard and free ale on a dwarf detective's birthday.

'I think I'm rather more guilty of that,' I finally admitted.

'Ah, yes: at last Truetouch is touched upon.'

'Yes, sorry for that, Thelen. I didn't really know who I should, and shouldn't, be talking to and I didn't want to put you in a difficult position either. Want to play catch-up now?'

I told her everything I knew about the dead elf. The 'when' and 'how' and the 'where', although I was far too unsure about the 'why'. She didn't seem too surprised, but elves never do. It's another reason why some folk so often want to hit them, but it's a very poor excuse for an axing.

Thelen then gave me her account. It transpired that it was Thelen herself who had seen Highbury returning the Gnada Trophy. She was out for an early surf one morning and spotted him with the trinket in tow setting out from the beach hut. She decided to snoop around a bit, and had found paints and leaflets as well. Incensed, she had confronted Highbury back on the Hill and demanded an explanation. She really could not believe that elves were capable of such behaviour. She got a lot more than she bargained for, and she found herself a prisoner. Thinking that she was working with someone else, they had not been too gentle in asking the questions.

'I do not know if Perry Goodfellow gave him the Trophy to return,' she added. I told her that Highbury had simply relieved me of it after I'd found it hidden under Perry's bed, and she agreed that this did not sound too rosy a prognosis for Perry's health. We both went quiet at this.

'Any chance with the ropes?' I wondered, eventually.

'Elfin ropes do not make a habit of coming untied,' she replied.

'Hey – I thought that was what made them magic!'

'Come on, Nicely. What would you think is magic; a rope that stays tied or one that comes undone?' I couldn't argue with that.

We lay on the floor listening to the rain come down and I gave her an abridged version of what else I had also found out over the last few days. She couldn't make sense of it either. If Mrs Hardwood had set me up for the Surf Elves, why all the fuss about the emerald? Had Leo Courtkey stolen the gem, sold it and gone west with the profits? Who had killed Truetouch? The Surf Elves? Thelen did not believe that they would actually go as far as killing one of their own. I was not so sure. And if not them, who? Petal had denied killing any elves, so who was to gain from a dead elf? I asked Thelen if she knew Truetouch. She did not know the name, but recognised the description. It seemed that he was always on the periphery at the beach, certainly was never seen surfing – the eternal towel-carrier, or maybe he was just happy to be part of the crowd?

A little while later Highbury came in and gave us a speech, what he called the Big Picture. It was full of stuff about the historic destiny of what he called the 'Old Races', by which he meant elves and the Men of the True Land, and, grudgingly, the dwarfs. How they were hampered in their Great Quest by the inferior races: trolls and ogres, gnomes and goblins and other degenerates and abominations.

'The gnomes, I admit, make excellent rugs and very good servants,' he continued, 'and I realise that the goblins, of course, were led astray by their dark masters in days gone by – but difficult times demand difficult, radical solutions. These peoples would be better off in their own lands, the goblins should go back east and the gnomes to the farthest north; compulsory repatriation is the only real answer, surely you see that? Multiculturalism has failed, separate development is the only answer.'

'So the gnomes try digging the tundra and the goblins get a one-way ticket to the pits?' I asked.

'There will still be roles for many here, naturally.'

'Oh sure, there's always enough crap jobs to be done; just that they won't be hampered by any additional chores, like having to vote.'

Highbury didn't have much time for irony and he gave us the pitying look. Now I've no particular fondness for goblins, mechanics aside, but some of my friends are gnomes. Quite frankly I almost wish he had beaten us up some more rather than give us this earache. Thelen hadn't said a word, but if looks could kill, Highbury would already be a Dune Dragon's appetiser.

Highbury finally left and we both let out a sigh. We did another bigger sigh for the continual folly that is the lot of the people of Widergard. This last one was joined by a sneeze in my left ear.

'What a little sweetheart,' said a small, deep, yet familiar voice. 'I get soaked to the skin and then hang around, freezing to death in a storeroom, while some jerk-off with more cheekbones than is strictly necessary on anyone's face gives some mouth-jabber straight out of the *Boy's Own Book of Bigotry*, and not once did he even mention the pixies.'

And from my shoulder hopped Wilmer. 'Old Races, pah, what does he know about Old Races? He wouldn't recognise a brownie if he found one asleep in his milk in the morning.' Wilmer's wet pointed hat hung limply from his head, and he wore a miniature trenchcoat tied tightly round his fat gut. Into the belt was thrust a small but very sharp-looking fruit knife. He shook himself to get rid of excess rainwater.

'Wilmer!' I said, with relief.

'The same.' He bowed low to us both and then poked his tongue at the door, accompanying it with a rude gesture involving one finger and a bent elbow.

'A pixie,' said Thelen, slightly incredulous.

'Yeah, how about an introduction to the lady, fat boy?' said Wilmer.

'How about you cut us free first?' I replied.

'Sure, I can help you with these here ropes.' The pixie set about the ropes with his effective blade, humming an old pixie song as he worked:

'Harden, harden, harden hamp,
I will neither grind nor stamp,
If you'd given me better gear,
I'd have served you many a year,
Thrift may go, bad luck may stay,
I shall travel far away.'

The first of my ropes fell away from my feet and I could feel some blood returned to where blood has every right to be.

'So that's the good news. The bad news is: I can't do much about your pointy-eared pal out there. Slightly punching above my weight.' Wilmer wielded his knife expertly, continuing his somewhat disjointed story as he went about the ropes around my arms and chest.

'So, I says to Arito, "I smells burning", and he says, "Must be supper", and I says, "Don't smell like no supper to me, not unless you've taken to cooking the bedroom." He goes to the bedroom door and then whoosh: the wall blows in before he gets there!

'I have to help us disappear double quick, which is something of a knack that us pixies have – don't ask, as it's a union thing. Anyway, Arito, he says: "I think maybe we should stay disappeared for a while, but you find that Nicely Strongoak, he should know we are safe, and warn him 'cos these same characters as set the fire in our hole, they might well be after him."'

Wilmer finished my ropes and set to on Thelen's as I massaged some life back into my hands and feet.

'So look for you I did, and find you I did – eventually. Which, I guess, could easily be construed as a perfect case of locking the cattleshed door after the dragon's eaten your cows, seeing the mess you is now in, but you are a hard dwarf to track down, even with pixie power! All over the Citadel I flies and then end up here! It's a good job I had a good sniff of you back in Little Hundred – and your aftershave is so distinctive – or I would have lost you completely, and then where would you have both been, huh?'

The little guy could talk the four feet off a fell beast and then persuade him to take up embroidery.

Finally Wilmer had finished his knife work at last and now Thelen and I were both stretching tired and aching limbs.

'Wilmer,' I finally managed to interrupt his flow, 'you have already done enough to keep you in nectar for life, but, if you want to go for tonight's big, Top-of-the-Tree, once in an elf's lifetime prize, I need to ask a couple more favours. Can you get back to Arito, double quick? Ask him to contact Ralph at the Citadel Guard – he knows who I mean. Tell Arito to warn Ralph to expect something big, very big, on the civil disorder front. It will appear as if it's gnomes responsible, but it won't be, that's very important; they are not gnomes doing this – no matter what it may look like!'

The pix saluted and made as if to go.

'Hang on, there's more. Ralph needs to contact Joss Corncrack at the *Citadel Press* and tell him the whole story, how certain factions are trying to stir up trouble for political ends. Joss needs to blow the whole thing sky-high. Take pictures of all the mess being caused by these Surf Elves and their friends, and if he can persuade them to get a scroll out on the streets, telling all, in less time than it takes a pixie to sneeze – no offence – we might still be able to keep the Citadel from falling apart.'

'Can do, Fat Boy.' One last salute and Wilmer turned, and then he was – gone. I must have blinked once and there he was – back again.

'Almost forgot, there was another message for you from Arito as well. He said you would understand: "There ain't no such elf!" Make sense to you? 'Cos it don't mean diddly to me.'

'It's beginning to, Wilmer. The fog is lifting, even if the path's not clear. Now go with our thanks, a lot depends on you!'

'I'm out of here. Just one thing, see if you can do something about pretty boy next door, will you? We got a problem child there. And I would prefer it if whatever you came up with involved a spank and the swallowing of a lot of teeth.' Wilmer tipped his hat to Thelen and was gone for good.

'Neat trick,' said Thelen.

She was still in a pretty bad state, feeling a lot worse than yours truly, as she had been bound for some time before my abortive rescue attempt. I got to my feet, not a moment too soon.

The door opened and in stepped Highbury. His mouth formed an 'O' of surprise and then he made as if starting to speak. I knew it was probably going to be some prolonged fable. It would probably mention 'Sons of Stone' a few times and maybe other stuff about race and such, and to be frank I had been powdered, half-drowned, beaten, maced and bitten and I was not in the mood for it. I wrapped his stomach around my fist and I will not say it did not feel good. I half caught him as he fell, and I did it again. That felt even better. Next I took his long straight nose and spread it all over his face a bit. This had the effect of sending him out of the storeroom, past his astonished compatriots and bursting through the beach hut door into the night and onto the wet sand. Handing off the other elves with closed fists, I followed him at speed. He was coming to on the strand and just drawing his shooter. I kicked it right into the ocean. It took the shine off my shoes, but it was some terrific kick.

Highbury shook himself around. The rain fell in sheets, making the night even darker, but could not wash off the blood pouring down his face. His eyes were murderer blue as he shakily got up, sand clinging to his fancy uniform.

'You should not have done that, dwarf.' The blood had reached his mouth, outlining those perfect teeth like a goblin's mouthwash. 'Now you are going to see an elf lord angry – very angry.'

The sudden flare caught my gloom-accustomed vision by surprise. An elf lord unmasked! I'd read all about that. I stepped back blinded, vaguely aware of the other elf lights behind me that had joined the party. I knew that these eldritch pyrotechnics were mostly for show, but it was a good show, and despite myself I was impressed.

'Amateur hour,' shouted Thelen, suddenly by my side and thrusting a convenient length of hardened driftwood into my bruised but ecstatic mitt, 'what better way to advertise their whereabouts?'

Thelen was right, they were like burning torches, even in the rain-filled night, while we might as well have been wearing invisibility caps. She didn't bother with any light show, she just got on with business and we proceeded to wreak some havoc with our land-and-sea-forged weaponry while they stumbled around in the dark trying to get to grips with our unhampered violence. I brought two of the away team down with axe-like swings to the knees that had kneecaps snapping like popping corn. For the home team Thelen was darting around in the sheets of rain like a will-of-the-wisp on Moondust, wielding her bleached branch like a quarter-staff and cracking skulls like it was going out of fashion.

The numbers game was not on our side though, as further Surf Elves soon turned up from other parts of the beach, and we soon found ourselves standing back-to-back on the sodden sand as the ring of light tightened around us. Any moment one of them was going to remember the rest of the shooters in the beach hut and then our goose was not just cooked, but well rested and ready for carving.

'Sorry, Nicely,' shouted Thelen, still keeping the Surf Elves well out of grabbing distance with her twirling staff.

'Hey, don't be!' I shouted back, brushing water from my face. 'I haven't had this much fun since I did door-keep duties at the Cross-dressing Goblins' Midwinter Ball and refused entry to a Hobgoblin queen in a tiara. How was I to know she wasn't in drag? Now that was a fight!' I caught a slight elf lad on the calf and sent him limping away.

'Oh, I'm not worried about the brawling – just remembered I never did teach you how to surf.' She punctuated her speech with a tremendous backswing that sent another elf flying back to the Hidden Lands. I landed a blow on an unprotected noggin that floored the elf but left me with a broken weapon. Fortunately I spotted a dropped sword in the surf and grabbed at it. A few swings of this gave them all something to think about.

Finally I heard the sound of a shooter bolt being pulled back, cutting through the wind and rain. It was beginning to look like our dancing days were over. The blast, though, went over our heads and I heard a familiar loud booming voice curse in a language I didn't understand, before an elf screamed as if falling from a very great height.

'Very nasty, very nasty. You all should know better,' shouted the still unplaced voice.

This was accompanied by what sounded like a mad swarm of angry bees, if bees came in luminous blue and darted and stung elves faster than the eye could follow. The elves were completely distracted now and thrown into ten different types of confusion.

'Curse you to the blackest Pit of Tallengore, dwarf!'

screamed Highbury through the storm and rain, as he batted off the stinging blue bees.

And then the surrounding lights and sounds were lost, like fireflies consumed by a dwarfsmith's furnace. Suddenly all the world was bleached white and a new voice, booming with authority and completely drowning out Highbury, cried out, first in elvish and then in common speech: 'I think this has all gone on long enough.'

23

ELF QUEEN

What happened next is hazy. It was like a physical assault – perpetrated via the eyeballs. I was blinded, staggering a bit and my head felt split, as if by an axe. We were led out of the rain and I remember Thelen's voice, asking something in elvish, and then a one-sentence answer in the common tongue: 'She awaits.'

At some point I was separated from Thelen: cool cloths were placed on my eyes; the sounds of many elvish voices, worried and concerned. Then I found myself on the back of a horse, of all things. Me, on the back of a horse! What age was this? I would have laughed, if the pain had let me. The horse sped through the rain. Time passed. It felt faster than my Dragonette with the ragtop down. I could hear the rain falling around me, but somehow we were not getting wet. Then finally, strong arms lifted me from the saddle and I was carried somewhere warm that smelled of every good thing you can remember from your childhood and every good thing you wanted when you was all grown up. Finally a deep brown voice I recognised said, 'Drink this, Master Dwarf, I seem to remember you have a taste for it.'

'Grove!' I said, swallowing the Tree-friend's gravy. 'Thanks, that's as good as I remember. I thought I recognised your voice on the beach, but what are you doing here? And where is here exactly?' I tried to get up, but was pushed firmly down again. 'Take these bandages off me, will you, I can't see a thing!'

'Ho hum, I think perhaps not. No, indeed not. You would be well advised to have these dressings on a good while longer, oh yes.'

Another recognisable voice joined in: 'He's right, Nicely. I have added a powerful lotion of my design, but it needs a few hours to take away the sting.'

'Tolly? Is that you?'

'Indeed it is.'

'Those blue stinging things … that wasn't down to you, was it? That wasn't actual wizardry, was it?'

Tolly laughed, with only the smallest trace of malevolence. 'Actual wizardry, in this day and age? Surely not?'

'Have either of you seen Thelen? Is she safe?'

'Safe, oh yes. Very safe,' Grove said. 'A fine fighter that one, very fine. I'd forgotten just how invigorating physical violence can be.' He laughed his rolling Tree-friend laugh. 'I haven't felt quite this young in an age.'

'I still say that you didn't need to throw him that high,' said Tolly.

'Need? No. But want? That is a different mater entirely.'

'Would either of you please assist with some explanations?' I said tersely, before I started hitting folk again.

Grove and Tolly, however, were gone, but another voice – elf this time – said: 'She is safe, she is with her mother.' Well, there's a relief – I'd been taken home to meet the family. I was distinctly ill prepared for house calls, though.

Then we were moving again. More horse transport; hadn't these elves heard about the steam engine? Then I half-walked and was half-carried, not unkindly, through tunnels that distinctly shouted 'underground' to my dwarf nose. The drink had eased the pain, but I still wanted to speak to Grove. I had a lot of questions that I thought he could help me with. It would have to wait, as I felt a seat arm pressed into my hand, solid and welcoming. And another voice, female, quintessence of elf, texture of polished gold, neither young nor old, spoke to me: 'Please sit down, Master Detective. You may remove the cloths now. Your vision should be restored, do not be concerned. The elf-light is never permanent.'

Carefully I did as she said and opened my eyes. Coloured after-images danced before me and then settled down. I could see I was in a room, sparsely furnished, the curtains drawn and only one shaft of early-morning sun let through to light the interior. I realised that the storm must have subsided. I'm quick like that.

The room had a feeling of not having been lived in for a long, long time. At one end, seated on a high chair, her back to the window, sat the elfess. She spoke again: 'Please excuse the curtains, I find the sunlight trying after all this time. Also I think perhaps this is better for your vision – no?'

I nodded my approval.

'It is not many who chance to see an elf lord unmasked.'

'Highbury?'

She laughed, a forest stream. 'No, I do not mean one of these latter-day elves, I mean a true elf lord from the Hidden Lands, the one who came to your rescue along with Grove and the wizard.'

'We weren't doing too bad.'

'No, Master Dwarf, you were not doing that bad.' A pause. 'Do you know who I am?'

I thought about it for a while. 'I believe I do. Can't say I'm any too sure of the proper form of address, though.'

That passed her by, she seemed to drift for a moment. 'I knew your famous forefather.' The change in tack caught me for a moment. 'Do you know of whom I speak?'

I shuffled in my chair slightly awkwardly, like a youngster caught stealing pies. Then I said: 'There were rumours, legends, but many families lay claim to that kinship.'

She laughed again. 'And many may be right. How do you say it now? He got around.' This time I shared her laughter.

'He looked rather like you, there is no doubting the family resemblance. And he was courageous and resourceful – characteristics you also appear to have acquired. He was devoted to me, and I, I for my part was, was very … fond of him.'

'This is all very pleasant, my lady, but it's history.'

'Not for me, Master Detective, not for me.' She brought herself back to the present with an effort – who knows what ageless paths she walked at other times? I had heard of the curse of the elves. How the memories of all those ages, those countless years of experience could overflow from wherever they were housed within those miraculous minds and begin to leak into everyday life, causing problems that the demented would pity if they only could.

Rising now with all the ease of apparent youth she walked behind her chair, resting lightly on its carved back. Her face was still in shadow when she spoke again. 'I suppose you know why I am here?'

'The dead elf?'

'Yes. The dead elf.'

'So, a dead elf?' I could see us playing this game until the sun had gone down again.

'A number of very influential people have been in contact with me, not least a wizard and a Tree-friend of your acquaintance, both of whom have made personal requests for my help. You have made some important friends, it seems, as well as important enemies. I do not lightly take the Sea Path back from the Hidden Lands to Widergard after all this time. Although, I must admit it is interesting, yes interesting, to see how things have altered.'

'How about the dead elf?'

'Your forefather was also very much to the point.' She walked slowly towards me and for the first time I saw her face lit by the dawn light. For a minute I almost stopped breathing, the resemblance to Thelen was remarkable; plus, of course, the experience of a fair fraction of the age of the planet. 'This is a difficult tale to tell.' She changed vein again in a manner I was beginning to find just a trifle annoying – but I was not about to hack off an elf queen.

'Let me first tell you another story, Master Detective. Do you know anything concerning evolution?'

'Not over-informed, though I do seem to be picking up a bit of late.'

'A wealth of new evidence concerning the evolution of the Peoples of Widergard is coming from discoveries of fossils found in the furthest south.'

'The furthest south, who would have thought it?'

'Who indeed? I am afraid all the rather colourful stories of our origins may indeed be nothing more than stories.'

'Even the ones the elves tell?'

'Yes, even the elves do not hold all the secrets.'

'Then why isn't this all making the daily scrolls?'

'It might not be expedient.'

'I never thought expediency was top priority for the parchment pushers – circulation's more the thing.'

'Perhaps some pressure has been applied.'

'Ah, pressure!'

'It is, of course, election year.'

'Of course. And what is so incendiary a story that this pressure is necessary?'

'That we – and by that I mean all people of Widergard – we may have had our beginnings in a rather undistinguished and now sadly vanished ape-like ancestor that once roamed the grasslands of the furthest south, scraping a living eating nuts and berries.'

'Yes, that would be a story.'

'So, strangely, it looks as if the furthest south may turn out to have some claim as being the ancestral home of all the peoples of Widergard.'

'Not west! Or north or east, but south?'

'Yes, scholars have found the fossil bones of a number of upright tool-using creatures. Two of the earliest forms of these creatures share similar characteristics, but one is a smaller, more graceful form, whilst the other is much larger, more robust. These creatures are thought to have travelled from the south to explore the northern lands. The gracile form is not thought to have tarried here long, but walked across a landbridge that once linked these lands to the Hidden Lands themselves. Once there, in its unique environs, they evolved to become the elves. Some of the most robust forms stayed in the forests of Widergard where they became the Tree-friends, whilst others of their kin journeyed further north, and in the harsh climate of the mountains evolved to become the trolls.'

I whistled quietly.

This was going to go down big with the Citadel Alliance Party.

'Meanwhile in the south there arose the line of men. An early form of man, larger and more brutal, left the south first and in the colder climate of the north and east evolved to become the goblins.'

'That's going to please Petal.'

'I beg your pardon?'

'Nothing. I'm sorry, please continue.'

'Next there arose the true men, many of whom remained in the south, although others again took the northern road. Coming to the lands already inhabited by trolls and goblins.'

'And the gnomes?'

'The gnomes seem to be a very recent branch of the Tree of Widergard. It is said that there is a race of gnomes in the furthest south, who consider themselves to be nothing other than smaller men.'

'Interesting. Assuming that nobody still has the slightest idea of anything concerning the pix and the fey, that still leaves one outstanding matter.'

'Yes, Master Detective: you dwarfs.'

'As you say, us dwarfs.'

'It would be simplest to think of you as a primitive off-shoot of the earliest elves.'

I had to treat myself to a snort – elf queen or not, this was not going to go down well with the Brothers either.

'But here all the recent theories appear to come unstuck. Were the dwarfs instead descendants of the robust creature that was cousin to the gracile elves and gave rise to the Tree-friends and trolls? However, there is no fossil evidence yet found to link the dwarfs to any of the other evolving creatures of the furthest south. No evidence of the dwarfs at all until they appear, as if by magic, in the hills of the north.'

'Which strangely matches the dwarfs' own stories of their origins.'

'Yes, perhaps your old stories really are old, even by elf standards. There is a theory that the dwarfs evolved in the farthest east, from a totally different ape-like creature, and that it is from the east that the dwarfs migrated to the Northern Mountains – perhaps because of an influx of primitive goblins. This would mean that the whole of evolution has occurred twice; that the random chance that has produced intelligence and consciousness has happened in two separate branches of ape-like creatures. In the same way that evolution has led then to the evolution of all the different races of Widergard.'

'A chance, you say?'

'That is how the scholars refer to it. An accidental event in the makeup of the body; nothing more than a mishap – a sport – but oh, what a mishap, to gain so much from so little. And who is to say that such accidents are still not occurring? Master Detective,' she looked straight at me. 'The elf you knew as Truetouch, he was not exactly as he seemed.'

I cut her off to save anybody getting too excited by all the suspense. 'I suppose that was because he was a man, one Leo Courtkey.'

Her voice showed surprise. 'You knew?'

'Only pieces, it only just came properly together, because that's just the kind of dragon-hot detective I am! I did have worries that I'd not managed to find a picture of Leo in his racing days. Of course, as a rider, he was generally the right size and build for a Wood Elf, but I could not make all the proper connections at that time, not without Arito's knowledge. It's still hard to believe; after all, I met him, talked with him, he seemed as much an elf as any I've met, more so than some.'

'I know, I have seen him, albeit dead; elvish, but not an elf.'

'Doesn't that just wet on the wizard's fireworks!'

'If you want to come down to the mortuary, Master Detective, I can show you. As you may be aware, hair does not continue to grow after death ...'

'Yup, just a myth.'

'There is, however, some contraction of the skin, though, that produces a similar effect, and I can assure you Master Detective, elves do not have dark roots.'

'Oh Leo, a bottle blond! But what about his ears and those cheekbones and more importantly his general, well, elfishness?'

'Reformational knife work to enhance the ears, cheekbones and some other, less noticeable, minor points. And as for the rest, well, it would be nice to think that there was something in his ancestry that could explain it; elvish blood that just needed some chance meeting of parents to be expressed, but the possibility is too remote. We checked. Leo Courtkey, it seems, was something akin to one of these "sports" the scholars talk about.'

We both let the implications sink in. It was enough to make a seer drop-kick his crystal ball. I couldn't help but think of the elf in the linen summer coat with the winning smile. Poor lonely Leo, I hope you were happy back there as Truetouch, for a while at least. The speech by Highbury came back to mind. 'An abomination,' I said out loud.

She misunderstood me. 'Who knows? Man is unique amongst all the races of Widergard. The shortest-lived and yet the most fecund. They are the stuff of evolution. Who can tell what their fate might be? It is, perhaps, a terrifying thought.'

'But that is no reason to kill Leo Courtkey.'

'No, most certainly not, even if his behaviour did not always match his looks.'

'Don't judge him too quickly, my lady. It couldn't have been easy. Think of his position: a stranger to his family, outcast by virtue of his looks and manners. He finds a niche for himself, riding horses, but there is always something else riding him, the desire to be something he isn't.'

'But he cut a lot of corners to achieve his aims,' she shrugged. A lifting of the shoulders that gave me gooseflesh in a place gooseflesh has no right to be. 'And dreams aren't achieved by putting powder up your nose.'

'Is it any wonder?' I tried to keep my thoughts on the subject at hand. 'Any wonder that he should search for better things, even hide himself in powder-induced dreams? Perhaps then one day there was a case of mistaken identity, or someone made a chance remark: "Hey Leo, you know, in this light you look just like an elf, but in a good way!"'

'Thank you.'

'And so he has an idea, he bleaches his already fair hair and loads up his treasure chest, by fair means and foul, and then after some reformational knife work, he can finally feel at home.'

I don't know why I found myself defending Leo. I mean, the chances were that his treasure chest was loaded thanks to a race-track fraud. Maybe I still felt like I should have helped him more; the deal that hadn't been struck, but I knew I was going to take the job.

'Could there have been sufficient reason for the Surf Elves to kill Leo?'

'Over a little reformational knife work? These are elves, Master Detective!' the queenly tones took on a tone of real indignation.

'How about an argument over a particularly valuable lost bauble?'

The elf queen looked at me strangely. 'Bauble? An interesting word that, Master Detective. No, not even a lost "bauble" would be sufficient motive for a death.'

'I wonder, my lady. I just wonder. Are you so very sure? Haven't you been told what else has been happening in the Citadel this summer?'

'I am aware, thank you and such matters will be dealt with. But now it is my turn to say to you, Master Dwarf, you should not judge too quickly. Do not think too ill of these latter-day elves that missed out on the Great Age of the Elves; times have changed and it is not unnatural that they occasionally rail against such changes. They expect wide sweeps of colour in their lives and some are not content with the delicate shades of grey they encounter.'

'Who exactly are these latter-day elves, then?'

'Why, they are our children, Master Detective. Did you not know? With the Departure, when the Higher Elves left Widergard and we gave the folk of Widergard the right to self-determination, we all took a vow to never return; a vow I now break at some cost to myself. For good or ill, Widergard was now the responsibility of those that lived there. We did not take into account our children, those we were yet to bear in the Twilight Kingdoms of the Hidden Lands. They only heard about Widergard in song, in tales of heroism and great deeds. They grew bored with the Twilight and the Hidden Lands, and longed for the vibrant colours and adventure of Widergard. And they had made no such vows.'

'So you sent us your juvenile delinquents?'

She said sharply, 'Your forefather would not have spoken to me like that, Master Strongoak. I am not sure I like your attitude.'

'I'm not sure I like it either, but it's the only one I've got and it seems to get me three meals a day, when I need them, and a glass of something sticky for when I'm home nights grieving about my attitude.'

The elf queen looked at me down the wrong end of the telescope of time, like she didn't really understand everything that she was seeing. Elves, hey, sometimes you just wanted to explain the modern world to them in very simple one-syllable words while dangling the whole lot over molten lava.

'It's like you said, lady, times change. And we are talking about a bit more than youthful high-jinks here.'

'I know, word does get back to us, even in the Hidden Lands. That is why I sent my daughter to keep an eye on things for me.'

'Ah yes, your daughter. How is Thelen?'

'Recovering, she sends her best wishes.'

'That's top-of-the-tree, really.'

This was accepted gracefully and she continued her story. 'You have to understand our position. Our vows could hardly be said to include our unborn. How could we deprive them of what we ourselves had loved so much? So in the end we gave them leave to sail to Widergard. We made a condition, though. They could come to Widergard, but only as long as they brought a gift, a gift that we thought would more than recompense for any problem their return might cause. A gift to put an end to all the fighting and conflict that had occurred in Widergard since our departure and the Death of the Great Kings. A gift to put an end to all the petty kingdoms, princes and chiefs that had sprung up; we gave you the gift of democracy.'

'Yeah, democracy is just top-of-the-tree too.'

'It is indeed "top-of-the-tree". Rule of the people by the people. No more kings and Emperors, petty despots.'

'Just councillors and aldermen instead.'

'No system is perfect, Master Detective. Like you, we work with what we have at hand.' She sat again. Good, she was giving me a pain in the neck – in more than one sense! I had me a speech to make.

'Now, let me tell you a story, my lady. It concerns a dwarf king called Azed the Sixty-fourth. He lived a long time ago, by our reckoning, though to you this may seem like last year. As the Prince, Azed was groomed for the succession and soon became ready and willing to rule the kingdom. Now his father, Kole the forty-third, was a particularly healthy and long-lived individual and Azed soon became bored waiting for his father's demise and so he took up a hobby. He became interested in fly-fishing. Almost to his surprise he was rather good at it, something of an expert; his book is still considered the definitive guide to the sport amongst my kin. He was never happier than when he was up to his waist in a mountain stream, casting his "little gnat" for some unsuspecting fish.

'Now eventually Kole the forty-third did die, and although there was general sadness at his passing, he had had a very long and fruitful life and everyone was rather interested in seeing how his son, Azed, would manage as a king. So, it was with keen anticipation that Coronation Day approached. Azed had taken the preparations seriously; he had been measured for the ceremonial robes and had practised with the ceremonial axe.

'Everything went well in the Royal Cavern on the big day. The palace had never looked more beautiful. A thousand, thousand coloured lights shone off a thousand, thousand shining mirrored surfaces and fountains laughed and great music played, bouncing merrily around the subjects' heads. Crown on head, surveying his subjects, Azed spoke his first words as king.

'"Am I your true king?"

'"Yes," replied the assembled throng, who liked this kind of thing.

'"And do you vow to follow me with all your hearts?"

'"Verily," lustily cried the assembled throng – that being the only way to cry "verily".

'"And is my word law?"

'"Yes," said the assembled throng, although there were now one or two murmurs, as this last clause had caused a few problems in the past.

'"Good," said Azed. "Now listen, all you assembled, for this is my first and only decree: there shall be no more kings."

'And with that Azed went off back to his fishing and never set foot in the Royal Cavern again. Now, these events caused a bit of an uproar in the court. Each day his courtiers would stand waiting in vain at the riverbank begging him for new instructions, since to choose a new king would be to break the king's law, and this they could not do. Each day they waited and each day they came away disappointed.

'Eventually something had to be done and so all of the dwarf provinces, from the most far-flung parts of the kingdom, each elected a wise and popular representative and sent him or her to the Royal Cavern. There they put their heads together to solve the problem of the king who said there should be no more kings. This temporary committee

284

could not solve the problem either, of course, as there was no answer. However they debated long and hard and whenever any other problems came up, these would be presented to the temporary committee, and being made up of the wisest and most popular dwarfs, generally they would make a fair stab at solving the problem, which kept everybody happy. And when one of the temporary committee members died, why, they just elected another one. So, when Azed the sixty-fourth, henceforth known as the "loved", finally died, without progeny, but with a veritable library of fly-fishing manuscripts to his name, they realised their problem was solved for them.'

'You tell a good story, Master Dwarf.'

'Except it is not just a story, my lady. The whole of dwarfdom is still ruled by the Temporary Committee. It is the oldest temporary committee in Widergard. So thank you very much for your democracy. We do not need your brand of dubious party politics.'

'I still say, Master Dwarf, do not judge them too hastily.'

I remained unconvinced and said as much, adding: 'What about Highbury?'

'He will be punished.'

'But will it be enough?' I said, with sufficient vehemence to make the elfess raise an eyebrow.

'And does he admit to killing Leo Courtkey?'

'No. He knows nothing of this act.'

'I didn't think so, but I needed to ask. How about Perry Goodfellow?'

Here her voice grew genuinely sad. 'That, it seems, was an accident.' I held my breath. 'After Perry won the silly trophy, there was a challenge from one of the elves.'

'From Highbury,' I interrupted.

She nodded. 'It seems they tried to ride one of the waves that come in from the Big Sea at Midsummer, the Great Curve they call it. Perry came off his board, close to the Troll's Teeth rocks; his body could not be found.'

'While Highbury on his enchanted board just managed to make it back again, I suppose. How come Liza Springwater never knew anything about this supposed challenge?'

'A contest between equals, a private matter.'

'Conveniently private!'

'Master Dwarf, I am not obliged to give you this information. I have been given the story and I have no reason not to believe it.'

'Ah, of, course – live elves don't lie! They still should have reported the accident.' I was getting hot and bothered and ready to bang a few tables and kick a few priceless antiques around the room. 'They broke Citadel law with the cover-up!'

'I know the law, Master Dwarf, I helped write it!'

'I know that too, lady, but it doesn't belong to you now and neither does the Citadel. Time, as has been mentioned, moves on, whether this is agreeable to you or not.'

For the first time I became truly aware of the huge gulf that divided us, almost countless years. I wondered what it must be like, where everyday life was like a dream and reality might be a thousand years ago. The room suddenly seemed to get very cold. I got up. 'If that's it, I think I had better go.'

'Of course. I would not wish to detain you.'

I could not think of an appropriate farewell, and she seemed once again to be lost in thought. I walked across the room. It felt like walking halfway across Widergard. Just as I got to the door, she called out my name; I turned.

'Nicely, you are very like your forefather, you know,' and she raised a hand in salute.

My jaw set grimly. 'The given name, My Lady, is Strongoak.'

'I know, I know, I gave it to you.' She raised her hand and a golden glow lit up the room and then she was gone – like magic.

24

ALDERMAN HARDWOOD

Outside the door, I met an elf lord. I guessed he was the one who had saved me from Highbury and his jolly band, but I did not ask and he did not say. At first glance he could have passed for a Surf Elf; on closer examination I realised that he was moulded from different stuff, hardly flesh and bone at all, more like polished marble. So, these were the elves that still lived in the Hidden Lands, the mothers and fathers of the Higher Elves of Widergard. Well, I for one kind of hoped they'd all stay there.

He led me silently through a maze of poorly lit tunnels, all of which looked vaguely familiar. We came to a small door, just ajar. I walked through, and turning, finally tried a few words of thanks, but he shook his head, as if to say it did not matter. That made me feel less gracious, so I just continued, and found myself back in Old Town, in the Citadel. I had been in another set of the vast network of tunnels that I now knew undermined the Hill. Something must have happened to my time sense, though, while I was blinded. I couldn't believe that there was a horse still living that could have got me back to the Citadel in the time my journey had taken, but here I was.

I looked in the Citadel walls for some hint of a door, but there was no sign even my trained dwarf eyes could see. Maybe they were tired, like the rest of me. I shrugged and went looking for a street-train. I was close to the healers where I had dropped off Telfine an age ago. I decided to check on his health before heading back to the Two Fingers. I could also get a dressing for the spot where I had been maced.

The drains and gutters were awash with water from the recent deluge, and although the sun shone again, the air felt far better and cleaner. People were dashing hither and thither, but no one seemed to know what was going on. A street-train was not to be found for rings or silver. I decided that if feet were the order of the day, I might as well go and collect a certain bearer's package that should be waiting for me at the office.

I finally made it to the door of the Healers' House and I ran straight into Ralph. He had been to see Telfine and looked tired, but elated. I was pleased to see there were no obvious signs of the young scout's hide under his fingernails, so he obviously hadn't ripped it off as he had threatened previously. Ralph paced and brought me up to date while a physic added some more stitches to my stitch collection. It was good news for once. The rain had come in time to prevent the fire from reaching the docks and industrial areas; it had saved the Citadel, but was too late for most of the Little Hundred. The damage there was probably far worse than the instigators had planned, thanks to the tinder-dry conditions; I credit them with that much compassion. Maybe I'm getting soft.

The Citadel mood was one of stunned disbelief; councilmen

were to be heard on every street corner promising compensa-
tion for the victims and new homes for the survivors. There
was still bad feeling amongst the gnomes; things were still
far from settled. Further up the Hill, wary High Folk were
boarding their windows and arms were being kept close at
hand.

'Did I ever tell you Strongoak's Third Law, Ralph?'

'I think you may have mentioned it a few times in passing.
Something about it taking very few people to cock things up
for a whole lot of people.'

'Yes. Well, I've just thought of a corollary, Ralph: when
things are cocked up it takes an awful lot of people to sort
them out again.'

Ralph had to agree. All Citadel Guard leave had been
cancelled indefinitely and there was talk of them calling
an emergency muster for reserves – which would probably
include me! The *Citadel Press*, with Josh's help, looked like it
might assist in defusing the situation. It had just hit the streets
and Ralph showed me a copy. Josh had done a remarkably
fast job, with some excellent photography of the despoiled
Little Hundred that really hit home. He'd probably end up
with some sort of award, which would really annoy him.
Lacking definite evidence, the *Press* put the conspiracy down
to 'subversive elements' within the Citadel Alliance Party.
Further support for this conspiracy theory was provided by
the Guard's discovery of a plot to blow up the First Level
Gate – the Elf Gate. It was an interesting choice; did someone
know that it was unprotected by magic? (Would this have
made a difference?) Whatever, it would have crippled the
Citadel. The perpetrators, small grunt goblins for the most
part, were in gnome dress and had orders to create as much
extra damage as possible.

'Congratulations, Sergeant-at-Arms Fieldfull.' I meant it.

'Make that Captain Fieldfull.'

'Double congratulations. They do say it's an ill wind ...'

'Yes, and this wind looks like it just might have blown away a few CAP sympathisers from the upper ranks of the Citadel Guard, not to mention many more in the lower ranks.'

I then filled in Ralph with details of my adventures and misadventures since we last spoke. He was impressed and he does not play that tune easily.

'A real live elf queen?'

'And not just any old elf queen. The Elf Queen, the one they write the stories and sing the songs about.'

Ralph shook he head in disbelief. 'Whatever next? Dragons and elf queens, you wouldn't think this was the modern age at all, with legends walking the streets of Widergard again.'

'They never went away, Ralph. We occasionally just liked to pretend otherwise.'

'This is really something though, Nicely. Please, just say you had a quill and got her to sign something.'

'Why would I do that, Ralph?'

'You could sell her seal for a hundred crowns down at the Old Town markets.'

I would have hit him, but the physic still had a needle in my skull.

'Just make sure you get it all down in writing for the gold badges, well at least enough so that the story has a beginning, middle and end – or maybe just a beginning and an end.' Then it was time for Ralph to dash off and help with the distribution of the *Citadel Press*'s special scroll and generally keep whatever peace the Hill was in the mood for.

Telfine, when I finally reached him, was in reasonable shape, although he could scarcely raise a whisper. He was still furious about being spotted by the elves and worried about exactly what his chief had in store for him by way of punishment. I tried to tell him that if it hadn't been for him Thelen might even now be taking the slow boat back west and I, and a certain elf queen, were both unbelievably grateful. This helped a bit, but I think he was more scared of Ralph than any number of elf queens. As I was getting ready to leave, he beckoned me close.

'I never did get to give the chief my full report.' His voice dropped even quieter as fatigue and a sense of the dramatic kicked in. I leant closer. 'That Highbury, before the elfess tracked him down, guess where he had been?' Telfine's eyes lit up through the dressings. I shook my head.

'Only to Hardwood House. The house of the high and mighty Alderman Hardwood himself. So what do you think of that?' I thought a lot about that, all the way to Hardwood House.

The house steamed discreetly after the summer storm. The battlements were still ravening-horde-free. The lawns were still immaculate, and, incongruously, after the rain, sprinklers made rainbows in the warm sunshine. The pool still waited, aching for a swimmer; perhaps Mrs Hardwood was nearby, working on that one-piece tan.

Goodenough opened the door. He gave me that same look; I didn't waste time on introductions. I'd already seen plenty enough of him.

I asked to see Mrs Hardwood. He went away a while and then returned, quietly asking me to follow. Follow I did, but not quietly.

'You know Goodenough, you've got excellent posture. I bet you were in the army.'

'Indeed,' he replied.

'Good for the posture, all that standing to attention.'

'Assuredly.'

'Very distinctive too. You can always tell a military man, whether he's on his way back from the beach or sitting in a seedy little bar with a couple of goblin types.'

This did not rate a response.

'Of course, I bet that sort of training makes you really handy with a sword, or an axe.'

Goodenough turned abruptly and I nearly walked into him. His normally grey pallor sported red spots of high colour on his cheeks. They looked as out of place as spats on a gnome, but there was no doubting his sincerity.

'Very handy,' he enunciated carefully.

'And you clear up all the little problems for the Hardwoods, don't you? For Mr Hardwood as well as Mrs Hardwood?'

'Yes, I clear up all their … little … problems. Just remember that.'

Goodenough didn't add anything else, but spun round again and walked on, faster this time as if trying to make a point. I stepped lively after him, speaking to his back.

'Want to know when you first gave it away, Goodenough? When you made the crack about soft-tops. How would you know I drove a soft-top? Was it you, Goodenough, or Petal and his gang, who swung the axe into Courtkey's unprotected skull? Did you delegate on account of the fact that Leo had been your workmate? Come on Goodenough, no snappy comments now?'

The rest of the walk was in a silence so intense that it would have made a lordly tomb sound like the practice room for the *All-Star Syncopated Gnome Home Jump Band*.

We passed through what seemed like the whole length of the rest of the house, using the corridors this time. The

293

walls were all hung with the regulation age-old tapestries, but this time I did not give the fittings my attention. When you've just been chatting with someone who probably saw them being woven, suddenly they did not seem so impressive.

Goodenough showed me into an archive filled with scrolls and books that would not have disgraced the Citadel Central Archive. The red spots on his cheeks still looked like tail-lights on a steam-train.

'Better watch that blood pressure, Goodenough,' I said under my breath. 'You don't want to go having one of those "on-purposes", do you?'

He shot me a look that could have pierced blue steel, but I was made of sterner stuff.

Everything was very quiet and very ordered in the archive; neither in the design nor in the trappings could I discern any trace of the lady of the house. At one end in a simple chair, with a small table next to it, sat Mr Hardwood. His beard was neatly trimmed, his pate was polished and the long hair at the back was pulled into a small ponytail. He sat reading in front of a very long window. It stretched from floor to ceiling and filled the room with evening light, picking out dust motes in the air, caught momentarily like moths in amber, but on the small table there still burned a small lamp.

'I asked to see Mrs Hardwood,' I said, even though I'd realised this particular meeting was inevitable. He looked up from his book for the first time. 'My wife, Master Strongoak, has been taken ill. She has been advised by her physics to take a holiday, somewhere cooler, with less excitement.'

'For her health.'

'Indeed, for her health.' He regarded me levelly. 'She has, however, left adequate remuneration to cover her contractual obligations.' He pointed to an envelope on the small table. Even from this distance I could see it contained bills, a lot of bills.

'I haven't finished the job yet.'

'The task however, is completed.' He started back on his book.

'Not by me. It may have been my axe, but I did not wield it, or pay for it to be done.' This did not faze him one bit, but I had his attention. He marked his page, closed his book, and carefully put it on the table.

'Master Strongoak, as you can see, I am an old man, old by any standards, thanks to my ancestry, but I am not a fool. I married my wife late, very late, and I was aware of some of her failings as well as her previous title. She likes beautiful things and what I believe is known as a "good time". I indulge her, an old man's whim. Sometimes these indulgences, they become expensive and, as she does not like to keep asking me for money, she gets one of the help to sell off a trinket or two, perhaps replacing them with something she hopes will fool me. As I said, Master Strongoak, I am not a fool and if I have ever been fooled by anything, it has not been for a very long time. I continue the pretence for her sake.' He folded his hands neatly in his lap, like a child at first school.

I was beginning to get a bit irritable. 'But what about if it's something really valuable that goes missing? Something that should not have been in your family's possession to begin with?' Hardwood waited for me to continue; he was not going to break down and start confessing a thing.

'Maybe it's stolen from you by one of the help, maybe the wife hocked it?'

'Master Strongoak, nobody and I repeat nobody, takes

what is mine and walks away with it. Now, if that is all you have to say, I think our interview is at an end.' He reached for his book. Whatever he thought I knew was not going to be enough to worry him, I could see that.

'It's been a wild time in the Citadel,' I began again.

Again the level look. 'So I hear, a terrible event to occur.'

'All sorts of things are happening.'

'Yes. But what is that to do with me?'

'I just thought you should know that it appears that this event was not as spontaneous as it might first have appeared.'

'I am not following you, Master Strongoak and I repeat, what is all this to do with me?'

'Orchestrating that sort of disruption takes a lot of organisation and a lot of time and a great deal of money; a gamble by somebody with a lot of power, for very high stakes; not far off from revolution. Now, it seems that it's not going to happen. There aren't going to be any race riots. No uprising by the gnomes, or goblins dressed as gnomes, so no retaliation, no chaos, no emergency elections, and no sudden swing into power for the Citadel Alliance Party. And most certainly no Lord Highbury Evergleaming to front said party. He was supposed to be the leader, your leader, I take it, at least as far as the population were concerned. What were you going to do, divide the Citadel down the middle?'

'I think an individual's politics are his own concern, don't you, Master Dwarf?'

'Unless they involve subverting the system, preventing democratic elections; not to mention inciting riots and racial hatred.'

'These are grave accusations, Master Detective; I hope you can substantiate them.'

'It doesn't matter, Alderman, because it's all been squashed, finished. All that's going to happen now is that a lot of councillors and aldermen – including yourself – are going to find themselves without a seat this fall. And although they are going to be the only people in the Citadel who will be upset by this, they will be very upset.' I gave him a big, wide smile. 'Yes, sorry, but I do not think the Citadel Alliance Party will be much of a going concern this year, or ever. You don't own the Citadel, no more than the elves do. I thought you ought to know that.'

Hardwood gently stroked his beard, his only sign of agitation. 'As I say, politics is a very subjective matter.'

I needed very much to see that implacable calm disturbed just a fraction, and as much as I wanted to do it, I felt that smacking a very rich and powerful old man on the jaw was not advisable. I had the next best thing, though. I took the Hardwood Emerald out of the bearer's pouch tucked into my jacket inside pocket and held it up high where it caught the last of the evening sunshine and sent out shafts of green light all around the book-lined walls.

'I do believe that is my property,' said the old man, his attention now well and truly won.

'I do believe it's not,' I replied.

I turned, leaving the folding money where it sat. It is probably still there, gathering a little dust, on the little table, next to the light, by the long window.

25

AFTER THE FIRE

I was right in my evaluation. The *Citadel Press*'s scroll did do the job. Josh's photographs in particular. The looks on the faces of the gnome mothers looking in anguish for their children melted many a stony heart and the sight of their burnt and ravaged pitiful homes caused an uproar that is still ringing around Widergard. On the Hill, people's anger gave way to shock and disbelief; their fear gave way to sympathy. Although there was a groundswell of desire for justice and the population cried out for the ringleaders to be brought to trial, it never happened. By the time the Cits reached the Surf Elves' hut, it was empty of everything and the case had to be dropped for lack of evidence. This was probably just as well, for retaliation against the entire elfin population of the Citadel would have been disastrous. The story was enough to do the trick though; it effectively defused a very bad situation. Petal and his gang were never found so nobody came to trial, although as I predicted, come fall, a lot of councilmen and aldermen suddenly found themselves with nowhere to sit.

And the outlook for Alderman Hardwood? Well, it would have been nearly impossible to do permanent damage to anyone of his standing, either financially or personally. So he was never going to end up begging in the gutter. Strangely enough, though, his business empire did dwindle. I suspect a certain elf queen dropped a few words into the right ears – and eventually he was replaced at the top of his various industrial concerns and Hardwood became a recluse, studying arcane law, but never crossing the sea to the promised land. Mrs Hardwood joined him in seclusion, which was some small measure of justice and a great loss to the Citadel social scene, apparently.

However, as I left Hardwood House on that warm summer's evening I did not feel quite as good as I would have liked. For one thing, I could feel Goodenough's staring eyes drilling holes in my back and following my every step as I walked back to the wagon.

Plus, I still had one very important call to make. I found her on that small bit of beach in the main Bay area that is still left unpolluted. She was with Thelen. She had left a message with my answering service telling me where they would be. Thelen did not approach as I parked my Dragonette by the strand and walked on down the beach. She sat on the sand hugging her knees. Liza was down at the water's edge, idly skipping stones across the barely rippling surface.

I sat down on the still warm sand next to Thelen.

'She wanted some time by herself. I've told her about Perry.'

I nodded and looked at her closely. 'You have your mother's countenance.' She shrugged and I did not pursue the matter further. 'She might find a good home for this.' I handed her the pouch with the Elf Gate Ring, most definitely no longer the Hardwood Emerald.

Thelen gave the pouch the shortest of examinations, as if she was afraid the sight might do permanent damage to her eyes. They certainly seemed to be watering suddenly.

'Thank you, Nicely.'

'All part of the service.'

'And I am not sure if I ever did really thank you properly for the rescue, Nicely.'

'Not much of a rescue. And it's Arito Cardinollo and Wilmer we should be thanking. Them and your elf aunts and uncles.'

'I didn't know they were waiting in the wings. Whatever you may think, I was not just following orders. Elves do not work that way.'

'Sure, Thelen. I understand.'

'So, this Mrs Hardwood is a queen of sorts?'

'Celembine Merrymead – hardly in your mother's league, but about as legit as you can get these days. Why, does that get her extra discount at the Her Majesty's All-You-Can-Eat-for-5-Crowns Hogget Bar?'

Thelen look at me and shook her head before replying: 'I'm not surprised so many people seem to want to play punchball with your head.'

'I always put it down to unbridled jealousy at my outrageous good looks.'

She continued gamely: 'But Queen Celembine was not content to live her days in the Desolate Wastes?'

'A title is all very fine, but as we all know, that's not where the power lies in these modern times, and she likes that smell of control, does our Mrs Hardwood.'

'And what was Leo Courtkey to her?'

I shrugged. 'A damn fine rider, powder supplier and discrete seller of unwanted jewellery – take your pick and see what you hit.'

'So she brought him with her to the Citadel?'

'And to a nice situation with Mr Hardwood, somebody with real wealth and power, where they continued their little arrangement.'

'So what spoilt it?'

'Our Leo was not as other men.' I knew that for certain now because Josh had finally come through with a photograph of Leo Courtkey, a rare snap of him winning a race on his beloved Rosebud. I didn't really recognise the face, but I knew the smile. I'd put the photograph in my purse, meaning to show it to the others involved in the case, but I never did. It didn't seem right to somehow. As Truetouch he died; let him find whatever peace he could with that name and face.

For some reason I looked hard at Liza standing at the water's edge before I continued. 'Let's just say he wasn't happy in the company of men. He wanted elfdom and all it entailed and when he saw a chance to get some gold corn of his own, from a racetrack fix, he grabbed at it with both hands.'

'And this gold,' Thelen began, before a small shiver interrupted her flow. 'This enabled him to pay for the adjustment surgery he so desired?'

'Pointy ears and raised eyebrows and chiselled cheekbones and the rest – fine if you like that kind of thing.'

'Which I do!'

I gave her a smile: 'On you they look good!'

'Still, it takes more than surgery to pass as an elf.' She hugged her knees. 'I saw him and I was fooled too.'

'Everybody was.'

'Why did he take the Elf Gate ring – the Hardwood Emerald, as it was then thought to be?'

301

'Well, he wasn't getting a salary from the Hardwoods any more. He had to leave there when he started the surgery. So Leo Courtkey the rider was no more and he only had "Truetouch" to fall back on. I think he was probably just short of money, and knowing Mrs Hardwood's habit of selling off her baubles to pay for her habit, he didn't think it would get commented upon. He just happened to pick the wrong bauble. The very wrong bauble.'

'Surely Perry would have recognised Truetouch as Leo Courtkey when he saw him on the beach?'

'Maybe he did. From what Liza has said, I don't think Perry was the kind of man who would have blown the whistle on a friend – which I am guessing Leo was.'

'Leo must have been beside himself when a dwarf detective turned up at the beach?'

'I don't think he was exactly happy, especially after I wiped the floor with his hero. Probably thought my looking for Perry Goodfellow was just a smokescreen. I'm not completely sure what he wanted from me. I think he was a little conflicted there, between asking for assistance in handing the Hardwood Emerald back and just wanting to pick my lock and see what I was hiding.'

'Mrs Hardwood hiring you to look for the emerald – was that a coincidence?'

'Probably – I am the only dwarf detective in town, which is the only true thing Mrs Hardwood ever said to me.'

'And so, Nicely. We still need an answer to the big question: who killed our elf that never was? Who did for Leo Courtkey?'

I got up and shook the sand from my seat. 'There's no doubt in my mind that Hardwood ordered it and Goodenough would have been his middleman. I'm sure he was in *The Twilight Alehouse* looking for Leo Courtkey when Truetouch and me arrived. I kind of reckon a goblin by the name of Petal probably did the actual deed and tried to put me in the frame for it at the same time. Judging by the way the Hardwood bauble ended up in his coffer. And that's the problem with the world today, too much delegation. If you want to do a job properly, nothing beats doing it yourself.'

'But you got the velvet glove treatment the next time you ran into Petal?'

'I don't know if I would call a nose full of Moondust velvet glove treatment.'

'A lot of folk would pay good gold for that sort of treatment.'

'Not dwarfs!' I said with real conviction. 'But by then Hardwood knew the Cits could find a connection back to his wife, a trail he didn't want the Cits going down. He hoped Petal would just scare me off with vague threats. Doesn't know anything about dwarfs, that man.'

'Well, not this one at least.'

We left it at that. I suppose we were not sure exactly who had been using whom and for what.

I went down to the water's edge to talk with Liza. Although Thelen had already broken the bad news about Perry, for what it was worth, I could at least tell her he was in the clear with regard to the theft of the Hardwood Emerald. I was never going to figure out all of the ramifications of this case. Hardwood had too many fingers in too many pies; the only consolation was that by now most of them had got burnt. I did not feel that this was going to be much consolation to Liza.

I walked towards the small, stocky figure of Liza, and

pictured those haunting eyes and stopped. I was suddenly struck by her essential dwarfish quality. There was no other word for it. The Elf Queen was right: what a wondrous thing this creature called man was. I thought of Slant, the troll-like man, and Clubbin – did he not have something of Grove, the Tree-friend, in his manner? Then there was that strange inn, *The Twilight Alehouse*, the one I visited with poor Leo 'Truetouch' Courtkey, the club that was not there the next day. Were those really dwarfs and elves – or goblins even? Perhaps there was a secret underground of these characters: misfits who were never at home with the race they were born into, meeting up in their own private places. Axes and blood, could Petal really be a man after all? Who was passing themselves off as whom? It was a sobering thought. I took a breath and carried on walking, trying to think of something I could say to the sad young lady on the beach, to help her try to make sense of it all.

Later that night I met up with a new group of drinking partners. Ralph smoked his pipe and told me that Scout Telfine, now undoubtedly a better man, would make a full recovery. I took a flagon of Mother Crock's finest and the Tree-friend brought some homemade gravy. The wizard did some tricks, the gnome told some stories, the pix fell off his perch and we all got good and stinking, but I never did go surfing.

CPSIA information can be obtained
at www.ICGtesting.com
Printed in the USA
LVOW08s2325310317
529236LV00003B/9/P